# THE DARK

## BY

## Emilio Iasiello

© Copyright 2022 Emilio Iasiello
All rights reserved.

No portion of this book may be reproduced in whole or in part, by any means whatsoever, except for passages excerpted for the purposes of review, without the prior written permission of the publisher.

For information, or to order additional copies, please contact:

Beacon Publishing Group
P.O. Box 41573 Charleston, S.C. 29423
800.817.8480 | beaconpublishinggroup.com

Publisher's catalog available by request.

ISBN-13: 978-1-949472-55-4

ISBN-10: 1-949472-55-4

Published in 2022. New York, NY 10001.

First Edition. Printed in the USA.

# THE DARK

*"The winds were wither'd in the stagnant air,*

*And the clouds perish'd; darkness had no need*

*Of aid from them – She was the Universe."*

*-Lord Byron, "Darkness"*

*For my kids who appreciate the magic of ghost stories and things that go bump in the night.*

# THE DARK

BY

Emilio Iasiello

# Chapter 1

Mark was a fast runner, the fastest in his class at school by far. None of his fifth-grade classmates could keep up with him. Like an Olympic swimmer whose strokes in the pool seemed effortless, Mark's running motion was natural and purposeful. No movement was wasted; his arms pumped in perfect synchronicity with his legs. Together, they made his 54-inch-tall frame a well-oiled machine that forecast future success in athletic endeavors.

Right now, though, he wasn't running to win a race or a prize or any event that would yield him some honor.

He was running for his life.

The woods were deep, and the terrain unsteady. He found it difficult to race past the intrusive trees and thick underbrush, especially when there was no clear path to follow. Thin branches constantly snagged his t-shirt or scratched the skin on his arm, trying to bar his passage entirely, or else, just slow him down enough to be caught. Roots sprung up in inopportune places looking to trip up fast, careless runners. The overhead canopy that blocked out the natural light of stars only further complicated matters. On a good day, the looming solitariness of the woods was scary; at a time like this, the woods were flat-out terrifying.

Away. He had to get away. That was all he knew and for the time being that was all that mattered.

Fight or flight.

Mark battled the urge to look back. A person's natural inclination was to see how close an adversary was gaining. But in all this murky mess, what was he going to see anyway? His vision constrained, he had lost any semblance of direction and subsequently, had no idea where he was headed.

Or where that thing was out there.

He paused briefly to catch his breath and looked around in the hopes of gaining his bearings. It was all the same. Trees and darkness and bushes and limbs and branches.

Except one thing was different. It was quiet. Not normal quiet where the only sound you heard came from the chirps and buzzes from a diverse insect ecosystem.

These woods were impossibly absent of any noise.

They were silent as a cemetery, just creepier and more terrifying.

He picked up running again.

If Mark had stayed put for a few minutes, he might have heard the distant calls from his father, Peter, who was desperately looking for his son. He was pursuing the boy, but he wasn't Mark's pursuer. That title was reserved for the malevolence that had plagued the family since they rented out the cabin for the summer. It had showed itself to his son, befriended him, and now it wanted him.

Peter hated himself for not listening to his son when he had the chance.

And now he was paying the price.

So was Mark.

And with this sad realization came the Noise.

And with that, Mark shuddered.

The Noise was distinct as it was familiar. It came to him that first night in his bedroom at the cabin. It started off small, creeping in through the cracked open window. It stayed in the shadows. Gradually, over the course of days, it grew larger and stronger. Mark tried to explain it to his father. He described the sound as a cicada's buzz and click, but afterwards, he realized that the description misrepresented what he had really heard. No insect made this sound. It was the darkness itself that gargled this communication. It did not take Mark long to understand that the Dark and the Noise were one in the same, its own perverted two-in-one unholy Duality.

It spoke to him in its own way, and in its own language.

It came across docile at first, like a timid expression that rose just above a whisper. It engaged him, and in doing so, it liked and understood him.

But then the Noise changed.

It became more aggressive. It bullied him. The more he resisted, the more the darkness pooled around his bed. The Noise became more persistent and agitated until it dropped the false façade, making its intention crystal clear.

It wanted Mark. Forever.

Mark's terror fueled his stamina. But it also drove him in directions that he might not have gone down if he thought about it. He didn't even try to block his face from the branches in his way, going full steam ahead without a second thought. And just when he thought his heart would burst in his chest, he stumbled face-first into a clearing.

He hit the ground hard, scratching his face against bramble and roughly edged stones. The wind knocked out of him, Mark lay on the ground, a painful scream trapped in his chest that gave no air for its escape into the air around him. The pain grasped him then slowly released its hold. As his breathing normalized, Mark got to his feet.

The clearing was a complete circle, too perfect for it to be anything but manmade and yet with little indication that such tools had been used to carve out and smoothly shape its geometry. The foliage and bushes seemed to have stopped growing in perfect symmetry around a single tree. There was no sign of periodic pruning or trimming. No debris on the ground left from careless workmen.

Furthermore, there was little evidence that this awkward location had been used as a campsite. The clearing lacked the tell-tale signs of camping – a circle of stones for a fire, ashes, casual litter scraps. The ground was completely void of any leaf, weed, or grass. It appeared that things just didn't grow in the circle and things that did, did not encroach its circumference.

But that wasn't the strangest thing about where Mark stood.

The tree that stood dead center in this circle was unlike anything he had ever seen. Mark had been a Cub Scout since the first grade and a regular participant in the Little Rangers that met on weekends and explored natural parks and learned of trees, streams, and general ecology. He had seen several varieties of trees, studied their leaf patterns, how their limbs grew out and spread from their trunks, and this wasn't one in the books.

The tree's base was composed of several gnarled roots that grew from the ground and reached upward. They were intertwined, giving the tree the appearance of being a massive section of tethered rope. The bark was black and strangely smooth and glistening as if lacquered by the night itself.

Transfixed, Mark approached the tree. Around him, the Noise travelled through the tree limbs, rippling the leaves as it grew closer to the edge of the clearing. Once it arrived it immediately dispersed, the ripple spreading around the circumference in synchronized harmony. The buzzing and clicking chanted in unified cacophony. Like a highly organized mob, the Noise increased steadily in volume and intensity until it hit a frenzied, fevered pitch.

The crescendo was not just a description of sound; it was a destination.

Tears silently rolled down Mark's face.

"Dad?" he whispered to no one in particular.

It wouldn't matter if Mark had screamed his father's name at the top of his voice. Neither the Noise nor the Dark that directed it would have allowed that. Mark's father didn't have a chance to find his son, at least, not in time.

As the Noise chattered, the Dark gathered on the forest floor, collecting until it formed an obsidian pool devoid of any light. Once formed, it crossed the clearing's threshold, steadily pushing in on the child like a steady consuming cancer.

Mark sat down with his back against the tree as he watched its merciless advance. Just before it reached him, the Noise set upon him like a tsunami, crashing into him before any sound of pain could escape his lips.

# Chapter 2

The cabin was a remote getaway upstate, tucked below the swell of a mountain and in the dense thick forest of pine and birch. It was large enough to comfortably sleep a family of five with two bedrooms, one complete with a bed and a bunk-bed, two-and-a-half baths, a back deck overlooking a modest-sized kidney-shaped lake, and a pier with a nearby boat shack. By any standard, the cabin was a necessary retreat for those that needed to unplug and refocus or just wanted to know what clean air felt like in their lungs. Inside, the cabin had an open living design with rooms seamlessly flowing one into another. The kitchen, like any domicile, was the focus of internal activity with both a wood burning stove as well as a gas-fueled one, depending on the taste of the patrons. All bedrooms and both full bathrooms were located on the second level. A door off the living room revealed stairs leading down to a small partially furnished basement used mostly for storage.

It could be whatever guests wanted it to be. That was the selling point according to the online ad. The cabin was chameleon-like in possibilities. For those wanting a glimpse into how people once lived, it was rustic in every sense of the word. There were no neighbors in a mile-and-half radius, and it was a good two miles to a sleepy town on a one-lane road that twisted and meandered like any careless river. Trout could be caught in the lake, and if rented during hunting season, deer could be tracked and shot if patience and determination were implemented. For those wanting more comforts than a pioneer lifestyle, the cabin featured enough amenities to keep children occupied, Internet geeks satisfied, and foodie chefs' content.

Summers upstate bore a strong resemblance to desert climates. During the day, the sun bore mercilessly down, and the heat could be so intense that they made dips into the cool lake a necessary refuge for cabin guests. At night, temperatures could drop drastically, getting down as low as the thirties, making the air crisp enough to show your breath and fires in the hearth a mandatory practice.

Despite its removal from civilization, quiet didn't persist in the purest sense; there were too many animals and insects that made this region their home. But after a day or two, even their cacophony ultimately blended into the surrounding serenity becoming part of the majestic landscape. Evening stars shone so brightly that the cabin's exterior lights were rarely required; lack of man-made pollution enabled the clear sky to magnify their luminance much to the delight of awe-struck amateur astronomers that directed their telescopes upwards.

The Dark

The cabin was idyllic in every sense.

***

"Is this something, or what?" Anne said as she got out the old Chevy Caprice and walked toward the cabin. Behind her, her husband, Jack, and ten-year-old son, Joshua, exited the vehicle that had seen better days as well.

She looked back at her family, trying to ascertain how they felt about their home for the next month by their reactions. Their faces were hard to read, and Anne thought that her son would make a hell of a poker player someday.

"Well, Joshua? What do you think?" she asked.

When he didn't immediately respond, Jack rescued his son from the lingering awkwardness.

"Sounds like a ringing endorsement to me," he said too quickly. He went to the car trunk and opened it. "Come here, sport. We work for our food. Help me with the bags."

Anne turned away from them and let out a sigh of exasperation. She was officially on the other side of her thirties, an unofficial milestone that came with its own set of challenges. She didn't mind getting older; that fact of life was expected as much as it was accepted. It was how getting older had affected her marriage that was the hardest to come to terms with. She had heard how matrimony rarely brought two people together over time, that physical intimacy waned the closer and longer two people lived together. Individual idiosyncrasies may have been charming in the beginning, but as she soon discovered, they quickly became grating, debilitating forces. The veracity of this was no more apparent than when she discovered after her birthday that she had amorous interests besides her husband in their next-door neighbor. What followed should have been exciting if it wasn't pure cliché. And when she realized that she and her husband had to talk about some things, their utopia in suburbia did not lend itself to figuring things out.

The cabin had been her idea. She spent the time pouring over options on the Internet, looking for a place far enough away from home to provide a neutral, new environment, but close enough that if they had to pull the plug, the ride back wouldn't be a long, uncomfortable examination of a love gone sour.

She watched her husband and her son walk past with bags in hand. Positive thoughts, she reminded herself. If this was going to work out the way she wanted, she needed to have positive thoughts and exude them no matter the situation. The cabin would grow on Jack and Joshua, the way it had on her when her father brought his family on "forced" vacations. She and her sister hated camping but by the third day, they both had fun gutting fish, cooking over an open flame, and telling endless ghost stories. When they had to return home at the end of the week, they had shed their girlie selves; their hair was knotted, their bodies smelled, but their smiles were larger and more genuine than they had been prior to <u>The Lord of the Flies</u> experience.

Anne hoped that the same would happen to Joshua. Even if things didn't work out with Jack, she wanted her son to have a good experience. There was something refreshing about uprooting yourself from the familiar. All the old ways could be let go of largely because they didn't matter. Being in the woods in a cabin had a way of peeling away the petty things like a banana so that the only thing that mattered was left.

It was the last shot to repair everything that was broken.

That she had broken.

Taking a deep breath and fixing a smile to her face, Anne went to the car trunk and removed two bags and carried them happily into the cabin.

***

She found her husband and son in the kitchen area. They had dug into one of the several grocery bags and were eating Oreo cookies.

"Where's my cut?" she joked.

Joshua smiled and tossed her one. She fumbled the catch, slapping at the chocolate disc before it hit the ground.

"Five second rule!" Joshua shouted.

Anne quickly scooped it up and popped it in her mouth.

"I'm a professional," she beamed proudly. "Olympic material."

Joshua went to the sliding glass door that led to the back porch and offered a sweeping view of the lake including their small pier. His reaction was all that she had hoped for.

"Can I go outside?" he asked eagerly.

She shared a look with Jack who just shrugged his shoulders. His superhero power was annoying her with failing to present an opinion one way or another.

"Porch only," she said. "If you take one foot off that wood, there's going to be hell to pay."

Joshua opened the lock and the door and bolted outside.

"He's a smart kid," Jack said, unloading some of the groceries from the bags. "He won't get into trouble. Where's he going to go?"

"I just want him to be safe."

Anne dumped her bags in front of the steps leading upstairs and walked around the interior of the main floor. There were few doors that could be open or closed; at some point, the owners removed them to facilitate an openness in the shared space without incurring the expense of knocking down walls. It really brightened the interior making it a more inclusive experience. She perused the kitchen, looking through drawers and cabinets and taking stock of what they had.

"We'll need some things," she said finally. "We brought a lot of the staples and there's some things here, but a trip to town will round us out."

She looked over at Jack. She wasn't sure if he hadn't heard her or had ignored her.

"Jack?" she said. "Jack? Earth to Jack!"

His head snapped to. She wondered where his mind was at that moment, and a sick feeling pooled in her stomach when she thought what that might be. He looked over at her.

"What?"

"Can you at least feign some interest in what I say?"

"'Some things,' I heard you," he said. "I'll get the rest of the things from the car if that's all right."

He didn't wait for her answer and went out the front door toward the dirty vehicle. It was old and showed the dents of wear and tear, a fitting symbol for their own relationship. Anne watched him leave.

She drew some deep breaths before taking the heavy bags upstairs.

***

Joshua inspected his bedroom the way most kids did when they first entered a new space designated as "theirs" – with a scrutinizing skeptical eye. He first looked for imperfections like peeling wallpaper or noticeable scratches in the wood furniture. The room was smaller than the one he had back home. Two amateurish paintings of the lake and mountains hung from two of the walls, a mirror on a third wall, and a series of hooks for coats or sweaters stuck out of the last one. A narrow bed ran along one wall near a window. There was an empty bureau, a closet, a night table, a bookcase with a variety of books ranging from picture books to something called Great Expectations written by a guy whose last name sounded almost like a swear word.

He missed his things. He missed his games. He wanted to go home.

Joshua went over to the window. The view looked out onto the driveway and the woods that bordered the perimeter of the cabin's south and east exposures. About thirty feet of grass separated the forest line from the house. Joshua wondered if his dad would let him mow it by himself, or if he'd insist on supervising him.

"How you like your room, sport?"

Jack leaned against the door frame with a weak smile on his face. He hadn't slept much the past couple of weeks, a testament to the dark circles that perpetuated under his eyes. Joshua knew his parents were fighting, even if they didn't expressly tell him so. There was just so much adults could do to hide their contempt, no matter how many fake smiles they forced on their children

Kids always knew more than their parents gave them credit for.

The parents of a boy in his class last school year divorced. At recess, he'd tell Joshua and anyone else who cared to listen what happened, how his parents acted toward each other, as well as how they treated him. There was a lot quiet talking during the day, loud talk at night after they had put him to bed. And always the overly-sweet discourse when they addressed him, large wide smiles and too – too bright eyes that said they were doing a poor job hiding something from him.

It was the same for Joshua.

The past couple of weeks, his parents followed a similar tack. What happened that prompted this change of behavior, he didn't know. His friend had said that his parents fell out of love with each other, at least that's what they told him. Joshua didn't know if the same had happened with his mom and dad, only that whatever the cause, it happened right after his mother's birthday. Before that, their home was filled with jokes, and laughing, and anticipation of a fun summer. However, after her birthday, an uneasy silence entrenched itself in the home. His parents didn't interact the same way, didn't touch each other the same way, and didn't look at each other the same way.

Joshua just wanted things to go back to the way they were before.

The boy sat glumly on the bed. "I want to go home," he said.

Jack walked into the room and sat down next to his son. He tried to change the subject.

"You have a better mattress than we do. Want to switch?"

"Ha-ha," Joshua said sarcastically.

"I thought I was funnier than that. I'll take it up with my joke writers."

He gave Joshua a goofy smile and ruffled the boy's hair.

"Come on," Jack said in a soothing voice. "Your mother spent a lot of time picking out this place for us. It's only fair that we give it a chance. Besides, you saw that lake. Lot of fish in there from what I understand. And have you ever swum in a lake? So cold and refreshing you come out like a new person. Nothing like it."

"When was the last time you swam in a lake?" Joshua asked dubiously.

Jack made a big production of thinking.

"Your age. But it was extraordinary."

Jack suddenly sprang to his feet. He scooped up his son into his arm and spun him around the room. Joshua tried not to smile but getting dizzy was one of his favorite things and the faster Jack went, the wider Joshua's smiles. Giggles soon followed until they both collapsed onto Joshua's bed, laughing hysterically.

"Dad?" Joshua said after the dizziness had passed.

"Yeah?"

"How long do we have to be here?"

It was an honest question. He purposefully was careful to make sure he asked it without a hint of malice or dissatisfaction. He just wanted the truth.

Jack looked his son in the eye and provided an equally honest answer without subterfuge or deception.

"As long as it takes, sport."

"Can I go outside now?"

"Sure, you can."

***

Jack and Anne stood in the doorway of the large master bedroom. It featured a large queen-sized bed, two large bureaus, and a small sitting area built into an alcove. Two doors led to a large walk-in closet and a private bathroom.

All of that was window dressing. The two were focused on the bed. It would be ideal if they were a unit; but both looked upon the sole bed wondering who would get the bed and who would have to find another place to sleep.

Anne spoke first. "I just think it's better if we try to keep this as normal as possible for Joshua. He sees us sleeping in separate rooms, I'm afraid he's going to have more questions running around his head than he already has. You can only use the excuse for grading papers for so long before he'll know something is up."

"That's good thinking," Jack admitted. "He's a tough kid, but you're right. He's feeling that something is off."

"Kids feel more than we think they do. I read that somewhere."

They set about unpacking. They moved with stiff formality, careful to not get into each other's way and risking accidental contact that might not be well received.

Anne broke the tension. "And speaking of our wunderkind, where is he anyway?"

"Outside."

Anne stopped dead in her tracks. Her face drained immediately, and her eyes flared.

"You left him alone? Jesus, Jack!"

"He's fine, for Chrissakes. We're not downtown, we're in the middle of nowhere," he said. "Give the kid some space."

"There's a lake right there. He can't swim! Or did you forget that?"

"He's not going swimming!"

She rushed to the window that looked out onto the lake. She saw Joshua near the dock. He was skimming stones on the lake. Anne exhaled heavily.

"I'm sorry, I'm just worried, okay? He could have an accident, Jack. Reach too far for a rock and fall in or something."

Jack groaned. He shoved the last of his clothes int the bottom drawer of one of the bureaus.

"He's not going to fall in," he said. "In case you haven't noticed, he hasn't done much of anything lately. He's timid as a rabbit."

"And who's fault is that?"

"What's that supposed to mean?" he asked, not liking the obvious implication of her question.

"I don't know, Jack. You're the English teacher. What's the subtext tell you?"

Jack opened his mouth to launch a counterpunch but thought better of it.

"I'm sorry, okay?" he said instead.

"You heard what the therapist said. You heard that, Jack, right?"

"I was there, remember? Two hundred bucks an hour, believe me, I'm taking notes and not wasting a word."

Anne shook her head. "Really? Are you telling me money is more of your concern than our son's well-being?"

"Of course not, Anne. I'm just saying that it's a lot of money to hear things you already know."

"And what's that exactly?"

"Something's broken. And I don't know if it can be fixed."

"He's our son, Jack. We have to try – for his sake."

With that, Anne exited the room. Jack walked over to the window and saw his son. Joshua had drifted to the end of the lawn and was facing the woods. Jack moved to get a better view of what Joshua was looking at. God forbid it was an animal or something that would send Anne through the roof. She was hopelessly overprotective of the boy. She was always looking for any excuse to lock him inside in the name of safety.

Whatever it was, it captured Joshua's interest. Moments later, Jack saw Anne go over to Joshua and escort him back in the house.

Christ, he thought. If this kid could get through the rest of his life without major psychotherapy, Jack would take that as a win.

He turned to leave the room but saw a calendar on the wall. He put the index finger of his left hand on today's date and counted the twenty days left until they could leave. So many days left.

He dug out a pen and made a blue "X" on the date of departure.

That couldn't come fast enough, as far as he was concerned.

***

Dinner was a strained and quiet affair. Conversation punctuated the silence instead of the other way around. The three of them ate their cold turkey and cheese sandwiches joylessly.

"I'm sorry about this," Anne said finally, breaking the silence that had settled. "I don't know where my head was at. I'll pick up some groceries tomorrow if that's alright with everyone."

"It's fine," Jack said. "It was a long drive and it's been a long day. Who has an appetite anyway?"

Anne watched Joshua dig a potato chip into a smear of ketchup on his plate. The boy had retreated into some game in his mind.

"You have any special requests, honey?" she asked her son. "Hamburgers or spaghetti and meatballs?"

The boy didn't hear her or didn't respond. He submerged a chip in the red mess, testing the sturdiness of the chip before it snapped in the dense condiment.

"I know," she continued. "How about cow brains and pig guts? Maybe a can or two of cat farts?"

Mention of the word "farts" elicited a response. Joshua looked up from the chip-dipping and met his mother's eyes.

"I hear they can them here," she pressed on. "All types: smelly, stinky, putrid, ripe, fetid…"

Joshua giggled encouraging her one-woman stand-up show.

"Also, there's rotten, rancid, and of course my personal favorite, malodorous."

Full laughter. It was a game they liked to play. Make lists of words that Joshua found funny. The other week, Anne ran through a list of synonyms for puke that made Joshua fall out of his chair he was laughing so hard.

"Okay, Dumb and Dumber," Jack said. "Let's finish up dinner. You can take your slap-stick routine into the living room for a second act."

"Your father doesn't appreciate our comic genius," she said.

Joshua looked at his dad.

"How come you don't tell jokes?" he asked.

"I may not be funny," Jack said, leaning in close to his son as if trying to impart a secret. "But I am funny looking."

He stuck out his tongue and made a crazy face. Joshua laughed so hard that milk came shooting out his nose. The suddenness of the expulsion caught everyone off guard. Jack couldn't contain his laughter and Anne had already lost it. Joshua mopped up his face with a paper napkin, giggling uncontrollably. It had been a long time since the three of them laughed like this, together.

Anne got up and got more napkins to help Joshua clean up.

"What do you say? Want to come to town with me tomorrow and get some things? I hear they have a place that makes killer homemade ice cream."

Joshua turned to his father. Anne noticed the look.

"What?" she asked.

Jack rescued his son. "Well, I promised him that he could help me get the canoe out on the water," he said trying to help his son out of an awkward position.

"Oh, well, that's fine," she said. She hid her disappointment poorly. "You help, Daddy, honey."

"Can I be excused?" Joshua asked.

"Of course," she said.

Anne waited until Joshua had cleared his place and went into the living room before she turned her anger at Jack.

"The canoe? Really?"

"It's a lake house. He wants to get out on the lake. That's why we are here, isn't it? Fresh air and all that jazz?"

"And you had no involvement in convincing him that's what he wanted?"

"He's a boy. Boys like canoes. They also like bugs, dirt, and everything that goes with it. What do you want from me?"

"I want us to work as a team when it comes to Joshua. No matter what personal issues we're having, I don't want him to be affected by it."

"That's fair. Yes. Of course."

"Just don't be a jerk, okay?"

"That goes both ways."

Jack pushed himself from the table and followed his son into the other room. Anne remained seated, breathing deeply to control the anger welling inside her.

***

Jack tucked Joshua into his bed and sat down alongside him with his son's favorite bedtime book. It was a simple story, one that a lazy or enterprising author had cobbled together from the greatest hits of nursery rhymes, fables, and abridged versions of fairy tales. It played on all the usual themes, paradigms, and symbols.

"…and so, the prince defeated the evil wizard. The thousand years of darkness was finally vanquished from the kingdom, and the people were free to live again in happiness, with the sun on their backs, and the bright future ahead. The end."

Jack closed the book. Joshua yawned. He was on his last legs.

"Good night, sport," Jack said, leaning over and planting a kiss on his son's forehead. "Sleep tight."

He gets off the bed and heads toward the door.

"Dad?"

Jack turned to see his son's face. His brow was furrowed, and a grim expression fastened around his mouth.

"Yeah, sport?"

Joshua wanted to say something but either couldn't articulate it or thought better of it.

"Nothing," he said.

"Get some rest. We have a big day in front of us."

Jack took a step out of the room.

Joshua bolted upright in bed. "The dark!" he exclaimed.

Jack paused and smiled. He dipped his fingers into his shirt pocket and removed a Bugs Bunny night light. He inserted it into the socket near bedroom door. Bugs' face lit up a bright orange.

"You thought I forgot? Come on…" Jack said. "What did I tell you about that guy?"

"No dark will ever dim this light," Joshua repeated from memory.

"I used this when I was your age, and you know what? It works."

"Thanks, Dad."

Jack blew him another kiss and shut the door, but not entirely, leaving a crack open.

***

Jack changed into his pajamas while Anne sat up in bed flipping through an old magazine that she found in the night table.

"How's he doing?" she asked him.

"Kid's got more guts than I ever had at his age," he said.

"You put in the night light?"

Jack shut the drawer and climbed into his side of the bed. He made sure not to encroach on her space.

"Some of us don't forget the little things," he said.

Anne tossed the magazine onto the floor. "It was one time, Jack. One time."

"Yeah, well, one time is all it takes."

Her eyes narrowed in anger. "Like you said, the kid's got guts."

"He was traumatized, Anne."

"Are we still talking about the night light?"

Jack turned to face her. "We're talking about whatever you want to talk about."

They looked at one another, but neither offered another word. When no one gave ground, each turned to their tables on their sides of the bed and clicked off the lights. Each laid on their backs looking up at the ceiling.

"I still love you, Jack," she said. "I really do."

"That's what you keep telling me."

"Do you still love me? Does some part of you still love me?"

Jack didn't say anything. He didn't know what to say. And because he didn't, he kept his mouth shut. The silence said more than any word could.

"Good night, Anne," he said finally.

# Chapter 3

The boathouse was more of a rectangular shack than a true edifice that stored smaller sports craft. A canoe and a rowboat were stacked neatly in the center. One wall was adorned with oars and paddles. It faced another wall on which hung several pylon-orange life jackets. Various tools were strewn over a built-in work bench.

Jack hoisted the two-seater canoe, balancing it over his head. Joshua stood near the door holding it wide open for his father.

"Okay, sport, watch your head."

Jack walked slowly out the door, banging off the frame before threading the bow through. He set the chipped green paint canoe on the grass near the dock. It had seen better days and needed a good scraping and a fresh coat.

"Will it float?" asked Joshua skeptically.

"I was thinking the same thing. Only one way to find out."

Jack picked up the canoe again via the center yoke and hefted it to the edge before plopping it down on the lake. He and Joshua watched it carefully, looking for signs of leakage.

"What do you think?"

Joshua scrunched up his face. "It's dirty. And it smells."

Jack frowned. "It's not pretty but she'll stay above wate. We'll clean it up a bit, get that gook off the bottom. Heck, we'll be out on the lake after lunch."

He rubbed his son's hair and went into the boathouse and came out shortly after with a bucketful of supplies.

As he waited for his father to reappear, something stirred behind the boy.

If someone had asked him what it was, Joshua would have had a difficult time describing what the sound was. It was neither a rustle of leaves nor a person's voice but some combination of both. Wind-stirred branches or a person's voice would have been distinct and familiar. And because of its familiarity, it would be otherwise forgettable. Of that Joshua was sure.

But this was different. This was nothing like he had ever heard before and that's what had caught his attention.

Joshua turned and looked at the forest's tree line, but all that was there was a series of spruce and hardwoods and thick, thick bushes. There was nothing there, yet…

"Amazing, isn't it?"

Jack placed a hand on his son's shoulder giving the boy a startle. His father gave him a reassuring smile.

"We have foliage where we live but not like this," he continued. "Out here, trees are dominant, and people take the back seat. I remember when I was a boy, I had to be around your age, my father used to take me fishing all the time. We'd go to his special place about an hour away from our house. There was nothing like it. It was just us guys, no women. We used to set up a tent, eat what we caught. It was really back to basics. At night by the fire, we'd drink hot cocoa and listen to the sound of the woods."

"The woods talked to you?"

"Well, not like you're thinking, but the woods have a language all their own."

"I thought you were afraid of the dark?" Joshua asked.

Jack let out a laugh. "Let me tell you something, sport. I don't care if you are five years old or fifty. Anyone tells you that they're not afraid of the dark is a flat-out liar. You don't think about it until you're alone or it's all around you, but yeah, you still get scared. But I'll let you in on a little secret. Something my father taught me."

Joshua leaned in close. He was looking for some magic in Jack's words.

"It may get dark," Jack said, "but out here in the woods? The stars never do. No matter how black the woods seem the stars shine brighter. You don't even need a flashlight. You watch tonight and see if I'm wrong."

"Okay," Joshua said.

"Yep. Any time you get scared out here, Joshua, just look up at the night sky. The stars will never let you down. Okay, let's get to work."

***

Remington was one of the smallest organized towns in the state, a reputation that locals wore on their chests like a medal from an unheard-of battle. Like most municipalities of modest stature, the heart of Remington lay in the intersection of two streets on which two cornerstones of most towns were founded – the First Congregational church and the sheriff's office. From there on out, businesses closest to these essentials were those most important to a community: drug store, hardware store, a small market where local farmers sold their produce, a clothing store/tailor, a shoe store, a schoolhouse.

French Acadians first settled in the area during the 17th Century and featured a few obsolete skirmishes that took place years later during the French and Indian War. Remington held onto its Acadian roots maintaining a working blacksmith shop and gristmill. Houses were built in the same architectural style, and while there were not many original structures left standing, many of the houses still had the original edifices in place, having been updated here and there along the way.

People were friendly amongst themselves. However, they kept a healthy skepticism directed toward outsiders, even those tourists that rented out the better places near or along the lake and pumped in much needed dollars during the summer so that the locals could survive the winter. This reality softened some opinions and hardened others. The one thing that all could agree on was that outsiders were welcome in Remington; they were just not accepted.

Anne walked up and down the aisles of Remington Supply, a general store that served as the town's version of a specialty shop, a necessary evolution as more upscale tourists came to spend time in the sleepy town. Things that couldn't be found on an everyday basis could generally be found at Remington Supply, and if the proprietor didn't have it, he certainly made it his business to be able to acquire it. Anne was surprised to find some of the items on the shelf, including sel gris, or gray salt. The Supply offered some of the other needed goods, saving Anne an unnecessary trip to the grocery store. She brought her basket to the checkout counter where an older man in his sixties wearing a John Deere baseball cap read the local paper.

He looked up and gave Anne a polite smile as he worked the old push-button cash register. It was an antique, but it was functional, the bell ringing up after each recorded sale.

"You must be the folks that rented out the Daniels place," he said, his voice accented in the unique tonal blend of the Northeast region and a rustic French dialect.

Anne smiled. "What gave me away?"

"You're the only cabin that hasn't come here rummaging for things that they forgot to bring. The folks that rented the Curtis place came in last week, and those at the Boufards and Maloshes are halfway through their leases."

"You sure got you fingers on the pulse of what's going on," she remarked.

The man paused ringing her up. He took off his cap and wiped his brow with the back of his arm.

"Small town," he said. "An ant doesn't fart around here without people two blocks away breaking out the Lysol, if you catch my meaning."

The frankness of the statement took Anne by surprise and she let out a laugh louder than expected.

"Excuse me," she said, covering her mouth in embarrassment.

"No need. My apologies, miss. Sometimes my rustic charm overrides my commonsense filters."

"It's a nice change of pace," she said. "Where I'm from people's idea of a joke is something off-colored and usually offensive on so many levels."

"Is that one of the benefits of urban living?"

Anne paused. "Well, suburban living," she said. She eyed him keenly. "You sure know your customers."

"I was born and raised here going on sixty-five years," the man said. "I know who lives here and everyone in a twenty-mile radius. Faces I don't know are just not from these parts."

"Are you telling me you've never left? What about vacations?"

"Well, I served four years in the military. Just missed Vietnam by a raccoon whisker. Was stationed in Germany for two years, then back in the States for two. I've seen enough to know that strange places don't excite me as they do other people. I'm more of an Oliver Wendell Douglas type."

"Excuse me?"

The man chuckled. "'Keep Manhattan just give me the countryside.'"

For the second time Anne released a loud laugh. It took her a second for the joke to register, but when she did, she immediately associated the line with *Green Acres*, the old sitcom about a mix-paired couple – the woman favoring a socialite lifestyle while her husband embraced a more agrarian routine.

The man nodded in the direction of two farmer-looking men outside, loading grain bags in the back of a pickup truck.

"Here, people say 'Kate Spade', you can bet your ass it's more likely they're talking about the latest shovel and not a lady's purse."

"I'm impressed you've heard of Kate Spade."

"We may be in the sticks, but we still get our fair share of those glossy magazines."

He finished ringing her up.

"That'll be thirty-two fifty," he said. He slid over two brown paper bags full of her items.

Anne dug into her purse and removed to twenties. "I don't even want to tell you how much that would have cost me in the city. Thanks, again -" She struggled for his name.

"Henry," the man said. "Henry Clay."

"Anne Mitchell," she said. She shook Henry's hand.

Henry helped her with the bag to her car out front. She climbed into the driver's seat and started the engine.

"See you around, Henry Clay," she said.

"I don't doubt it," he said. "Oh, and one more thing? Keep an eye on that little one of yours out there."

Anne's face betrayed surprise. "How'd you know we had a son?"

"Small town," he replied, then explained himself. "Boys and woods. You know. They get curious about things they don't understand, they're apt to go down paths that ought not be gone down."

"Thanks again," she said.

Henry gave her a curt nod and a wink. "You betcha."

***

Joshua checked the latch on his overstuffed lifejacket. He felt like a grotesque marshmallow; the padding was so thick that the blocky foam came up to his ears. He watched his father set the canoe into the lake and with the rope he had tied to one of the yoke's, dragged the canoe to the dock so that they could climb aboard.

His father steadied the canoe and looked back at his son.

"Ready, sport?"

Joshua nodded and walked over to him. His confidence waned when he saw how unsteady the canoe seemed on the water.

"You're going to love it," Jack said, sensing his son's apprehension. "Come on, I'll help you aboard."

The bow of the canoe had one of the two places for rowers to sit. Jack lifted his son into the air, placing him onto the metal seat. The boy's hands grabbed the sides of the canoe when the boat started to rock under his weight.

"Hold on," Jack said. "No sudden movements or you're going to take an unexpected dip."

Jack steadied the canoe and in one fluid motion hopped into the back seat. The boat rocked as it pushed away from the dock, gradually steadying as it adjusted to the weight of the two bodies. Jack got his paddle and put it into the water.

"Hey sport," he said. "This isn't a free trip."

Joshua smiled and picked up his own paddle and put it into the water.

They gradually made their way to the center of the lake where they could get a good panoramic view of the surrounding environment. On this side, theirs was the only cabin visible. The Boufaurd place was a mile or so away down from their place. Jack had done a little research on his own after Anne had told him about booking the place for the month. Crescent Lake was approximately 700 acres in size with a maximum depth of 100 feet, give or take, and an average depth of 35 feet. An overhead view of the lake depicted a conical shape, hence the name. Small and largemouth bass were plentiful for skilled anglers.

Jack rested the paddle across the canoe and let the boat drift. The lake looked really large to Joshua, and it wasn't until now did he realize that the cabin in which they were staying was  on the edge of just one section of a large water mass.

"Have to say, I don't envy those suckers stuck in some  cubicle downtown," Jack said finally. Joshua noted that since his mother went into town for groceries, his father seemed more relaxed. Jack opened a small cooler and pulled out a beer for himself and a soda for Josh. Josh drank too quickly causing him to burp.

"What's a cubicle?" he asked his father.

"Dante's Third Ring of Hell," Jack said matter-of-factly.

For a second time Josh didn't understand his father's cryptic remarks. He couldn't' be certain if his dad thought Joshua was older than he actually was, or if his careless use of vocabulary was just his way of trying to address his son as a peer and not someone numerous years his junior.

Joshua turned around. "Who's Dante?"

Jack finished his beer in two more gulps and crushed the can. He let out a loud belch that echoed, soliciting laughs from Joshua.

"Someone who never had to deal with middle management."

It took his mother a few calls before he heard her. Joshua looked around and saw Anne at the end of their pier. She was waving an arm in the air to get their attention.

"Mom's calling."

Jack gestured for to hold on and got paddling. In a few minutes they pulled up alongside of the dock. He steadied the canoe and helped Joshua before climbing out himself.

"Didn't you hear me?" she asked.

Jack gestured to the lake. "It's farther out there than you think."

"Dinner's ready. My men hungry?"

"Starved," said Joshua.

"I could eat," Jack said. "What's on the menu?"

"Tuna casserole. Wash up and I'll put food in the dishes."

She walked away. Joshua saw his father's expression change as he led the canoe to the shoreline and hoisted it out of the water.

"Dad?"

"Yeah, sport?"

"What's tuna casserole?"

Jack stuck out his tongue and made a distasteful face. "Dante's Fourth Ring."

***

Dinner proceeded without fanfare. Joshua relayed his day working with his dad. There was a genuine enthusiasm in his voice as he relayed working with tools and describing in excruciating detail the gunk they removed from the bottom of the boat. Despite the current problems between the parents, both Jack and Anne appreciated seeing their son the way he was before the great unpleasantness.

When Joshua finished his debrief, Anne took her turn and described what she saw in the small but quaint town that, in her own words, "had more charm than utility." She told them about Henry, the friendly store owner that reminded her of her Uncle Zeke, the one person on her side of the family that never left the hometown in which he grew up.

After dinner and dessert, Anne handed Joshua an apron. He set up a foot stool near the sink and filled it with water and soap as Jack bussed the table and stacked the dishes and silverware next to him. Anne popped in to check on his progression.

"How's it going, kiddo?" she asked.

"I hate chores," he said.

"Who doesn't? But it builds character."

"What's character?"

"An ambiguous term that grownups use when they make their children do things that they don't want to do."

"Oh," he said. "What ring of hell is this?"

"Excuse me?"

"Dad calls things he doesn't like 'rings of hell'"

"Your father has a strange sense of humor."

She watched him a little bit longer. He was fastidious when he concentrated on a task. He got that from her side. Jack's side were more creative, free thinkers. Getting things done was squarely from her side of the family.

***

Anne found Jack outside on the back porch. She handed him a glass of iced tea, taking the seat next to him.

"Dante, Jack? Really?

Jack smirked. "Kid's smart. I'm just nurturing his intellect."

"More like his tendency to be a smart aleck."

"There is that."

She paused to consume the view of the lake. The water was still, a perfect mirror of the sky above. "Have to hand it to that vacation site. It is beautiful out here. So quiet and peaceful."

"I'm going to get some fish tomorrow. There are some big ones in there," Jack said. His eyes never left the lake.

"How are we doing Jack?" she asked.

"Fresh air. Wide open spaces. What could be wrong?"

"Jack." Her voice regained its edge.

He sighed and drank his iced tea. "What do you want me to say, Anne?"

"Something. Anything."

He scoffed and turned back to the lake. "It's not that simple."

"It's not that hard, either. Nothing happened that night. See? That wasn't difficult at all."

"Sure," he said. "Whatever you say."

"Nothing happened," she repeated. "That's what I say."

"An hour, Anne. I don't know, that's a long time."

"I went out for cigarettes, Jack. That's all. Cigarettes. I still smoke one or two when I'm not home. You know that."

"An hour though? Where'd you drive, Connecticut?"

She groaned. "You're insufferable."

"And Dave Selznick? What about him? Why'd you need him to go with you?"

"I couldn't drive. I'd had a few drinks."

Jack's eyes narrowed. "Well, that's convenient."

"People kept my glass filled because of my birthday. I was drunk. Pardon me for trying to be responsible."

"So, you got drunk at the party when you had your son with you?"

"It was poor judgment, I admit. But we were just next door."

"And the cigarettes? What were you going to say if our son saw you smoking them?"

"Again, not my finest moment, I admit it."

"That would have been better than what he did see."

"I explained that" she said. He misunderstood what he saw. The light. The situation. He has an aggressive imagination, Jack. You've said so yourself. Tell me I'm lying."

"Oh, no, I couldn't do that. You seem to have all the answers."

"That's because they're the right ones. I'm not lying to you," she said, swallowing hard. "I've never lied to you."

"Our kid says differently."

"Our son is an impressionable ten-year-old who doesn't understand the things he sees."

"He understands a kiss, Anne. He's seen people do it in the movies. He's seen us do it."

"Not for quite some time, Jack."

"Well, that's a good excuse for making out with the neighbor."

Anne got up off her chair, exasperated. She walked over to the edge of the porch and leaned her hands against the banister.

"I can't talk to you when you get like this."

"Then don't."

Anne walked back into the cabin. Jack remained seated, staring at the lake. He took another sip of the iced tea. Then, remembering the beverage came from her, Jack tossed the contents on the deck floor.

***

Joshua stood in front of the sink. The window that overlooked the back porch was open and he had heard his parents talking. He hated that his parents were fighting, and he hated it more that he was the cause of it all. If he hadn't walked out of the party to sneak a quick cupcake, he wouldn't have seen his mother and Mr. Selznick in the front seat of the car.

Making out. That's what he heard the older boys call it. Making out. When you put your open mouth on a girl's open mouth and touched tongues. Joshua had never done that. He didn't understand why boys or girls for that matter did that at all. It seemed so gross and unnecessary.

But his mother did it and she seemed to like it. She looked like an animal feeding on a carcass the way she attacked Mr. Selznick's face.

Joshua folded the apron and draped it on one of the kitchen chairs. He walked past by his mother who was on her cell phone. She didn't notice him or was too preoccupied to say anything when he walked past. He went to the front and looked through the glass in the storm door.

Joshua regarded the forest line. The woods seemed lusher at night. Maybe it was the way the darkness billowed around the trees making their limbs seem heavier and fuller. One massive limb caught Joshua's attention. It didn't conform to the others, not that it had to. Tree limbs did their own thing, at least that's what that painter guy said on television. And Joshua knew from the Forest School that trees grew dependent on their access to light, and even grew sideways to do that. Photosynthesis was how green plants generated their energy.

But this limb looked strange. And eerie. None of the other limbs jutted out like that, stretching toward the driveway, and by extension, the cabin. Based on the other tree configurations, sunlight didn't hit the back driveway. The limb should have twisted like the others, stretching straight upward, thirsting for the light, not hiding from it.

The thin branches that forked at the end looked like bony fingers. And when the wind caused them to rustle, it looked like the fingers were trying to grasp and hold onto something.

Or someone.

A chill crawled down Joshua's back and he shut the front door.

He didn't like what he saw. He didn't like to think bad things before he went to sleep in the dark.

He would have liked it even less if he had noticed the windchimes that hung off the front porch did not sound.

They didn't make a noise because there had been no wind.

# Chapter 4

Anne sat in bed. She knew that Jack wasn't coming upstairs. She could kick herself for pushing back so hard outside, but whenever he got that snide tone in his voice it just set her off. He had a holier-than-thou attitude that just made her want to blast him in the face. Who was he to pass judgment on something he never saw with his own eyes? Anne caught him several times checking out other women. He wasn't very subtle about it either. At a local restaurant, a waitress in a short skirt walked by and his eyes were pulled by the sway of her hips. The teller at the bank couldn't be more than a year out of high school, but that didn't stop him from dropping his eyes to the swell and depth of her cleavage.

Yeah, he might be able to point a finger at her, but it was a short one.

Still, as much as she wanted to bring him down to her level, there was a fundamental difference between looking and doing.

She had done the latter.

Anne blamed it on the booze, but she was simply bored with the marriage. Dave Selznick was no prize. Of all the guys to have an affair with, Dave Selznick wouldn't register on most people's radars. He was slightly shorter than Jack and had more gray hair and a larger paunch. He wasn't terribly funny or good looking. He was simply there. Being close and easy to pick up and drop made the affair seem like a temporary indulgence like a box of chocolates. You didn't eat the whole thing all the time, just certain moments when you were looking for a treat or just to be bad. There was no chance of it being anything more than what it was – an exchange of urges and secretions. She even giggled when she compared herself to Hugh Grant when he was arrested for picking up a prostitute. How could someone that went to bed with Liz Hurley bargain-basement shop like that?

Well, now Anne understood.

It would have ended soon, that was the natural conclusion. It was going nowhere largely because there was nowhere to go. There was safety and reassurance in that reality. Like a kill switch, the affair could end with a snap of a finger. Her finger most likely. Selznick would have protested it, tried to convince her otherwise. She was a step up for him, but there was nothing there for any long-term haul.

If she was honest with herself, she didn't regret the affair as much as she regretted how she got caught. It made her sick when she recalled seeing Joshua's face staring at her as she sucked Selznick's face like a horned-up but inexperienced high schooler.

Yes, she denied it and would deny it until the end of time. There was no percentage in coming clean. She just needed to weather the storm, so to speak. She thought that Jack would come around. There was just enough doubt to give her plausible deniability.

Did she want to preserve her marriage? Yes.

Did she want things to continue before her little indiscretion? Yes.

It was a mistake. It was reckless. Now it was over. The questioned that lingered – did she want her marriage to be over?

That was an unequivocal, 'no.'

Anne sighed and rubbed her face with her hands.

Not her finest moment, indeed.

***

The couch sucked. It looked comfortable the way rustic furniture did at first glance, but the plump-looking seat cushions hid the fact that some of the springs were out of whack and poking up through the coarse fabric. They either dug into his lower back, or if he switched sides, the back of his thighs. Worse, the couch's length was just short enough to prevent Jack from stretching out. He either had to lie on his side and bend his knees; prop up his head on the uncomfortable arm rest; or set his feet up on the other arm rest. None of these options was conducive to a good night's sleep.

Jack glanced up at the ceiling where the master bedroom was. He wondered if Anne was up or if she was sleeping soundly without a care in the world.

He didn't want to get a divorce. That was the farthest thing from his mind. Yet, that's what people did when they found out their spouse had side action. You got mad, you said mean things, and you got divorced. That was the scorned spouse playbook, page by page.

Could he live with it? That was the only question that mattered.

Yeah, probably. For the sake of his son, he had to. Jack was the product of an early divorce and it wasn't fun. He grew up hearing his mother and father bad mouth each other nonstop. God, he didn't want that to happen to Joshua. It was a horrible thing hearing the two people that made you, that loved you more than anything, say the most disgusting, vile things.

Forgiveness came hard in his family. And even now, looking back at that time with wisdom and distance, he saw himself doing the same thing his parents had. Apples and trees.

Fact was, he wanted his pound of flesh. He wanted her to suffer the way he was suffering. Since

Joshua told him what he saw that night, every time he saw Selznick, Jack felt like a fool, a cuckold.

He was going to have to come to a decision. If he couldn't let go of the indiscretion, then he needed to end the marriage quickly. Staying attached would not end well. Hatred was a cancer. If it wasn't addressed and stopped, it would grow and spread and affect people that didn't deserve to be affected.

Jack stood up and made his way to the stairwell. He leaned forward and listened to see if he could hear any motion in the rooms upstairs. When he couldn't, he went to the cabinet near the fireplace and removed a bottle of bourbon. It wasn't his; it had been there for God knows how long. He uncorked it and took a tentative swig. It was hardly high-end, but the taste was still there. He found a glass and poured himself three fingers worth and sat back on the couch, staring at nothing in particular as he drank and thought what the hell he was going to do.

***

Joshua never liked the dark. He didn't know why exactly, but he knew he wasn't the only one. Kids in his class were afraid of the dark, even if they talked big like their hearts didn't skip a beat when their parents clicked off the light. Anyone could talk tough when the sun was still out. Once it fell, well, that was another matter. Joshua remembered when his friend Kenny Gilbertie had a sleepover for his birthday. He had invited five friends over including Joshua. When it was time to go to sleep and Kenny's father turned off the light, the six of them instinctively huddled close together in their sleeping bags fighting to be the one in the center, and therefore, better protected. No one talked like a tough guy that night. None of them got much sleep either. The bragging and trash talk returned the next day, but the kids had shared an intimate experience. Because a secret had passed between them, the boys would never call each other out for it in front of others. Even the way they looked at each other changed, especially when they were alone and could let down their guard.

The dark was a powerful thing largely because it couldn't be defined. It simply was. There was light and there was darkness. Middle ground did not exist between these extremes. There were also levels of dark, depending on where you were experiencing it. The dark in the city was different than in the suburbs. Shadows ran longer and corners were more easily saturated. The darkness in the sticks took blackness to a whole new level.

In bed, Joshua struggled to stay awake. Sleeping in new places was often difficult. It usually took him a night or two to adjust to the unfamiliar surroundings. The running joke in the family was that by the time Joshua got used to new beds, the vacation was over.

This trip he was going to have plenty of time to get used to things. They were there a month – that translated into four weeks, or thirty-one days, or how many countless hours.

The time was there; the trust wasn't. That was earned little by little.

Joshua regarded the bright face of his Bugs Bunny night light. It was the color of orange soda burning powerfully in the surrounding darkness.

It was originally his father's when he was a boy. Jack bought some old Loony Tunes DVDs at a house sale and showed them to Joshua. The cartoons were unlike the ones that he watched today. The outdated artwork made the cartoon seem old, but there was something oddly compelling about the crazy duck and stuttering pig that made Joshua laugh. And the rabbit was infectious. Like most children his age, Joshua was drawn to a smart aleck persona, and Bugs Bunny had that in spades. Plus, he was smart. He always tricked his opponent. Joshua liked that. He tried to be clever like the rabbit.

The comfort of his night light helped ease the unfamiliarity of the new environment, but for Joshua to sleep soundly, he needed a deeper sense of security. Sleep in a new bed, was a different animal altogether.

The Noise didn't help matters.

To be fair, he didn't hear the Noise at first.

It was low and native, just one of the many sounds remote locations made. Insects made the most peculiar of sounds; ticking, chattering, and clicking non-stop. And because it seemed natural, it was easy to disregard it.

But when the Noise changed timbre, a chill flooded Joshua's veins.

The Noise assumed a more familiar sound. Later, Joshua would wonder if the Noise wasn't trying to communicate with him in a variety of echoes and reverberations until it found the one that Joshua could understand.

But at that moment, the Noise became a voice, a whisper at first, but one that became more distinct every time the breeze stirred the leaves outside so that they rustled and chattered in a language only that they understood. Only when it swept through the half-open window did Joshua recognize the sound of a child's voice. Young and clear, a boy probably around his age.

It said one word. His name.

"Joshua," the voice said, ushered in with the wind through the partially open window.

Eyes wide, Joshua bolted upright in bed. He looked around the room but saw no one.

"Hello?" he asked to the emptiness.

"Joshua, won't you play with me?"

Joshua scrambled to turn on the lamp on the night table, almost knocking it over. The light was low wattage and its frail brightness seemed to succumb to the encroaching darkness. Confident that he had carefully surveyed the room of any human that might have whispered his name, Joshua got out of bed and crept to the window, peering outside. The sky was covered in clouds, blanketing the stars. No natural light penetrated causing the forest line to be absorbed in a thick mud-like blackness.

He shut the window, turning around to get back into bed.

Joshua froze when he saw the bedroom closet open just enough to make his heart race and the blood thump loudly in his veins.

He knew nothing was inside the closet. He had checked before his father came in for his bedroom story, and it was closed then. Well, it looked closed. It was very possible that he had simply not made sure it had closed properly, listening for that click when the door was put in place.

Still.

Open was open. It didn't matter if it was an inch or a foot. It represented access, a point of infiltration.

And that meant that it needed to be checked out.

He walked slowly to the closet. Joshua suddenly felt the need to go to the bathroom. His bladder filled quickly when fear coursed through his body.

His hand raised and trembled slightly when it touched the doorknob.

God, he needed to piss.

Joshua held his breath, steeling himself in the dimly lit room. He flung the door open to find only his clothes hanging from the rod and his suitcase and bags on the floor.

He shut the door immediately, waiting to make sure the door didn't pop loose.

When he was confident that he had done it right this time, Joshua jumped into bed. He was going to hold it as long as he could. He didn't want to leave only to come back and repeat the same steps.

Joshua pulled the sheets up over his head. If he had taken the moments to catch his breath, he would have seen the night light start to flicker, teetering on the edge of going out and staying connected.

# Chapter 5

The next morning gray storm skies gathered in the early hours and had entrenched themselves by the time the light of dawn had formed and begun its morning ascent. Rain threatened until it could not hold back its formidable presence any longer. By the time Joshua had finished his breakfast and was ready to go out and do some fishing, the sky had opened up and a steady pour ensued.

Rainy days in a cabin by a scenic lake were very similar to rain in the city. In addition to throwing the proverbial monkey wrench into any outside plans, if the storm was substantial enough, it impacted indoor activities as well. The cabin's advanced wiring and recent equipment, while a modern amenity, was also susceptible to outside forces. Subsequently, any heavy rain put a kibosh on watching TV. Reception was spotty during conditions like this, and even the wireless Internet connectivity dropped intermittently or was stuck in a constant state of buffering.

The brochure boasted of getting back to rural living. There was nothing like nature to ensure that guests enjoy that experience on some level, whether it was embraced by them or forced on them.

Joshua rummaged through a slim selection of DVDs. Finding an extremely worn copy of an old Disney movie, he inserted it into the player. The machine made a whirring noise. When an image finally came up on screen, it immediately froze, then skipped, then froze again.

"Dad!" Joshua said.

Jack came into the living room. He was still working out the kinks of a divided night between sleeping on the couch and the floor.

"What's the problem, sport?"

"The DVD won't work."

Jack stretched out his back. Once he heard the "crick" he went over and inspected the machine. He was about as technical as his son, but his role and title of Dad didn't allow him to be anything short of an expert in just about every field. He made a show of pushing some buttons, ejecting the disc, cleaning the disc with his shirt tail, reinserted the disc, and fiddling with various settings before tossing the remote back on the couch.

"DVD won't work," he said, repeating his son's words, providing his final report. "How about we play a game? There's got to be something around here. A deck of cards maybe?"

"Did you bring my Nintendo Switch?" Joshua was hopeful.

"Sorry, sport. You spend enough time on that thing. Your mother thinks so. And to be honest with you, so do I. We're out in the country. We're here to get some fresh air into our lungs."

Joshua turned to the window. Rain thundered down.

"It's raining."

"Well, you know…"

Jack walked into the kitchen as Anne poured a cup of coffee. She took it to the table and watched the rain.

"Thank you," she said.

Jack retrieved a white ceramic mug from the cabinet above the sink and got some coffee.

"For what?" he asked.

"For backing me on the Nintendo. You didn't have to, but you did and I'm grateful."

Jack shrugged. "I agree with you."

He pulled up a seat across from her. "He plays too many video games," he said. "When I was his age, I was always outside."

"You didn't have video games," Anne countered.

"Um, Atari ring a bell? Intellivision?"

"Wow," she said. "You just dated yourself."

"Pinball was my real game."

"That doesn't make it better."

Jack gave a small smile. He watched the rain. It came down straight. The drops looked big and sloppy. "It is nice out here. I don't know if I could live here full time or anything, but it is nice, I'll give you that."

"You sleep okay last night? I hoped you would make it to bed."

Jack couldn't look at her. "I'm not ready," he said.

"When will you be?" It was more of a plea than a sincere question.

"I don't know," he said honestly. "Let's just take it one day at a time, okay?"

He knew it wasn't the answer she wanted to hear, but it was one that held a kernel of promise.

"That's all I'm asking for," she said sincerely.

Jack got up and walked to the sliding door that led to the porch. He looked up at the sky. It was one solid sheet of gray that showed no sign of breaking. He set his mug on the kitchen counter and returned to the living room to look for Joshua, but the boy wasn't there.

***

Joshua paused in the doorway of his bedroom. He had tried not to think about what had happened the previous night. He practically ran out of the room once he woke up, throwing himself into the morning routine – going to the bathroom, brushing teeth, getting dressed. He thought about telling his mother when they were in the kitchen but decided against it. Even at his age, he knew that telling adults a story like that – any adult including your parents – especially your parents – would not be taken seriously. They would pretend to show concern, even try to say the right things, but in the end, the belief just wouldn't be there.

The room looked unremarkable in the light of day. Even under a gray sky, enough light streamed through the window to keep him at ease. The Bugs Bunny night light, the ultimate test, didn't even register the dark. No, all was clear. For now.

Joshua opened the closet door and found the bag that held his books and toys. It was a product of his own invention, something he called his "survival kit." Anything longer than an overnight stay required the kit to accompany him.

Inside the red and yellow bag, Joshua rummaged until he found what he was looking for – an old Gameboy. It was an outdated portable video game console to be sure, but he had traded for it with a friend on his soccer team who was more interested in Joshua's Pokemon cards than archaic technology.

The Gameboy was gray and square and bland, and the graphics weren't terribly impressive.

Compared to his Nintendo Switch, it was like the difference between writing on a computer and writing on a chalkboard.

But it was a video game, and any video game was better than no video game. That's why he had made this private transaction – in case of emergency – and this was nothing if not an emergency.

He tucked the Gameboy under his shirt and left his bedroom, closing the door behind him. Joshua paused before heading down the stairs. He returned and opened the door – wide. Feeling better about that decision, the boy headed down to the main floor.

***

Fortunately, his parents were nowhere to be seen when Joshua got down the stairs. He heard his mother in the kitchen putting dishes into the sink, and his father was in the bathroom, judging from the light under the closed door. Joshua made his way to the front door and opened it. The rain had finally passed, intermittent drops falling. The sky revealed the gray clouds moving past. The sun was making its presence known.

"I'm headed outside," Joshua said to anyone who was listening.

"Can't you wait until your father's out of the bathroom?" his mother called back from the kitchen.

"I'm just going out front," Joshua said. Then he paused. "Don't worry. I'm not going into the woods."

"Let him go, Anne!" his father called out from the bathroom. "Stay in the driveway, Josh! Once I'm done here, I'll meet you and we'll see if we can nab some fish."

Joshua didn't wait for his parents to finish their debate. He bolted out the door and down the front steps.

The driveway was well soaked. There were puddles where there were potholes, and anything that was once dirt was now full-fledged mud. Joshua walked over the gravel driveway looking at the tree line that sagged under the weight of damp limbs and leaves.

Joshua wiped down the door of his parents' car with his hand and then removed his Gameboy. He leaned against it as he played the game – something called Double Dragon. It didn't come with directions, so Joshua was learning as he went, finding the right combination of button presses to deliver a series of punches, kicks, and flips.

For whatever reason, Joshua paused mid-play and looked at the strange tree limb that reached out over the driveway. It unnerved him how much the branches limbs looked like the frail withered digits of a witch. With one arm, he mimicked how it looked, reaching out and making his fingers curl and jut out just like the limb. It was an odd tree, one that he couldn't readily identify despite what had learned at Forest School earlier that summer. Granted, the school was more of a day camp, his father's attempt to show him a different life outside suburban monotony. Jack grew up in a suburb and had attended summer camp in Maine when he was Joshua's age. He'd tell Joshua all the things he learned there – shooting a rifle, how to skipper a sailboat, how to start a campfire without matches – all this fun stuff that kids who didn't live in high-rise apartment buildings did. The Forest School provided a different education, that's what his father said. It got him away from the sterility of civilization.

Joshua hated to admit it to himself, but he liked the Forest School. They gave the kids a chance to explore on their own, which was a welcome reprieve from constant supervision. The teachers did a good job balancing structured instruction with ample free time to let the kids be, well, just kids. In the meantime, he learned some interesting things like how forests covered 4 billion hectares (a cool term that measured land) of the Earth's surface and how 70 percent of the world's animals depended on forests for their homes.

The sway of the trees had a meditative quality about them. Back and forth. Back and forth. They moved in subtle harmony.

All except that one jawed limb. That remained fixed in place, straining to grasp something Joshua couldn't quite see or understand.

***

Jack exited the mud room with his fishing vest and tackle box. He saw Anne standing at the front door with a mug of coffee in her hand. Something had caught her attention, and she was standing with a puzzled expression on her face.

"What are you looking at?" he asked.

"Joshua," she said.

"Why, what's he doing?"

"I don't know… Looking."

"Looking?" he asked. "Looking at what?"

She turned to her husband. "As far as I can tell? The woods."

Jack went over and stood beside his wife. Their shoulders barely touched.

"Huh. That's the second time he's done that," he said.

"What do you mean?"

"Nothing. The other day I saw him staring into the woods is all."

"Staring? Why?"

"I don't know. I didn't see anything. Maybe he saw a squirrel or something. You know kids. Things easily distract them. I'm sure it's nothing."

Anne frowned. The answer seemed trite but then gain what interested ten-year-old boys and what interested her was not the same thing.

"I'm worried about him, Jack."

"He's processing a lot of stuff. We all are. But kids are more resilient than we give them credit for. He'll get through it."

"I hope he does. I hope we all do."

Jack didn't immediately respond. "Let me get him and go fishing. We'll have a talk."

***

They paddled to the deepest part of their side of the lake, a depth Jack estimated to be 60-70 feet. Jack used to fish a lot with his father, but since getting married and moving to suburbia, his fishing trips were regulated to one or two times a year. Lake fishing didn't require a lot of equipment as much as the right equipment. Typically, Jack liked to use a pole with a 10-12lb test line with a size 2 circle hook, especially if he was going after catfish or bass. A foot leader was usually enough to get the job done. Worms and rooster tail lures were perfect for catfish, crank bait for bass.

He had read that lake trout were the predominant catch in Crescent Lake and was able to adjust his fishing repertoire accordingly. He had purchased two light-action rods with 4-6lb test lines. Jack didn't know if a live bait shop would be close to the cabin and opted to buy a couple of spinners with weightless lures, just in case. Since the best lures were ones that closely replicated the individual food preferences of the trout, a Spring Frog flatfish lure was what the online experts said.

Father and son dropped their lines, gradually jiggling them to mimic the actions of a wounded baitfish. Jack instructed Joshua to watch the line carefully; lake trout had a habit of slowly swimming away after they inspected, and in some instances, sampled what you were offering. That's why patience was essential to catching trout. That's what an over exuberant boy needed to learn. So, they repeated the process – casting, jiggling, reeling, and recasting.

"How are you doing, sport?" Jack asked. He was careful to abide by the unwritten rules of fishing: talking was allowable; eye contact was not.

"Haven't gotten a bite," Joshua said. He had only fished a few times with his father and was trying to regain the rhythm of the act that fishing dictated for success.

"I don't mean that. You getting used to being out here yet?"

Joshua made an unintelligible sound.

"What's that?"

"Nothing," Joshua said. "It's okay, I guess."

"The camp I went to when I was your age was a lot like this."

"I know. You said that."

"Well, it was. And if I'm being honest, as much as I wouldn't have thought so, your mother did a good job picking this place," Jack said. He let the compliment sink in a bit before he continued. "You know, we never really talked about what you saw that night with mom. I mean, talked like two regular guys, not father and son."

"Okay," Joshua said. Jack could tell from his son's expression that the boy wasn't picking up what he was trying to put down.

"How'd you feel about what you saw?"

Joshua didn't say anything for a while. He frowned as he worked something over in his mind. Jack was about to prompt him when the boy finally something into words.

"I never saw that before," he said finally. "Kissing like that. I don't know. It was weird."

"You've seen mom and I kiss," Jack offered. "It's not that weird."

"Not like that. It was like they were eating each other's faces. It was gross."

Jack's stomach jerked. "Well, it was a one-time thing. Grown-ups sometimes do gross things. Kind of like you."

This prompted Josh to turn and look at his father. "What?"

"Your smells, your sounds, you're just, I don't know, totally ewwww…" Jack teased. Joshua smiled and giggled a little. "When did you get so much gas?"

Joshua laughed out loud, and for a moment, father and son bridged any lost territory that had separated them since Anne's indiscretion.

"Sport, can I ask you a question?"

"Sure."

"What were you looking at?"

For the second time, Joshua turned around to face his father. "When?"

"This morning. Your mother and I saw you looking into the woods. Did you see an animal or something?"

"No. I was just looking at the trees."

This provided Jack some relief, but it also piqued his curiosity. "Any particular reason?"

Joshua shrugged. "They were moving. Well, one wasn't. You know the one I'm talking about. That looks like a woman's hand."

Jack didn't know what Joshua was talking about, but merely nodded his head. Before he could ask a follow-up question, Joshua's line pulled. His face registered the turn of events.

"Dad!"

There was nothing Jack could do from his position in the canoe. Going to the front risked knocking his son into the water or distracting him enough to lose the fish on the line.

"Stand up, Joshua," he directed his son. "Lift the rod high."

Joshua complied with his father's instructions.

"Jerk the rod!  Jerk the rod! You want to make sure that sucker's hooked!"

Joshua jerked the rod. The movement was awkward for the boy. The rod was already too big for his son's size and the strength of a trapped fish was a surprise for anyone the first time they experienced it. Jack could tell from Joshua's eyes that the fish was hooked.

"You got him, Josh, don't let him get away. Let him run a bit. Use your drag. You want to tire that sucker  out."

Joshua concentrated on reeling the fish in. It was a struggle, but he kept after the fish. He'd dig in and work the reel, playing the game. Jack watched his son. He was doing well.

"Stay with it, Josh."

The boy did. The struggle lasted nearly thirty minutes but, in the end, he watched Joshua reel in a 20 incher. At that point, Jack was able to make his way to the middle of the canoe and catch the fish in a net.

His son's eyes blazed with the success born out of his own sweat and determination.

"That's a monster!" he said, breathlessly.

Jack hefted it in the net as the trout flopped about. "Heavy too. Three pounds I figure."

"Can we eat it?"

"Definitely. Now let's catch another so everyone can."

***

There was nothing like eating the very fish you caught four hours earlier. It simply didn't get fresher than that. Jack showed Joshua how to properly gut and fillet a fish. He first took one of the fish in hand and used a sharp folding knife to slice the fish from anus to front. The second incision was right below the jaw line to separate the tongue from the jaw. Then Jack held the upper and lower jaw with two fingers, and gripping the tongue, pulled down hard enough to rip out the gills. Since the intestines were attached to the gills, the further he pulled down, the more the innards were released. Joshua watched intensely as the guts came out in one piece. Jack used his thumb to push the remaining blood "stuff" out of the hallowed carcass. What was left was to rinse it out completely. The filleting was more surgical than anything else requiring use of a thin-bladed extremely sharp knife. Jack sliced down neck gill until he hit the spine and simply sliced down to the tail, surgically removing a pristine panel of meat. *Voila.*

Anne prepared the fillets simply with garlic lemon butter and herb sauce and some one-minute rice and steamed broccoli. The men ate hungrily, polishing off their plates and asking for seconds on everything. Joshua saw his mother smiling with pride. He knew she took great pleasure in having people enjoy what she prepared, but even he knew that she got extreme satisfaction when she saw her family eat. His mother was more receptive to nonverbal accolades. The proof was always in the pudding, to use an expression of hers.

Joshua regaled them talking about the fish he caught. In true fisherman style, the fish was bigger, the fight was longer, the struggle, more grueling. He made it known to his mother that he and he alone reeled in the larger of the fish they caught that day, and he did it without help. Jack corroborated his son's statements, rubbing his hair.

For the first dinner in a while, things seemed normal again. The conversation was natural, the laughter unforced. There was even a moment when

Jack instinctively reached out for Anne's hand on the table, placing his palm over her it and patting it affectionately.

Joshua didn't even need dessert. The dinner was that good, the day was that long, and he was that tired that he wanted nothing more than to go upstairs and get into bed.

Jack took him upstairs and tucked him in.

Joshua lay in bed staring up at the ceiling. His mind did not once think about the woods or the strange boy's voice he had heard the night before.

Had he imagined it? Maybe. He certainly did not hear it now.

His thoughts were reliving the moment he felt the fishing pole pull when the trout took the hook, and the loud whirring sound the line in the reel made when the fish tried to get away.

Most of all, he thought about how good dinner went. How his mother and father were like themselves again.

For the first time since they had arrived, Joshua thought the vacation actually might be a good idea. It forced them to be with each other, to see each other, to listen to each other.

To be a family again.

The boy fell asleep with that sappy thought in mind. He was so content that he didn't even notice

Bugs Bunny's face flickering like a warning that something was terribly wrong.

# Chapter 6

The next day wasn't as successful. If Jack thought the day before showed the promise of what two steps forward could be, today was the result of three steps back.

Jack showered and dressed and searched for his phone. When he couldn't find it, he saw Anne's phone on the kitchen counter. He thought calling his phone would be his best bet to find where he had misplaced it.

The first thing he saw when the black screen cleared were three text notifications from Selznick. He didn't have to get into the text application to read what the adulterer had typed:

*Where are you?*
*Is everything okay?*
*Call me. Please.*

There may have been more. That's all he saw, all he could stand to see, but it was enough. Jack's stomach dropped. His pulse throbbed in his heads. His blood pressure immediately escalated. Like a fuel injected car, the blood shot through his veins. He felt his face grow hot. He felt dizzy.

She said it was a kiss. This said it was more.

He didn't hear Anne come down the stairs or even enter the kitchen.

"You're up," she said as she went over to the coffee maker. She replenished the water and scooped coffee into the filter. "You want some eggs and toast?"

When he didn't respond, she turned toward him. "Jack?" she said.

Jack looked up and showed her the phone.

"I didn't mean to look at your phone, "he explained. "I was trying to find mine by calling it," he said.

"What is it?"

"I wasn't snooping. I swear to God, I wasn't."

"Jack…," Anne said. She didn't seem to understand. But then her face suddenly changed when her worst fears were realized. "Jack, let me explain. He's worried you're taking everything out of context."

"There's nothing to explain. It's my own fault, really."

"I told him not to contact me, Jack. I swear to you I did. He's worried. He's our neighbor. He's our friend."

Jack set the phone on the table and left the room. She may have said something else, but he didn't hear her. He found his phone in between the sofa cushions and looked for someplace to escape to. Like a cornered rat, his eyes darted in various directions looking for options.

He saw the cellar door. He hadn't been down there since they arrived and now was as good a time as any to see what was down there.

Anne called out to him one more time from the kitchen. Jack opened the door and went down the stairs.

***

Joshua found his mother on the back porch, drinking coffee. Her cell phone buzzed on the outside table, but she didn't pick it up. There was a distant look in her eyes. She may have been physically sitting in front of him, but even the ten-year-old could see that her mind was somewhere else, far away from the idyllic views of a lake in the middle of nowhere.

"Mom?"

She was slow to acknowledge him. When she did, he could tell that something had happened in the hours between when he went to bed and right now.

"Yes, honey?"

"Everything okay?"

"I'm fine," she said. "I'm great. Everything's great."

Her tone was too measured and calm to be reassuring. It wasn't genuine, and therefore, it wasn't real. Her phone buzzed again, and for a second time, she did not pick up the phone. He looked at her questioningly.

"Mom? Your phone."

"It's okay, honey. It's nothing important."

Another buzz. She picked it up this time, glanced at the notification, and turned off her phone. When she saw Joshua watching her, she tried to explain.

"It's Mr. Selznick. He has questions. We all have questions."

He didn't understand what she meant but she didn't elaborate, and he wasn't going to ask her for any further clarification. Joshua turned to leave but asked her before he went inside.

"Have you seen Dad?"

"Too many questions, darling," she said, shaking her head. "Too many questions."

***

The basement was larger than Jack had expected. Semi-furnished, more than half of the ample space was naked cement and unfinished with exposed beams and insulation. A little less had a large dirty throw rug on the ground and two musty winged-back chairs. Three sets of shelves held a variety of books and games and knick-knacks that get regulated to dark spaces when there isn't a clear place for them.

Jack wanted a cigarette badly. He had quit when Joshua got to be the age when he could recognize what his parents did. Anne couldn't make the full commitment, but she had done well in sneaking cigarettes when Joshua wasn't around. In order to prevent their son from mimicking his father's actions or later assuming a bad habit, Jack had quit cold turkey. It was tough going, but Jack would be damned if he was going to use a crutch to get him over the hump. He didn't believe in nicotine gum or the patch or any pill designed to curb impulse. If he was going to beat the habit, it would have to be with guts and determination. During those first few weeks, Jack smelled his fingers constantly. Nicotine was set firmly in the digits that held his cigarettes while he smoked. He relished those smells in the beginning. It was a way that he could still partake without crossing any set lines or boundaries.

After the series of twos passed (two hours, two days, two weeks, two months), the desire to ingest tobacco waned, and finally went away altogether. Since that time, he relapsed only twice and only for a single cigarette in each instance. The first one he didn't enjoy at all. He had it at a Super Bowl party about a year after he officially quit. It hurt his throat and didn't taste good at all. The second one he had after he got promoted, and he and buddy went out to the work smoking pit to celebrate. That one went down better, a reminder that such habits could be quickly reacquired under the right circumstances.

There were five boxes of light bulbs in the corner. They represented different sizes and shapes, each box housing a larger, more powerful wattage.

Jack quickly inspected the shelves. The books were random and covered a variety of subjects and genres. There were quite a few romance novels, a couple of westerns, and some legal and serial killer thrillers. All were far from current. Most were severely creased, and some had their paperback covers falling off. Jack didn't know if these were the literary preferences of the cabin's owners, or if they were contributions from people that had been guests who didn't like what they found and wanted to leave something else for the next visitors.

The games didn't offer much better options. Board games consisted of *Sorry!*, *Monopoly*, *Payday*, *Life*, and of course, *Clue*. There were a few card games like *Uno* and *Old Maid*, and a board that could be used both as chess/checkerboard, and if you flipped it, a backgammon board. Whether all the pieces were there for them was up for debate.

Jack was about to leave the basement when he saw a lump under the *Monopoly* game. He leaned over and pulled the game off revealing a leather-bound journal book. It had dust on the parts not covered by the game and bore the faint but unmistakable smell of mildew. He took it out and flipped through the pages quickly. Handwriting scrawl in different colored inks flashed by. He flipped to the first page that featured one word written in a manic style with large letters in heavy black ink that was underlined several times.

DARK.

***

Joshua wasn't a proficient soccer player. He liked the game, and he was athletic enough to be just good enough at it. But this past spring, the players on his rec team had gotten noticeably better, and Joshua was nothing if he wasn't competitive. His dad agreed to sending him to soccer camp after they got back from the cabin. For now, he practiced on his own, doing a series of exercises that his dad had down-loaded from the Internet, mostly little ball tricks and juggling and drills to improve his touch.

He took the ball he had brought and went outside to the front where the land was flatter. The backyard sloped too much to the lake and didn't replicate the true playing conditions of a real soccer field. It was late afternoon; the sun was well into its descent and the day's humidity was lessening with the approach of dusk.

Joshua warmed up with toe-touches and knocking the ball back and forth with the insides of his feet, something the coach in the video called "making popcorn." He found some sticks and made a makeshift obstacle course six feet long with three piles of sticks set at two feet intervals. Joshua dribbled the ball slowly at first working his way up and down, gradually picking up speed every time he completed a pass without losing control of the ball or hitting a stick pile.

After twenty minutes, he had worked up a sweat and took a much-needed water break. He purposefully avoided looking at the weird claw-hand tree limb, and instead stared at the woods as he drank. The tree line seemed different, as crazy as that sounded. Closer somehow. Joshua knew that if not tended, nature will reclaim the land. But that took a lot of time. No, it was probably just the way the pines and white birch looked at this hour. Plus, he was closer now and the large trunks loomed large, hovering over him, their limbs outstretched and awake.

He set the water bottle down and picked up the ball and started to juggle on his thighs when something or someone called out to him.

*Joshua...*

The boy looked around. The ball ricocheted off his thigh and bounced toward the woods.

Did someone just call his name?

"Dad?" he said. "Mom?"

No answer. Joshua started for his ball.

*Joshua... Let's play...*

The boy froze, dead in his tracks.

The Noise. It was back again.

Joshua took a tentative step forward. His ball was right at the edge where forest met grass.

*Let's play...*

It was clear this time. It wasn't the wind, and it wasn't the leaves rustling in the trees.

It was a voice. A child's voice. A boy's voice, no older than Joshua.

"Hello?" Joshua called out to the forest. "Is someone in there?" He peered inside the thick under-brush looking for a face to match the voice but couldn't make out anything but the thickly inter-twined brambles. The branches of a nearby birch rus-tled happily.

*Joshua...* the voice said again, and then gig-gled.

"Where are you?" he asked.

No answer. Joshua looked up at the sky. It had grown suddenly darker over the past half-hour.

The branches rustled again, taunting him.

*Come find out...*

***

Anne found Jack in the living room watching a ball game on the television. She didn't say any-thing, hoping he'd acknowledge her first. When he didn't, she knocked on the doorway.

"Have you seen, Joshua?" she asked. She tried to hide her concern, but as recent events had shown, she wasn't good at hiding things.

Jack didn't look up from the game and shrugged.

"He was out front last time I looked kicking around the soccer ball," he said.

"You didn't want to play with him?"

Jack made a face. "The game…," he said.

"What time did you see him exactly?" she asked, annoyed.

Jack muted the television. "Why the third degree, Anne? The kid's playing, let him play."

"He's not there, Jack. That's why I'm asking."

Jack looked up now. "What are you talking about?" He went to the window that outlooked the driveway. Joshua was nowhere to be seen. Anne stood beside him. She released an audible gasp when all that she saw was her son's soccer ball by the tree line.

"Jack," she said.

She didn't need to say another word. Jack's long legs strode to the front door.

"Let's go," he said.

***

Twigs and dried dead leaves crunched beneath Joshua's feet as he walked deeper into the forest. It got denser the deeper he got. Branches from bushes and vines frequently snagged his shirt, trying to keep him from going farther, or else trying to hold him in place.

Joshua had followed the Noise (or was Voice a better name at this point, Joshua wondered?) into the forest. But since then, the calls had gotten softer and seemed farther away. The deeper he went, the less he could make out from where the boy was calling out to him. Whoever this kid was, he liked playing games.

When Joshua realized that he hadn't heard the boy's voice for a few minutes, he stopped walking to gain his bearings. An ice ball started to form in the pit of his stomach as he looked around and realized that he was lost. He hadn't thought he had gone so far from the edge of the driveway, but every direction was a mirror of the one he had just seen.

"Hello?" he said, trying not to sound afraid. "Are you there?"

There was no answer. In fact, there was no sound. Not a bird. Not a chirp. Not a weird insect noise. It was quiet as a graveyard. That's what his mother said when things were too quiet for her taste. Quiet as a crypt. Quiet for the dead.

Panic grew in the boy. It flooded down his neck and across his shoulders.

Before it subsumed him, the Noise spoke again.

*Where are you?...*

"Where are you?" Joshua said, his voice breaking. He heard a rustle in front of him and saw movement of some bushes.

The unseen boy giggled again. It seemed to say, Tag, you're it.

Joshua pushed forward, not noticing the farther he got, the darker it became. Any light from the sky was blocked under thick canopies of trees, forming an intricate interwoven tapestry of foliage.

***

Jack and Anne looked all around outside the cabin, calling out their son's name. Finally, the two parents met at the front of the house when the search of the immediate area did not turn up their son. Concern quickly gave way to worry.

"What did I tell you, Jack?"

"Joshua! Come here! I'm serious! No games!" he called out in desperation, knowing fullwell it was no better than a Hail Mary. The lush vegetation around him absorbing the loud, baritone voice.

They waited a few moments but were only met with silence.

"I'm scared," Anne said.

Jack looked up at the sky. Light was at a premium.

"Get two flashlights. Hurry, Anne!" he directed his wife. She sprinted inside the house.

***

Joshua knew he was on the right path when the sound of the boy's laughter seemed closer. He hadn't yet seen the owner of the voice. He was elusive, always one step ahead like a rabbit disappearing before the fox catches sight of him. But the voice drew Joshua, and the more he heard it, the less afraid he became. Joshua was going to give that kid a piece of his mind when he found him. Then they would set up a play date.

Joshua paused to realign himself. Everything seemed to shift slightly. The trees, the bushes, the branches. And in that shift, the forest suddenly became new again, all familiarity vanished.

The giggling permeated through the dense folds.

It was an odd contrast to the dark that loomed heavy in the heart of the forest. Without the laugher, this would be the scariest place on earth, his worst nightmare. The shadows were more threatening; they were longer, scarier, darker.

But the laughter, a boy's laughter, made it more manageable somehow.

He was someone like Joshua. A boy in the forest.

A boy looking for someone to play with.

A friend.

*Closer, Joshua… closer…* the Voice called out to him.

And because of this, Joshua pressed on.

***

Jack ignored the wild blackberry brambles and the sharp prickers that drew blood in long streaks across his legs. He moved with purpose, and therefore, ignored anything that wasn't directly related to the focus of his search. He turned on the flashlight waving it around as he called out for his son.

"Joshua! Where are you? Joshua!"

Anne followed her husband's lead, shouting out for her lost son in between her husband's monolithic shouts. Together they sounded like an unharmonized a capella duo.

As they continued, Anne couldn't help but think how it felt that the deeper they got, the more it seemed that the forest was ingesting them. It was an odd sensation to be sure but one that she couldn't shake free. The fuzzy green throat of the forest was swallowing them up whole, gulp by gulp.

"Joshua!" she yelled, shaking herself free from that horrible visual. If she was this worried, she can only imagine how scared her son was.

No one liked the dark. But Joshua was absolutely terrified by it.

And if she was being honest with herself, now she was as well.

***

Even with limited light to aid general visibility, Joshua saw the shoe. It  poked out from underneath a fallen branch. It was as if the shoe wanted to be found, but not in any forthright way. Just enough of it was exposed. It was a teaser, a lure. And Joshua bit. He reached out for it and pulled back the branch.

It was a child's shoe, a sneaker to be exact, white with a blue zig-zag on the outside. Two initials – "MR" – were written in black marker along the heel. It was an odd find. There was nothing else lost or discarded, no other odd stray piece of clothing or food wrapper or random object in testimony of another person's presence here at one time.

People lost things all the time in the woods. Joshua remembered that from the Forest School. His group found some crazy, inexplicable things on their weekend jaunts. Mostly old water bottles and a few beer cans. There was even a license plate of all things. A plate and no car. Go figure.

But something about the shoe felt strange. A lone shoe seemed... abandoned. Vulnerable. Why wasn't there a match to go with it? And more importantly, where was it?

Whose was it?

If he had found the sneaker down at the lake, the discovery could be rationally explained. But out in the middle of the dense forest, well, that raised a whole set of different questions. Uneasy questions.

He turned the sneaker over in his hand. It was approximately the same size as Joshua wore. And in recognizing this fact, Joshua shivered.

Why would a boy leave the shoe here?

Where was the boy?

Joshua's heart raced. It was all too strange. His breathing picked up. The panic had returned. Joshua started to feel lightheaded. Fear was such an injection to the bloodstream.

*A little farther, Joshua...* the Voice beckoned.

*A little farther...*

For a dense forest that offered no easy passage, up ahead seemed suddenly to part enough to provide a path that led to what he could only guess was a clearing of sorts.

*A little farther...* the boy begged.

Joshua did not move. He didn't want to go any farther. He didn't know where he was. He didn't know how he was going to get back. So, he did the only thing that a boy his age could do.

He screamed.

***

Jack and Anne froze in place when they heard it. It was a solitary scream and one that originated from fear rather than pain. When you raised a child from infancy, you recognized the distinct nuances in their cries. They knew Joshua wasn't hurt; he was scared. And for that, they were thankful. Judging from the sheer volume, he must have been some distance away, maybe a hundred yards. But they both heard it. Their son was out there and still alive. Nothing else mattered.

They moved quickly, fueled by adrenaline, and didn't bother using the ineffective flashlights to guide them, letting the sound of Joshua's voice dictate their path.

"Joshua! Joshua!" they yelled.

Anne tripped over a root and sprawled face-first across the uneven ground. When Jack paused to help her, she waved him on. A sprained ankle was immaterial. Their son needed them.

"Go! Go!" she commanded.

Jack didn't offer a rebuttal. He continued his mission. Anne found her feet and awkwardly limped in pursuit through the dense underbrush.

They weren't that far. They found him promptly after that.

The expanse of the forest was a deceptive trickster. What seemed close, turned out to be far, and vice versa. It was little wonder that people died in the woods when they were lost because they couldn't trust their senses. They couldn't trust their senses because they couldn't contain their fear.

Jack found Joshua where the boy had found the shoe. He was crying and clutching onto the white sneaker like a life preserver. When he turned and saw his parents, Joshua sprinted for them. Even though Anne knelt first with her arms open for him, Joshua bypassed her for Jack, nearly knocking him over. He needed a symbol of protection, a knight, a father.

"Take it easy, sport. I'm here, I'm here," he said, holding him close and stroking the boy's hair.

Anne turned from him. Her flush of embarrassment would have been more apparent if the darkness didn't conceal it. Jack knew she was embarrassed, even angry that their son had reached for him first and not her, but what could he do? If Joshua had caught him in a lip-lock with a neighbor, maybe the roles would be reversed.

"Give your mother a hug," he told his son. "You had her out of her mind."

Joshua wiped his eyes and went to her mother and gave her a tight hug. She nuzzled his neck, but her eyes were looking straight at her husband. Even in the dark he could feel their heat burning holes into his head.

"You okay? You're not hurt, are you?" she asked Joshua. The boy didn't respond, shaking his head in response.

Jack walked over to them. "You gave us a good start, sport," Jack said, kneeling and holding him and his wife in his hands. "I swear the left side of my head is covered in gray hair."

Joshua tried to speak but couldn't muster words. What came out was an expulsion of fear and relief and sadness and every other emotion under the sun.

"Everything's fine," Anne said. "We're all good now."

They waited until Joshua's breath normalized before they started to head back. That's when Jack noticed the shoe in his son's hand.

"What do you have there, sport?" he asked.

Joshua looked at the shoe he still clutched in his hand.

"I found it over there," Joshua said, pointing to the spot near the entrance to the clearing.

"A sneaker. That's odd. Who lost a sneaker out here?" Jack wondered aloud.

"Who cares?" Anne said. "Let's get back home."

"The city or the cabin?" Jack asked

Anne gave him a snide look. She turned her light into the forest and put her arm around her son guiding him back to from where they came.

Jack bit his lip, immediately regretting what he had said.

Sometimes he just wanted to avoid fights; other times he liked to start them.

***

Round two found Jack and Anne in their bedroom. Anne was relieved they found their son. That went without question. But part of her, a big part, did not like the fact that Joshua ran to her husband first. She was his mother, for Chrissakes. She gave birth to him, nurtured him, took care of him. She was always the first line of defense, the go-to parent whenever the boy was sick or hurt…

Or scared.

Jack came out of the bathroom. He had showered and was in his pajamas and Celtics t-shirt. His hair was still damp.

"Poor kid was terrified," he said, continuing the conversation they had had since they put Joshua to bed. "So, he went to me first. So what? I'm his dad. What's the problem?"

"Nothing. I'm fine," she said. There was more to it, but how could she punish her son for something like that? "I'm his mother is all."

"This wasn't a nightmare, Anne. The kid was lost in the forest. That's pretty damn scary for most adults. I can only imagine what it felt like for him. What did you expect?"

She shook her head. "You wouldn't understand," she said finally.

"I think I do. You don't like the fact that he chose me first. You have to ask yourself, Anne, why did he come to me first? I think that's what you should focus on. Not that he did it, but why."

"What's that supposed to mean?"

"It's what you think it means," he said.

"It was a shoe, not a Grizzly Bear," she said, trying to dodge the focus of the talk.

"In woods that big to a kid who's more comfortable in an Uber than on a bicycle? That's a lot."

She didn't like the way he said it. His voice was too smug and sanctimonious. Her voice dripped with venom.

"You're liking this too much, Jack. You're exacting punishment for no crime. Not a serious one, anyway. He kissed me. I let him. And then I pushed him away. We had too much to drink and were flirting too much. But in no way did anything more happen. I'm sorry it happened, but it happened. And nothing came from it, okay? End of story."

"If you say so."

"I didn't sleep with Dave Selznick. I don't love Dave Selznick," she said, then took a chance. "Talk to him, Jack. You'll hear the same thing coming out of his mouth. You'd know if he was lying."

Jack studied her face. She could feel his eyes penetrate hers and crawl inside her body.

"Selznick might not lie well," he said. "But Anne, you've got a face to bluff a winner-take-all pot."

"I'd take a lie detector if I could."

"What good would that do? You'd pass it."

"Because I'm innocent, Jack. Well, you know what I mean."

"Here's what I can't figure, Anne. You say you only kissed him."

"Joshua saw it, yes."

"But what about the other forty-five minutes?"

"What do you mean?"

"You left to get cigarettes, you said. You needed a ride, you said."

"That's right. That's why Dave needed to come with me. So, I didn't get a DUI. I don't understand what you're getting at."

"What I'm getting at, Anne, is the amount of time you were gone. You didn't bring, Joshua. There must have been a reason."

"Because he was playing with Stanley at the house. There wasn't a need. There were plenty of adults." Stanley was Dave Selznick's son who was a year younger than Joshua.

"Right. The rest of the neighbors were there. The Stewarts, the Ryans?"

"Yes, so?" She wasn't following his logic.

"You stop at 7-11 or Sherman's market, that's two miles tops. It's seven o'clock at night? Even with reasonable foot traffic, you're back in the house after smoking two butts in thirty minutes. That leaves me to ask, what did you do all that time?"

The implication was clear. Anne's face lost its confidence.

"There was traffic," she said weakly.

"Just a kiss, Anne?"

"I was drunk, Jack."

"That explains the tongue down your throat," he said. "What about before? Where was his tongue then, or shouldn't I guess?"

Anne's face smoldered.

"Go to hell, Jack," she said.

Jack thew up his arms. "Can't you tell? I'm already here."

***

Joshua couldn't sleep. After his father tucked him into bed, the boy went down quickly and soundly. He was that physically, mentally, and emotionally exhausted. The body needed to shut down and repair itself, and that's just what his body did. Once his head hit the pillow, it was lights out. He didn't even hear his father leave and didn't wait to confirm the night light was in place before surrendering to fatigue.

But the body's a resilient healer. After two hours, Joshua woke up. He wasn't refreshed as much as he was restless, his mind working over the events of the previous evening. Thinking about them now, they seemed to have transpired days ago rather than less than twenty-four hours. Time and distance had lessened the tightness of that fear that had gripped him and wouldn't let go. The previous night was not so much a memory as much as a point of time that had been officially recorded and marked.

One thing was clear – the boy was back.

At least his voice was. He had still not seen the mysterious boy, but there was no doubt in Joshua's mind that he was real, and he was out in the woods somewhere. Alone, definitely. Helpless, maybe. But still there.

It was possible that he had misinterpreted the sound the first night. There was so much new; so much going on that even Joshua had to admit that what he thought was a boy calling out to him was something else entirely.

But last evening solidified the boy's existence. The voice was clear and distinct and couldn't be written off as the wind or the trees or any other plausible natural alternative.

The boy was out there and knew Joshua's name.

What Joshua did not know was where the boy was, or if he lived nearby. He remembered his mother telling his father that the nearest house was a few miles away. He couldn't have wandered that far by himself, could he?

If he did, that would explain Joshua's discovery of the sneaker. If it wasn't the boy's, then whose could it be?

So many questions. The more he tried to answer one, newer ones emerged and remained unanswered.

And this got his head warm and his heart racing.

And he felt that grip tighten around his throat.

His bladder immediately filled, and he felt like he was going to pee the bed.

Joshua reached for the lamp on the table near his bed and turned it on. The bulb illuminated briefly, a dull light that barely shed an ochre glow before burning out, allowing the darkness to gather in deep folds in the corners of the room.

As he got out of bed, Joshua froze when he saw the orange Bugs Bunny night flickering like heat lightning. It was like it was fighting its own war against the blackness, winning and losing battles as it fought for supremacy. Every time it went out, it took longer to flicker back on.

Urine ran down Joshua's leg. He didn't even feel it puddle around his feet.

Joshua didn't look out the window. If he had, he might have seen that jawed tree limb waving menacingly over the driveway in the windless night. What's more, if he had seen it, he might have thought it was goading on the darkness to extinguish the night light once and for all. And then Joshua might have collapsed in mindless terror.

But he did not, and the night light finally caught and held the socket's electrical current. The face of the wascally wabbit burned a bright carrot orange. When working properly, it was a powerful light in a very small, very dark room.

Joshua took advantage of the victory and bolted out of the room, tearing down the hallway to his parent's bedroom. He didn't bother to close his window or shut the door, and because he had failed to do so, Joshua missed the subtle tittering of a ten-year-old boy giggle from somewhere near the forest's tree line.

# Chapter 7

Anne was never the kind of girl growing up that took chances. She always played it straight, going with the grain, and always in accordance with the rules. Even in elementary school she exuded a maturity far beyond her age. She never disrupted class, always abstained from passing notes to or for anyone, and if the teacher needed someone to hand out assignments or clean the chalkboard erasers, her hand was the first raised. In middle school, she would be called the "teacher's pet." This type of behavior ultimately earned her the nickname "Pristine Anne" in high school, a moniker well-deserved because she rarely dated, never missed a class or a day of school, and delivered homework on time and near perfection. If it weren't for her general likeability, Anne would have been ostracized by her classmates. The fact that she wasn't was testament to being able to connect with people. It was little surprise that she earned two superlatives in her graduation yearbook – Biggest Sweetheart and Most Likely to Rescue [Insert Animal of Your Choice].

College was a different animal altogether. A salutatorian, Anne had her choice of institutions of higher learning, having been accepted to five, including her first choice, and waitlisted on one. Contrary to her teachers and friends, she chose a state school instead of the liberal arts college in New England that was considered "Most Competitive," a classification usually reserved for Ivy League schools. At State, she didn't suffer the same fate as most expected kids who went away from home for the first time suffered. After getting the hang of college scholastic rigor after the first semester freshman year, Anne didn't receive a GPA lower than 3.7, and ultimately graduated with a 3.85 double majoring in Art History and Psychology.

But going to State was not about excelling in the classroom. She was confident that regardless of what college or university she attended she would excel when it came down to hitting the books. No, State to her was about experiencing a side that up until then, she had only heard about on Monday mornings from friends in high school that attended parties, and rallies, and beach gatherings. So, as much as she refused to ignore academics, she made a point to promise herself to embrace all things non-academic as well. And so, she played seasonal intramural sports, joined a sorority (Kappa Delta), lost her virginity to a boy; lost her inhibitions with a female sister; and learned how to drink SoCo and Tequila without any chasers.

Anne didn't sleep around often but slept around enough. She refused the temptation of one-night stands, even with those guys she thought "freaking hot." She maintained the illusion of commitment, dating men just long enough so that she could enjoy the physical pleasures of sex and explore boundaries she didn't know existed or where they were. In four years, she had five relationships (not including her sorority sister – that was her lone non-commitment indulgence) with guys she liked but knew she could never love. Some of her friends attended State solely in pursuit of their MRS degrees. Her sorority sisters were notorious for that. Some purposefully pledged the same sorority as their mothers just because that was how they had found their banker/lawyer/doctor future husbands, and usually in one of the fraternities on campus.

She met Jack right out of school when she worked as a paralegal in a corporate law firm. Cheryl, a sorority sister, set them up. Cheryl's brother and Jack went to school together and over one too many glasses of Pinot Grigio at happy hour, informed Anne that she had found her husband. At the time, Jack was teaching at an inner-city high school literature, a labor worthy of Hercules, she told him over their first date. He was intellectual and easy-on-the eyes, a combination most did not have, especially men. Jack wasn't an athlete, but he carried himself like one. His body was lean and muscular, the result she would find out later from outdoor activities and not sports. Love was quick and easy. Saying it was like a whirlwind seemed too Harlequin to her. But it was intense. After six months, they were married. Nine months later, they had Joshua and moved from a loft in the city to something more manageable in the suburbs. Jack got work at the community college, and Anne, well, Anne did part time work to help the household. It wasn't until Joshua was four that Jack encouraged her to find something permanent for herself, something that she enjoyed doing.

She dabbled but could not find anything that suited her, at least, not in the suburbs. Jack encouraged her to teach, to put that summa cum laude to good use. There was the community college and two high schools that would be lucky to have her.

She'd think about it. Jack tried one more time to gently prod her but when she didn't respond to the hints, he stopped, much to her relief.

In the beginning, Anne was genuinely happy to serve as the primary caregiver for Joshua. This freed up Jack to teach another class and serve as the faculty adviser to two clubs.

Watching Joshua grow was an interesting scientific experiment. Anne was fascinated as she objectively watched his development, curious to see how he learned, and how he applied such learning to his activities. What's more, it was all mommy all the time. There was little that Jack could do to satiate the boy's needs. While she felt bad for her husband, she privately enjoyed the attention.

But as he grew older and developed his personality and his own likes, the boy explored interests that did not jive with the things that she liked. By the time Joshua was four, she was taking him to soccer practice and climb parks and things that boys liked to do. When Joshua turned eight, she had had a lifetime of schlepping the boy to all sorts of academic and athletic practices, birthday parties, and playdates.

Then there were her son's night terrors. They didn't help matters any. They put a strain on the family, mostly because there was no foreseeable solution. Anne didn't need any more incentive to put space between her and the men in her life.

She didn't know what possessed her to go to that site online. She had heard two other mothers talking about it. Online personals were nothing new. But this site had all sorts of people looking for services, for used goods, for romance, for sex.

Sex with Jack had been good at first. Real good. But the old adage often joked about by comedians, couples, or anyone else who danced around the topic of commitment and fidelity was true; sex with the same person was flat-out boring, and not because

a partner wouldn't role play or use toys. Human be-
ings – and Anne believed this to be true – simply
wanted to fuck or be fucked by different partners.

Anne checked out the website mostly out of
curiosity at first. Maybe it was the psychological/be-
havioral aspect of the personals that attracted her.
Many of them titillated her even if the particular
"bent" wasn't her cup of tea. The website provided
an anonymous medium for people to expose their inner likes without fearing attribution or embarrassment. If you were into something that seemed –
weird – chances were that someone out there was
into it as well. Unsurprising, there were many more
posts in the "Man Searching for a Woman" link than
the "Woman Searching for a Man" (she read both to
see if and how they differed).

She perused the titles and read a few that interested her. She finally picked one, drafting and re-
drafting a response. The idea of meeting a stranger
for intercourse was still too foreign for her, an un-
touchable taboo. No, she wanted to experiment without making a firm commitment, to dip her toe in, so
to speak. She created a new e-mail account with a
fake name and sent it.

The man replied two hours later. She studied
the text, using her psych background to see if she
could tell how abnormal this man was. Nothing in his

words alarmed her; he seemed polite and straight forward to what he wanted for himself and her.

They went back and forth a couple of times, getting to know each other without providing too many details. If she was married chances were that he was too and it was best for both parties to respect the anonymity, use the fake names they had adopted, and just go for it when both felt comfortable to move in that direction.

Anne met him at a coffee shop on a Wednesday. Joshua was at school and Jack was teaching. The man – he had signed his e-mails "Bill" – had taken the day off from his own job.

She was super nervous sitting in the back room. She had ordered a latte but didn't feel like drinking it. Her heart jumped every time she saw someone come around the corner with a coffee looking for a place to squat.

He finally showed. He was taller than she imagined, with an average build. He was dressed in a blue collared shirt and khakis. His hair was short, recently cut, that was just beginning to gray at the temples. He wasn't handsome, but he wasn't ugly either. A regular general guy.

Bill was as nervous as she was. They shook hands and he sat down. They made small talk, covering a wide variety of topics that didn't link them to any specific place, person, or area that could be used to identify them. Finally, the time had come to put up or shut up. Did she want to come with him and do what he wanted to do?

They drove in separate cars to the back of a supermarket where deliveries were made. At this hour of the afternoon, no new shipments came, and the back was empty. She got out of her car and climbed into the passenger seat of his Buick.

"Go on," she said, trying not to sound too excited. "Show me."

Bill fumbled with this belt and undid his pants. He slid them down to his ankles and adjusted his seat to lean back a bit.

"Do it," she said. "I want to watch you."

"Tell me to jerk off," he said. The voice was husky. He was very turned on and his cock immediately got erect.

"Jerk off," she said. "I want to see you make it cum."

It didn't take long. Bill stared at her face as he went to town on himself. She alternated watching his face and watching his hand pump up and down. It was hot and he didn't last long, soon shooting the white fluid all over his hand and stomach.

Bill thanked her as he got himself together. He didn't even bother cleaning himself off.

She got back into her car and drove away. She didn't know if he had tried to contact her for a repeat performance because she immediately closed down the e-mail account.

That night she had sex with Jack, and it had been the most satisfying since they had been married.

The next incident happened about two months later. Again, she turned her attention to that website and scrolled through the wants, fantasies, and desires of men desperately seeking a kindred spirit for their kinks.

She settled on two possible ads – one from a man seeking a public thrill, the other looking for straight anonymous sex. She chose the former and they met at a motel two towns over. He was more forthcoming than Bill, said he was married and that his wife didn't like to explore the sexual paths he was dying to go down. The public thrill was simple. He left the blinds open on the first-floor room he had obtained while she gave him a handjob. If someone walked past and saw, so be it. It would add to the excitement, make his orgasm intense.

Anne felt like she had in college when it was all open to her. She knocked on room 7 and he let her in. He was her height with more of a paunch than Bill. She opened the blinds wide. The two-level motel was horseshoe-shaped with rooms facing the parking lot. Anne ordered him to undress in front of the window. He immediately complied. Anne asked if he wanted her naked or not. He readily accepted and she removed her clothing slowly, carefully folding what she took off and laying it on the table. He got immediately hard. She ordered him not to touch himself and to sit on the bed. She adjusted him accordingly on the edge of the bed, so he faced the window. She sat down beside him, fingers wrapping around him. She started in long even strokes. His pleasure was apparent in his face and the moans crumbling out of his mouth.

When he said he was getting close, she picked up speed and looked at the window. The sound of a maid's cart was just out of view. Anne tried to time it right and for a newbie at such acts, she hit a home run the first time at bat. The Hispanic maid pushed her cart, instinctively looking into the window. She was in her forties and plump. She did a double take when she saw them. Anne gave a lascivious smile as he made her new friend spurt. The maid was too shocked to do anything but watch the finale shoot high in the air and over Anne's hand.

While these tête-à-têtes served their purpose, they were ultimately unfulfilling. What she craved was sex with someone new. She couldn't remember what drew her to Dave Selznick other than his proximity next door, married, and otherwise unattainable. He was a year younger than Jack and worked as a personal trainer at the local gym where he taught cardio-aerobics to supplement training income. After seeing him a few times helping out various middle-aged women through a series of squats, cowbell lifts, and various planks, Anne decided to flirt and see where things took them. She was in good shape and had a good figure for someone who had just crossed the other side of thirty.

It was playful banter at first, the kind where friendly innuendo and off-the-cuff remarks planted seeds that could be interpreted in any way you wanted to take it and cultivated to bear forbidden fruit. Anne thought she could control the situation. Dave may have had a tight body, but his looks were average. He was married to Betty Grace, an older bleached blonde Hooters waitress with fake tits and Botox lips. She was positive that she could keep the affair casual, and most importantly, discreet.

And she was careful – at first. She made sure she left no digital or financial trail. No calls or texts were made to or from her phone. Cash was king, and when she left the house, credit cards were kept safely in the drawer in the kitchen island.

They met in areas far enough not to run into someone they might know, but close enough to avoid questions about mileage on the car and to respond to a call from Joshua's school. They had sex in each of their cars, at Dave's friend's place when he went out of town and asked Dave to feed his cat, and in a careless heat of desperate passion, the changing room of a low-end department store.

Discreet activities like this required a clandestine touch, and the most successfully clandestine operations were short, limited engagements. The longer the operation, the more it was vulnerable to detection. She originally saw the thing with Dave as a two-week bender. But he was close by and Jack never seemed the wiser, so what was the harm?

The party at the Selznicks served two purposes. It was primarily in celebration of Betty Grace's promotion to night manager. Her birthday which had passed two days prior was an add-on. Jack attended briefly before returning home to grade papers. Betty Grace invited Anne to bring Joshua to play with their son and some of the other neighborhood children. The Selznicks understood the difficulties of finding babysitters so it was easier to hire two out to watch the collective group of children than for parents to compete to find babysitters for their children alone.

Thirty people mingled about the kitchen and living rooms. Eighties music pumped through the speakers in each room, causing people to relive their youth and try dance moves they hadn't replicated in years. Without Jack, Anne felt unencumbered. Joshua was in the basement playing games leaving

Anne the ability to hop from group to group at will. When she found Dave in the game room playing pool, she had had three gin and tonics and was getting that familiar tingle between her legs. After a couple of games and another drink, Anne needed the accompaniment of a cigarette. She always liked to smoke when she was having a good time and even though she had officially quit, a cigarette now and then was a reward for her pretty good behavior.

When Dave saw her digging in her purse for her keys, he asked if she was leaving. She told him that she needed to get a pack of smokes. He said she was tipsy and shouldn't drive. Tim Goldman, a police officer that lived a block away, wasn't at the party and wouldn't appreciate such carelessness from a neighbor, he told her.

Anne followed Dave into the garage, and they drove out. They didn't tell anybody. She didn't think they would be longer than fifteen minutes, twenty tops. She did get cigarettes, that much was true. Anne just didn't smoke any. She and Dave got busy the moment she got back into the car. He drove them to an empty parking lot. She had removed her panties and climbed on top of him as soon as he turned off the car.

When they got back, they continued making out, their horniness not quite abated. That's when she saw her son standing on the front lawn. The only thing she could think of was how negligent the babysitters were for letting her son leave the house unsupervised. But he had seen Anne kiss Dave, that much was sure. The babysitter came around the corner moments later, along with two other children. They had been playing flashlight tag, she would find out later.

# Chapter 8

They had been at the cabin only a couple of days, and aside from a few bumps, the change of scenery had begun to work its magic on them. Even Joshua seemed to acclimate himself better. He didn't wander too far off the property, but at least he wasn't moping around like he sometimes did back at home. Things finally appeared to be on the right course.

Anne made a trip to town to pick up some propane gas for the grill. She took Joshua with her enticing him with ice cream for his help, giving Jack a free morning. Since he promised his son some fishing when he got back, Jack made himself some scrambled eggs and toast, and fixed a nice strong cup of coffee. He took his breakfast on the porch listening to the sounds of the birds in the trees. Moments like this were rare when he could just do what he wanted to do without running into Anne and getting into yet another fight. Moments like this allowed him to weigh the pros and cons of staying married to a woman that he was pretty sure had had an affair with their next-door neighbor. He may not have had incontrovertible proof, but there was enough circumstantial evidence – her denials, the texts that he saw, the sheer improbability of a 45-minute trip for ciga-rettes – to persuade him that he knew the truth even if Anne would never come clean.

Depending on his frame of mind when he listed the pros and cons of preserving his marriage, he found himself on both sides of the argument. As much as he didn't want to admit it to himself, the fact that he didn't repeatedly come to the same conclu-sion told him not to rush the decision.

Had she hurt him? Definitely. Did he want some measure of punishment, realize some measure of revenge? Absolutely.

Did he want a divorce?

That question kept rearing its ugly head and that was one that couldn't be answered quickly.

After rinsing his plate and fork and putting them into the dishwasher, Jack refilled his coffee and headed downstairs to see if there was a good book or something that might take his mind off things. His only foray down in the basement revealed some in-teresting things, and Jack thought that he would bring up a couple of games for the family to play that even-ing. He set a few to the side when he noticed a door that he must have missed before. Inside was a kid's bike, a tire pump, some rain gear, a can of gasoline, and some other things that the previous guests must have left behind. He inspected the bike. An orange Schwinn Firehawk, it was a fairly new model that, aside from two flat tires, otherwise seemed in good working order. Jack grabbed it and the pump and placed them near the stairs.

When he went to get the games, he noticed the leather-bound journal. He grabbed that as well. As an English lit teacher, the personal diaries of people of history were a passion for Jack. They blurred the line between literature and record, providing a time capsule of a specific place and time. He taught a course the previous semester Memoir as Historical Record, filling the reading list with such esteemed authors as Nabokov (Speak, Memory), Hemingway (A Moveable Feast), Angelou (I Know Why the Caged Bird Sings), Thoreau (Walden), Wiesel (Night), Orwell (Down and Out in Paris and London), Broyard (Kafka Was the Rage), and some unexpected ones from Anthony Bourdain (Kitchen Confidential) and Keith Richards (Life). He thought that the students really responded to the books. Jack made sure that they understood that such recollections were subject to bias, but that the direct access to events personalized the experience in a way that the cold objectivity of historians simply could not achieve.

He quickly reviewed the pages again. The author had filled much of the ledger and Jack wondered how long the person was here, and what made him leave such a personal book behind?

Jack kept this at the back of his mind as he first brought the games upstairs before making a second trip down to retrieve the bicycle and pump. He wanted to clean up the bike and give his son an unexpected gift to balance out whatever treats he was getting from his mother.

***

Joshua usually despised running errands with her on weekends. Anne smiled subtly as she watched him looking around at the passing scenery, absorbing everything he saw. Though the town was small, seeing new faces and cars driving in the road was strangely reassuring. Anne walked leisurely down the sidewalk of the main thoroughfare, glancing in the windows that she passed. She wondered how small businesses in remote areas made enough money to stay open. In the summertime, the town probably saw a noticeable increase in foot traffic with people summering by the lake. If they had rented the cabin after Labor Day, the price would cost one-half less than what they were paying now. The town likely followed suit, raising prices accordingly with the temperature once spring turned to summer.

She stopped to get Joshua's promised ice cream before heading down to Henry's store. It was a small wooden shack at the end of the street that intersected with the road that led to the lake properties. A freshly painted sign promised *Homemade Ice Cream!* Two high school girls worked the counter, which made Anne think of her own summer jobs when she was that age. Both were on their cell phones, talking to each other as they typed furiously with their thumbs. It was comical to see the dual conversations going on. They never skipped a beat.

Joshua got a scoop of coffee and vanilla in a cup; Anne got pistachio in a sugar cone. Her son was like an old soul; she hadn't known many kids that didn't like their ice cream out of a cone, but he was one of them. Also, coffee was a peculiar choice, but he liked to mix the two flavors together. Anne smiled as she watched her son go about his process, making sure he scooped just enough vanilla to balance the coffee already on the spoon.

"How you been doing the past couple of days?" she asked him as they sat down at one of the picnic tables near the shack. She wasn't sure how to bring up the topic without making her son feel uncomfortable.

"Good," he said, spooning a large amount of ice cream into his mouth.

"Other night," she continued. "You gave us quite a start."

"I know. I'm sorry."

"You know better than to wander off like that," she said, trying to keep a non-judgmental tone in her delivery. "But I have to know why you did."

Joshua took another carefully crafted scoop of ice cream.

"The boy," he said.

Anne frowned. "Boy? What boy?"

"I don't know. I heard him and went to see," he said.

"Did you find him?"

"No. But I think the sneaker is his."

"Why do you think that?"

Joshua shrugged. "I just do."

Anne didn't know what to make of this. She certainly hadn't heard any boy when she was out in the forest. The idea that a boy would be out there alone at night was difficult to believe, and she wondered if this wasn't more the product of Joshua's overactive imagination than reality.

"Tell you what," she said. "Next time you hear him, come get me. If he's out there alone, his parents must be worried sick."

"Okay," he said. "But I don't think his parents are around."

"What makes you say that?"

"He never mentioned them once."

The response from her son was so matter-of-fact that it sent a chilling sensation down Anne's spine.

***

Remington Supply had gone through their inventory of propane gas tanks. Usually, Henry Clay did a good job anticipating ordering based on the season, the holidays, and the weather. He doubled his stock of corn near the 4th of July and Memorial Day, and once the summer season was in full swing, he always had tiki torches, lighter fluid, and grilling starter kits on hand. For some reason, the renters bought gas tanks in twos and threes rather than one at a time. Most city folk tended to use their grills a lot when on vacation, probably inspired by those food television shows with those hotshot chefs preaching the benefits of barbecue.

Henry left the back of the store and met Anne and Joshua at the front.

"I'm embarrassed to say it, but we're out," he told her as plainly as he could.

"Oh, no," Anne said. "When do you think you'll get more?"

"I'm going to put a call into the surplus store in Larson, the next town over. I'll see if I can have them delivered tomorrow or the next day."

"Okay, that's not too bad. The boys have been fishing and they want to cook it themselves on the grill." She mussed her son's hair.

Henry chuckled. "Of course, they do. That's man stuff right there." He leaned over so that he was eye level with Joshua. "You get some of those trout out of that lake yet?"

Joshua nodded. "Yes, sir," he said. "Caught a big one too."

Henry feigned surprise. "Well, how about that. You say you come from the city?"

Joshua nodded again.

"Not many people catch a fish like that, and certainly no city folk," Henry teased, removing his hat and scratching his head. "You must be a natural. I know some people around here can't catch a cold, no less catch a big lake trout."

Joshua giggled. Henry stood erect again.

"Tell you what," he said to Anne. "When the tanks come in, be glad to run them to your house first thing."

"That's very kind of you, Henry, but I don't want to put you out."

Henry waved her off. "No trouble at all. Even an old dog like me has to stretch his legs once in a while. Besides, it's one of the perks of a small town – door-to-door service."

Anne beamed. "Thank you so much."

Henry tipped his cap.

"Can I have a quarter?" Joshua asked his mother.

She rummaged her pockets. "Sorry sweetie," she said. "I don't have any change."

Henry dug into his pocket and poked through a palmful of coins. He found a quarter and handed it to the boy.

"Thank you, but he has enough stuff, trust me," she said to Henry.

"It's alright. I suppose he wants to get a prize from that machine out front."

Joshua looked at his mother, who nodded her approval. Joshua ran out the door and to the machine.

"Kids are kids," Henry said. "Times change, kids don't."

"You can say that again. Speaking of which, can I ask you a question?"

The old proprietor flashed her a wink. "Remington Supply supplies more than household goods. Information is free though."

"It's about the family that was in the cabin before us."

Henry's expression suddenly changed. "Oh? What about them?"

"The other night my son found a shoe in the woods, and –"

"What was he doing in the woods?" Henry asked, a bit too quickly.

"Well, it's tough not to," Anne said. "I mean, they are all around."

"I meant by himself. Was he by himself?"

"Yes, but not for long," Anne lied. "Anyway, he found a sneaker, and…" she paused, realizing how silly the question was going to sound if she asked it. "Forget about it. City folk…"

But Henry didn't smile. The joviality so present in his face moments earlier had all but vanished, replaced with a stern, hard look.

"Ma'am, a word of advice? Those woods… best to keep your son on a tight leash. I mean that in the nicest way possible."

"That's the second time you've said that. What aren't you telling me? What is wrong with the woods?"

The old man sighed. He looked at her and bit his lip. "They're deep," he said finally. "Awfully deep. At night – in the dark especially – they seem like, well, like they could go on forever. If you're not watching…"

A chill ran down her spine. "What are you saying?" Are you saying that kids have gone missing?"

"I'm saying a child that gets some ideas to go exploring, well, that's a child that might not find his way out, if you catch my drift."

"I think I do."

Henry sighed. "Remington's a good town. With good people. Our sheriff, he's just one person. And those woods…"

"I know, they're deep," she said, a little annoyed with Henry's tone.

"I don't mean to worry you none," he said apologetically. "It's always best to err on the side of caution."

"Yes, you're right, of course. Thank you. Really."

"I'll run that tank out to you as soon as I can. My word."

Anne smiled and nodded. She left the store and picked up Joshua who was showing her a small rubber ball. He bounced it as they headed back to their parked car.

***

While Anne took a much-needed bath, Jack took Joshua to the dock to see if they could catch some trout. He wasn't sure if they would catch anything this late in the day, but the fact that the only other house on this part of the lake was clear across the other side, there was little traffic on the water frightening fish to other, less congested areas.

If truth be told, Jack didn't like fishing at first. His old man politely forced him to accompany him on weekends during the summer. They didn't speak much during those trips. But when they did it was about important things, not idle chit-chat used to fill in lulls in conversation. Interaction was done mostly through looks and gestures and Jack grew to understand his father's nuances. Even though they rarely spoke, Jack felt that he got to know his father better when they fished. The old man was more prone to sharing things with him then, and Jack learned some of the most important things from his father while they fished like about his father's first marriage and his terminal lung cancer. Jack had long wanted to bring Joshua fishing, but things never seemed to work out that way. Now, he had the chance, albeit, not under the best circumstances.

He handed his son his rod and watched him fix a lure on the end and cast it.

"Look at you," Jack said. "Not here a full seven days and you're already a master. Just remember to keep your pole straight when you cast. Bring it slowly back, then release the catch. See."

Jack cast far into the lake.

Joshua didn't say anything. His face was fixed on the water. There was something on his mind, and Jack thought it best to let the boy work it out on his own. This time when Joshua reeled in his line and cast again, he made sure his pole was straight.

"Dad," the boy said finally. "Can I ask you a question?"

"Sure, sport," Jack said, casting his line again. "Ask me whatever you want."

Joshua bit his lip. "Are you going to leave Mom?"

The frankness in the boy's delivery surprised Jack, and he felt his flush with embarrassment for the first time in a long time.

"Why do you say that?" he stammered.

"I hear you two talking," the boy said, then paused. "I hear you fighting."

Jack sighed. "I'm sorry about that, Joshua. We need to do better at that. Both of us."

"It's because of what I saw, isn't it?"

Jack looked hard at his son, determining if he should lie or not. Children had a way of digging out the truth, even if parents did their best to hide it.

"Yes, sport."

Joshua looked away from his father.

"I wish I never saw that. I wish I never went over to their house. I hate myself."

The frankness of his son's remark struck Jack in the heart. He set his pole down and knelt by his son.

"Joshua," he said. "Don't say that. Never say that. This isn't your fault. Your mom made a bad decision. And she feels really bad about it. But it was her decision. Not yours."

"She's sorry?"

"Yes. I think so," he said. "I hope so."

"So, why not forgive her? When I do something wrong, you tell me to say I'm sorry and to not repeat the mistake. Can't she do the same thing?"

"It's not that easy, sport," Jack said.

"Why not?"

The simplicity of the question stumped Jack. There was an obvious difference between playing ball in the house and breaking a vase and sleeping with someone outside the marriage, but when reduced to its fundamentals, a mistake was still just a mistake.

WWJD – What would Jesus do?

Jack struggled to answer but was saved by a pull-on Joshua's line.

"Flick your wrist!" Jack ordered.

The boy quickly switched into fish-catching mode. He flicked his wrist as his father directed, making sure that hook got lodged in the fish's mouth good and tight. The line thrashed about in Joshua's hands.

"Dad? I need help."

"You're doing fine. Stay with it."

"He's strong."

"You know what to do. Let him run a bit but when you start to reel him in. Let him tire himself out. Once he's lost his fight, he's yours."

"You mean, ours."

Jack laughed. Joshua followed his guidance. Teeth gritted, his face sweaty, Joshua gradually brought the fish in closer to the dock. That sucker was giving him a hell of a fight, but his son stayed with him. Jack readied the net. Joshua arched back hard. The fish broke the surface, flopping chaotically around. Once out of the water, the large trout lost half of his strength. Joshua took two steps back brining his catch closer to the net.

Jack scooped the fish.

"Look at the size of this guy," he said.

The trout was one of the largest Jack had ever seen. It was going to be good eating.

***

Anne apologized for the propane but promised that they would have it in a day or two. It didn't matter because everyone scarfed down the fish hungrily, oven baked or not. Joshua did not even put up a fight when it came to bedtime. He was exhausted from the day. Jack easily tucked him in, making sure the night light was functioning and the bedroom door open enough.

Jack and Anne sat together on the living room couch. They had agreed not to re-investigate the Selznick incident until they had something constructive to say. There was a lot of sense in what Joshua asked Jack on the dock about forgiveness.

From the mouths of babes, Jack thought.

After an hour of television, Anne announced that she was going to bed. She lingered briefly to see if Jack was going to follow her. He said that he was going to catch the sports scores, and that he might be up later.

She nodded and wished him a good night.

***

The next day, Anne made another trip to town under the pretense of checking in on the propane order, but Jack sensed that she was looking to get out of the cabin. Whether she wanted space or to talk to Dave, he didn't know, and didn't really care. If this marriage, this family, was going to remain together, it would be because Jack decided it to be so. Leaving him alone let Jack really go over the pros and cons of staying married. When he mentally filled the columns with every benefit and detriment, he cleared them and started from the beginning.

In between trying to make up his mind, Jack focused on chores. In the morning, Jack cleaned up the bicycle and put air into the tires. After an hour of light maintenance, it was road-ready, and Joshua was excited to take it for a spin. Jack set up the parameters for its use.

The front of the house, the side of the house, and the road before it bended around a cluster of pine trees were all fine. Anything else was strictly verboten. And the woods? Forget about it. They were a definite no-no.

"And if that kid calls you again, you tell him to come over here," Jack said.

"Okay," Joshua said.

"Your mother's looking for a gym or something in town, and I'm going to be in the living room reading. You need anything…"

"I know, come inside."

"If you see a bear?"

"Come inside."

"If an ice cream truck should come down the road?"

"Come inside."

"If a clown wants to give you a balloon?" he teased.

"Scream my head off."

"So, we understand each other?"

"Yes, Dad."

"Good. Have fun."

Joshua hopped on the bike and biked around the gravel. It was difficult at first, but he got the hang of it, pushing the muscles in his thighs to increase his speed. As he got acclimated to the terrain, Joshua tried to pop a wheelie. When he couldn't leverage enough to get the front wheel off the ground, he really threw his back and arms into it, nearly sending him ass-over-tea kettle. He was able to catch it before the momentum made him flip. His face flushed with excitement and his heart thumped fast.

Joshua got off his bike and made a makeshift ramp with a couple of bricks and a piece of flat plank wood he found along the side of the cabin. The first two runs didn't yield the thrill he was seeking so on the third pass he pumped his legs and gained a full throttle of steam. His front tire went up and over the ramp and he captured a good amount of air, landing solidly on the ground. He made a long hard skid, sending gravel flying into the grass.

The boy paused when he looked to see how far he sent out the small rocks. Bushes at the tree line rippled from the spray. Normally, such a feat would make Joshua proud, but there was no way he was going that fast or skid that hard to make the gravel reach the tree line. It was too far away, or at least, it was supposed to be.

Joshua looked at the trees. They were the same birches as yesterday only they seemed closer somehow. The boy then got off his bike and walked to the edge of the driveway. The section of grass that served as demarcation line between the driveway and the forest seemed smaller, narrower than the previous day. He knew that couldn't be possible but there it was anyway.

The trees swayed and the leaves rustled in such a way that caused a perfect fluid ripple that started at one end of the tree line and flowed to the other.

Joshua couldn't help but think that the forest was beckoning him to enter, like the voice had before, to get lost in the woods, to explore.

And then he remembered the shoe he had found, and Joshua picked up his bicycle and ran it back over to the other side of the driveway.

If he dared to have looked back, he might have seen the face of a timid boy poking through the thick leaves, watching him closely, wanting so desperately for him to play.

***

Inside the cabin, Jack found the black leather-bound journal and took a seat on the couch. He sipped his coffee, then opened up the book, flipping past the opening page with the word 'DARK' underlined in thick black ink to the title page.

"The Summer Journal of Peter Rothman by Peter Rothman."

Although he wouldn't classify himself a literary snob, Jack sighed. The banality of the title did not promise exciting reading.

"May 2," he read. "This entry marks the beginning of the Rothman summer vacation. God willing and the creek don't rise, as they say in these parts, this journal will track the progress of my novel…"

Jack set the book aside and took another sip of coffee. He momentarily considered adding a splash of bourbon in order to make the read more digestible.

He idly flipped through the pages. Entries were written in several different types of ink, and in various styles of penmanship. It looked like Ol' Petey got lazy the longer he recorded the events of that summer. Later, Jack would realize that Peter or somebody had gone back to the journal and added sections that weren't part of the original text.

The writing varied from straight prose to erratic rambling.

These are the events that he read.

# Chapter 9

(Note: The following excerpts serve as an interpretation of the events written down by Peter Rothman. The writing style varied from fluid prose to more choppy observances and recollections of events that had transpired.)

May 3

Beer in hand, Peter Rothman sat on the back deck of the cabin. It was a little after ten in the morning, but this was vacation. He didn't need to conform to the same societal constraints of his normal routine. It was just a beer, but more importantly, it was a symbol of the start of his summer vacation. All year he saved up time to take a month off with his family, in a remote spot near a lake and far away from an office.

He had his shirt off, exposing his mayonnaise-white skin to the summer sun. He didn't even have a farmer's tan. A corporate accountant rarely got out of the office. He was always processing some executive on the seventh floor's expense forms. Peter saw where they went – the steak houses, the cigar bars – expensive places where the firm allowed them to run up large bills in the name of "customer engagement." They liked Peter for his discretion, and they rewarded him at the end of the year in under-the-table bonuses. The firm might not provide such gifts as company policy, but the partners did, especially when it concerned the people who kept the right side of their bread buttered.

Peter watched his son skim stones in the lake. Mark was ten years old and was starting to come into his own and push boundaries with his parents. Toward the end of the school year, his wife Karen had found a half-pack of cigarettes in a box under his bed. Neither of them smoked, and where he got the cigarettes remained a mystery. They sat Mark down the day Karen made the discovery and questioned him without passing judgment, just like the books said to do. Despite their approaches (empathetic, good cop-bad cop, laid back), Mark held firm and did not provide the name of the individual.

When Mark got in trouble with another boy for pulling a prank on a younger student's locker a week before school let out, they knew they had to nip this behavior problem in the bud. They didn't want Mark starting the new year as a bully or a trouble-maker or a kid that became so much of a nuisance that teachers did even try anymore. In public school, it was a numbers game. Teach who you could, anyone else, let go.

It was Peter's idea to come to the cabin. He had been going through his own version of a middle-life crisis. Work was work, the money was good, but the soul satisfaction wasn't there. He often laughed with friends who asked him how he got to be an accountant when he had majored in History in college. It was an odd profession for a major that didn't require the tabulation and rectification of numbers and balance sheets.

He wanted to write a novel. Ever since he was a kid, he saw himself as an author when he wasn't imagining himself a solider or a gangster. He had tried at various times in his life, but the blank page was an imposing obstacle. Getting words down – the right words – was not as easy as he thought, and his drawer soon collected hundreds of pages of "first starts" but few with anything more than a few paragraphs.

This time he was ready. He had outlined an idea and filled in some key bits of information and scenes that would propel the story. And most importantly, he based it on what he knew – corporate accountancy. The story was a fictionalized thriller, but rooted in the reality of corporate shenanigans, less than ethical business practices, and with the names and places changed accordingly to protect the not-so-innocent.

Karen opened the sliding glass door that led to the kitchen holding a glass of white wine. Peter turned to her and smiled lifting his beer bottle in a makeshift toast.

"Vacation, right?" she said sitting in the seat beside him.

"This is just what the doctor ordered," he said, breathing in deeply. "Got to love the feel of sunshine on your face."

"You can get that at home. You just need to get out more."

"I'm out now."

"Yes, you are," she said, giving his arm a squeeze.

They both turned and watch their son running along the bank, chasing birds.

"He's going to be alright, isn't he, Peter? Mark's going to be fine?"

"Yes," he replied. "He's just a boy is all. Just watch. He'll be a new boy by the end of this trip."

"You were like that when you were his age?"

"Worse. I think I still hold the record for most suspensions at Tillerton Middle School. If they had a plaque for that behavior, my name would be on top in bright gold letters."

"So, that's where he gets it from."

Peter laughed. "He's fine. He's doing what boys do at his age."

"Drive his parents to drink?" She smiled.

Peter looked at his bottle and drank the rest of the contents down. "See?"

Karen laughed. It was a snort, the kind of sound she made when she had one too many and Peter wondered if that was her first glass of wine.

"I'm being silly," she said.

"No, you're not. I'm not worried, but we did the right thing. We are getting ahead of the problem."

"Problem?" she asked, concern returning to her voice.

"Not that way. He made some mistakes and we addressed it. Plus, getting away for a month will keep him away from that Freeman kid. You know it was his cigarettes. I mean, Rothmans? Of all cigarettes to pinch, only a small percentage of the parents in his school smoke, and smoke English cigarettes at that."

"That kid has a mischievous eye," Karen said with a playful sneer.

"You thinking what I'm thinking? Two to the back of the head?"

Karen raised her free hand and mimed a gun with her thumb and forefinger.

"Pow-pow."

"That's my girl," he said. He turned his attention back to his son. "Three and a half weeks. All he has is us so we can re-indoctrinate him."

"Like Manchurian Candidate."

"Worked for them."

She scooted her chair over closer to him and leaned her head against his shoulder.

"I'm glad we're here," she said.

"Me too."

***

Mark turned to look back at his parents on the deck in time to see his mom give his dad a quick peck on the cheek. He bent over and dug out a flat-looking rock from the soil and cleaned it off. He looked at the lake and picked the smoothest part of its surface. He cocked his right arm, imagining his throw before he launched the rock. Then he fired it off. The velocity and angle of the throw perfectly bounced the rock's edge off the face of the water. The stone propelled forward, skipping three more times before plopping down fifteen yards from where he stood. It was his best shot of the morning.

He didn't want to come to the cabin. He wanted to spend the summer with his friends, play ball, do things. Now that he got accepted into the cool kids' clique, Mark was afraid he'd lose that status if he wasn't around, and it took too long to get in the first place. He didn't want to be replaced simply because he wasn't there to assert himself in the pack. His parents knew about the cigarettes and the incident at the end of the school, but he had gotten away with two or three others that escaped their attention including egging his math teacher's house and stealing a box of candy bars from a truck making a delivery to a neighborhood store.

Mark slapped at a mosquito around his ankle. He hated being out here. There was nothing to do. Maybe if Jerry or Tommy came with him, it'd be different. But being alone with his parents… well, it just sucked. Even the present of the Schwinn Firehawk didn't make things better. Riding bikes was only fun if you had friends to ride with.

The boy wandered along the banks of the lake. He picked up a stick and whacked at bushes and low tree limbs, pretending to be a swashbuckling pirate. He was still in his parents' sight but barely. The grass that dominated the yard behind and around the cabin gave way to more untamed terrain. Large pine trees were clumped together littering the ground with their needle droppings. He paused before the massive tree line that bordered the property. There were no formal paths or even those made by constant food traffic. It was wild and Mark wondered if the trees that stood before him were hundreds of years old.

It was almost ninety degrees, but a sudden and unexpected breeze blew out of the forest, chilling Mark's skin, giving him goosebumps. The nearest tree limb rocked back and forward. Bereft of any leaves, the small naked think branches at the end looked like gnarled fingers. Unnerved, Mark took a step back. If he didn't know any better, he would have said that the tree was trying to grab him.

Convincing himself that it wasn't fear but a proactive measure not to hear his father yell at him to get back, Mark hurried away from that tree.

The woods were just creepy.

***

After lunch, when his dad retired to the small room that he converted into a makeshift office to write, Mark went outside. His father had found a lawn game in the basement closet. It was a take on horseshoes, only it used blue and yellow darts and two red hoops. His father explained the game and set it up on the front lawn that bordered the forest. From where he stood, Mark could see his bedroom window on the second floor.

Mark tossed the four darts at the target. He got three out of the four in the circle and decided to increase the distance. He picked up the hoop and walked it another ten feet back to make it more of a challenge.

When he drew near to them, the trees that bordered the property rustled in place. Mark made his four tosses, missing them all and walked over to retrieve the darts. As he drew closer to his wayward throws, the trees along the line rippled, following him until he bent down to retrieve the darts. Then the rustling stopped. Mark made his next four throws, and again, when he walked, the Ripple followed him. On the third retrieval, Mark caught something out of the corner of his eye. He glanced over and saw the Ripple tracking his movements. When Mark stopped, the Ripple stopped. When he moved, the Ripple did the same.

"What the hell?" Mark said. The woods commanded his full attention now.

He knew that this was impossible, should be impossible, but there it was anyway.

And then there was the unpleasant smell.

It was acrid and pungent and seemed out of place. Mark had smelled wet leaves and black mud before. While strong odors, they were fitting to the environment, if that made sense. They belonged in forests and wetlands.

But this was different. The closest thing Mark could think of was that it smelled like the rat his father caught in a trap he had set out by the back of their house but had forgotten about.. For a relatively small creature, the stench of corporal decay was all-consuming, overshadowing whatever power the rodent might have had in life.

His father had to wipe Vicks under his nostrils and tie a bandana around his face so that he looked like a bandit. He slipped on heavy work gloves and ended up throwing the rat (whose own face had been gnawed off by his brethren exposing the bone of the skull) and trap into a heavy-duty garbage bag. It took three days of a combination of ammonia and Lysol before that stink dissipated.

This stench made the former one look like a bouquet of roses.

The wind picked up and rustled all the trees except for one without leaves on one of its limbs. That stretched out like a skeleton's arm toward the cabin. It was the only limb that did so. It looked like it was bestowing a spell or curse or something supernatural and other worldly. It was also immune to the wind, unaffected by the cause-effect of nature.

Only when the breeze died down did its limbs move.

Mark looked around. The front door was only twenty yards away but seemed like a million miles. The toughness that he had been trying to cultivate for the past six months immediately drained from his body.

He shrieked and took off.

Mark felt like he was running through a thick mud that was trying to keep him in place. In reality, he took off so fast, he ran out of his shoes.

When he got inside, he slammed the door shut so hard, his father came out of the room.

"What the hell's going on?" Peter asked.

Mark didn't respond to him. He looked out the window at the forest. The limbs swayed naturally back and forth, but Mark knew there was no breeze.

The limbs were laughing at him.

***

May 9

Peter pulled the covers up to his son's chin. He walked softly to the door, careful not to creak the wooden floor. He looked back at his son before leaving. After four stories and three songs, the boy was finally asleep. Mark never had a problem going to sleep before, but this was an extenuating circumstance. Peter had to promise to leave the hallway light on and the boy's door open to ease his concerns.

He then walked down the steps and found his wife on the couch. She had showered and was now relaxing in her pajamas and college sweatshirt. She handed him a glass of red wine when he walked over and took a seat beside her.

"Thanks," he said. "I needed this."

He expelled a heavy sigh.

"Rough?"

"Yeah," Peter said. He took a big gulp and swallowed. "I mean, I wouldn't want to go to sleep after that either, but still."

"He made a mistake," she said. "Kids make mistakes all the time. We should be thankful it wasn't worse."

"That's true. He's shaken up pretty bad."

"He's not the only one." She gestured to his glass. It was nearly empty after two trips to his mouth.

"He wandered off into the woods for Chrissakes," Peter said. "Jesus, he knows better than that."

"He should. He does." She let him get it out.

"I get the rebelliousness. I really do. But there's pissing off your parents and getting seriously hurt."

"Potentially seriously hurt," she corrected.

"Whatever. You know what I mean. How long do you think it would take this Podunk town's sheriff to get a search party together to grid-search these woods? God, who knows what you'd find."

"Grid-search? You're being a bit excessive; don't you think?"

"Over cautious, yes, but…," he stopped himself. His wife scooted closer to him.

"You're a good dad. We're good parents. We may not be the only ones that have had a kid wander off on his own. But we're definitely one of the ones that got him back. You found him, Peter. That means something."

"He was so scared," Peter said, shaking the image of pure fear on Mark's face when he found him.

The last time he had seen Mark was an hour before dinner. He was out in the front of the house throwing rocks into the woods. Peter wrote for about an hour and came out for something to drink and to check on dinner. Before he went back to writing, he peered out the window, checking on Mark.

Not seeing Mark wouldn't have sent that cold jolt through his body. He could have been anywhere, playing or exploring, or just, well, being a kid.

What made that chilling hand gripping his heart was spotting Mark's ballcap on the grass. It seemed so out of place, so terribly alone, that it pushed Peter's fears forward.

It just didn't feel right.

He found Karen and they searched the house. Then they searched around the house and down by the lake.

There was no sign of their son.

Fear spiked the hearts of both parents. Without a word they both turned to the tree line and the dense forest behind it.

"Oh, God," Karen said.

He told his wife to stay put in case Mark returned. Like a first responder, Peter ran into the forest without a second thought or expectation of what he was going to find when he got inside.

Every ten seconds he called out for his son, listening in between shout-outs for a reply or a sound of struggle or pain. When none materialized, he thrust himself forward. Peter wasn't a stranger to the woods. He had been in a few over the course of his life. But he couldn't recall one that was so thick and heavy with undergrowth. It made him think of a book on dinosaurs he used to read to his son. There was a photo of the Cretaceous period where everything was lush and thick with overgrown vegetation. This wasn't quite that dense but close. His legs ached with the effort of pushing forward over uneven terrain.

Besides his difficulty cutting through the bushes and saplings, Peter noticed that it was suddenly darker. A glance at his watch reinforced his belief that, while early evening, the sky shouldn't be this black. Not at this hour in May. And yet the farther he made his way, the deeper he got into the woods, the murkier it got, like when he was swimming in the muddy waters of the Mississippi River hand fishing for channel catfish.

It was strange but the woods seemed to have its own force. The unstable terrain, the defensive thorns, the creatures that scurried and hid in between the moss-covered rocks and within rotted, fallen trees, watching you with eyes that flashed menacingly.

And it was upon this realization that Peter started to become afraid.

"Mark! Mark!" he shouted to the looming trees that swallowed up his voice. In this way, a large forest was very much like the open ocean where a person or a boat was insignificant in the presence of a much larger presence.

He found his son thirty minutes later at the entrance of what appeared to be a clearing. The boy was crying and shaking involuntarily. Snot streamed down Mark's nostrils and spittle dripping down his mouth. The boy's face was colorless.

Peter scooped the boy up in his arms, wrapping his arms round in an attempt to soothe Mark's trembling body. He pressed the boy's face to his, as he stroked his hair, whispering in his ear.

"It's okay, it's okay," he purred. "Daddy's here. Daddy's right here."

He took the boy away from the clearing's entrance. The nearby trees rustled angrily, although Peter didn't notice it. A Ripple through the vegetation tracked Peter's exit but gradually subsided, returning the forest to its natural state.

"It took a lot of reassuring tonight," Peter said to Karen. "But that's a lesson he won't soon forget."

"You didn't happen to pick up his sneaker, did you?" she asked him.

Peter shook his head. "No, sorry. I didn't even notice it was off his foot."

"Forget about it. He has another pair."

Peter nodded. His mind was elsewhere, and he didn't even notice his wife refill his glass.

"What are you thinking about?" she asked.

"Something he said. I mean, he was pretty shaken. We both were. But he kept on mumbling something. Ah, skip it. It doesn't matter."

"No, go on," she said. "What'd he say?"

"I think," Peter said, "I think he said, he saw a boy."

"What boy? In the woods?"

Peter nodded.

"Well, did you see a boy?"

Peter shook his head.

"I wouldn't worry about it," she said. "His mind must have been compensating. He was terrified."

***

May 12

Peter entered the cabin carrying an armful of boxes containing light bulbs of various sizes and wattages. Karen raised a questioning eyebrow at his purchases.

"When you said you were going to town to pick up some things, I was kind of hoping it would be ice cream," she said.

Exasperated, he set them down on the coffee table. He wiped sweat off his brow. It was humid outside.

"Mark's afraid of the dark," he said, taking a dishtowel and blotting his face.

"You can't be serious. The dark? Mark? Since when?"

"The last couple of nights. Every night he has the same nightmare, and he wakes up screaming bloody murder, shouting 'the dark, the dark." It's freaky, Karen. You don't hear him?"

"I've been taking some sleeping pills. The cicadas are noisy as hell." She paused, thinking. "He's never done that before. Not even when he was younger."

"No, he didn't. Hasn't done that at all. Well, not since I found him cowering in the forest."

Karen shook her head. "Jesus, Peter, what happened out there? What did he see out there?"

"I don't know. He said a funny thing tough. He said that he thought he heard a boy calling out to him. That's what made him go into the woods in the first place. A boy called out his name and he wanted to see who it was."

"But you said that he didn't see a boy."

"Right. Just heard his voice. Supposedly. And he said something else."

"What?"

"He said the boy knew his name."

"How is that possible?"

Peter shook his head. An unsettling chill came over both of them.

"Well, did he see an animal or something? A wolf maybe?" she asked hopefully. But her voice was weak and devoid of confidence.

"No, nothing like that. And for what it's worth, neither did I. There weren't even any noises that you'd expect a forest to make. Chirping, bird calls, insect ticks. Actually, it was pretty quiet. Like, too quiet. And dark. It was so unbelievably dark, even though it was, what? Five o'clock? Strange."

Karen nodded. "Whatever, it made an impression on him."

"You think?" he said pointing to the boxes. "He won't go to bed now without a light being on in his room. I have to change all the light bulbs. He wants brighter light. Much brighter light."

***

## May 13

Peter screwed in the lightbulb into the light on the table by Mark's bed. He turned it on, and the light beamed brightly, even with the day's sun streaming in through the window.

"How's that?" he asked his son. Mark looked skeptically at the glow.

Mark studied the luminescence. "Not strong enough," he said to his father.

"Buddy, if I use a higher wattage, a fuse will blow when something else is plugged into a socket in here. That's a safety hazard."

The boy's face frowned in thought. "What if I only turn it on at night? Nothing else would be plugged in then."

Mark's eyes pleaded, and it tore at Peter's heart.

"Tell you what," Peter said. "Let's see how this one goes. If it doesn't work for you, I'll put in another, okay?"

"Okay," Mark said reluctantly.

Peter walked over to the window. He peered outside and looked at the sky. The clouds had begun to gather threatening to bury the sun in thick grey stratus. The last two days the days had started off sunny and warm only to turn gray and cold by noon.

It was an odd weather pattern, but they only had another seven days there. Having once been promising, the vacation now bore all the signs of turning into a bust. Peter's novel had not really gotten off the ground as he had hoped, and Mark's anxiety and neediness certainly didn't help matters.

So much for getting away from it all. Peter seemed to have brought it all with him.

He turned back toward his son who scrutinized the light. He ruffled the boy's hair.

"Everything's going to be fine, Mark. I promise."

The boy didn't respond. He kept fixed on the lamp and removed the shade completely. Then he turned on the light. The bulb burned fierce white. .

Peter's face furrowed. Something had made an indelible mark on his son and he didn't know how to make it better. When they got back, he'd make a call to his old college roommate, a psychologist at some hotshot clinic in Massachusetts and ask for recommendations about what to do.

***

Later that night, Peter and Karen took their wine on the front porch. They were bundled up in sweatshirts and the light jackets they had brought. The cold was an unexpected turn of events. The porch light buzzed, emitting a dull opaque glow. It didn't shed much light in the encroaching darkness.

"I thought you changed these," Karen said, looking up at the bulbs.

"I did," Peter replied. "I think there must be a short in the wiring or something."

Karen nodded and sipped her wine. "It's like the light's being consumed," she said, and then shivered. "Spooky."

Peter stood and walked down the steps and looked up at Mark's bedroom window. In the end, his son had made him put in the higher wattage bulb in agreement to get in bed. The window burned like a beacon in the endless night, like the perpetual beam of a lighthouse.

"Jesus, it's dark," he said to Karen as he looked up at the sky. It looked like an amorphous mass of blackness. Neither the moon nor one star could be seen.

"Fourth night in a row," Karen said. "You think that's some kind of record around here?"

Peter shrugged and just shook his head.

A noise sounded along the tree line. Peter's head snapped to attention. Although he couldn't see it, Peter heard the swishing and crackling of leaves.

"Hear that?" he asked.

Karen looked at him and followed his gaze into the forest.

"Hear what?"

"Shhh," he said, and paused. Again, the trees made the unusual sound. "There! It's coming alive," he said.

"What's coming alive?"

"The woods. Moving out there. Rustling. You can't hear it?"

"Trees move in the wind," she said.

Peter ignored her and kept focused. Karen stood up. She licked a finger and held it up to the air. She suddenly frowned. She licked her finger deeper, getting it wetter. She thrust it up and moved it around in the air.

"What is it?" he asked. When she didn't respond, Peter stood up and licked his own finger and imitated his wife. He also frowned.

"Jesus," he said. He walked around the gravel driveway holding his finger in different places and at different heights. The tree line came alive, swaying back and forth, the lone distinct naked limb swiping at him when he came close. After a brief reconnaissance, he came back to the porch.

"There's no wind," she said.

"I could have sworn I heard it," he said. "I don't know, it's just weird."

"You've been saying that a lot lately," Karen said. And for the first time, he heard the undertone of concern in her voice.

"I'm not much of a meteorologist," he said finally, trying to bring levity to an awkward situation.

His goofy humor and delivery didn't bring a smile to his wife's face like it usually did. Karen sat back own and scrunched the jacket around her neck.

"I think I want to go home," she said.

Their son's shrill scream was almost primal. It was unexpected and the blackness of the night only accentuated its abandoned desperateness.

Peter's and Karen's eyes immediately met. They suddenly felt their son's fear. It crawled up their spines and dug into the base of their necks, terrifying them to their very cores.

# Chapter 10

$J$ack shook his head. He couldn't believe what he had just read. The story was remarkably similar, too eerily similar to be a coincidence. And yet, it seemed just too impossible to be true. How could it? Since the fires of civilization kids had feared the dark. And lots of kids wandered off into woods. This shouldn't be a big deal, all things considered.

And yet it was.

Jack flipped the page. One sentence was written in big block all-in-caps letters.

"There's something wrong here," Jack read aloud.

The next few pages contained crazy drawings. They resembled the scribbles of a madman than any serious attempt at a real drawing, impressionistic or not. In each, the lines made by the ball point pen were deep, as if Peter, or whoever the artist was, bore down on the tip with a heavy, frantic hand. The lines were jagged and violent and if scary was an appropriate word for art, these drawings would fit neatly under that mantel.

The first image was a mess of twisted lines and chaotic scrawl. It was as if the artist tried to make a black tornado or an eddy. Large circular swirls spun over and over and over again. If a child made this,

Jack wouldn't think twice about it. But he was pretty certain that Peter's son Mark did not make it, which left Peter or his wife. And that made it disconcerting.

The second image was clearer, but equally dark and menacing. It depicted a familiar tree line. The slender base of pines stretched up but disappeared behind heavy black pen scratches. The top of the page, someone had scrawled:

*The stars DON'T shine through the forest.*

Jack got up from the sofa and went to the window. He compared the drawing to the line near the house. Peter's drawing was remarkably accurate, and he wondered how long ago was Peter at the cabin? A year ago? Two maybe? Three? The journal gave him dates not years, but if the bicycle he found was Mark's then it had to be last year.

The third drawing was difficult to make out. Both sides of the page were colored black except for the center that was purposefully left unmarked. It resembled a hole, or a door, or some destination maybe?

The final drawing was just up and down scribbles. *What kills fire?* was written over and over again underneath it.

Jack closed the book and looked out the window again. Joshua stood on the edge of the driveway staring at the woods. Jack wondered what his son was looking at. He didn't see anything out of the ordinary. Just the trees and bushes of the forest.

The trees whose branches bowed under a mysterious breeze that never seemed to blow.

***

Something wasn't right. He was sure that the trees looked closer today than the previous day, like they were trying to sneak up on Joshua. That wasn't possible, even Joshua knew that. Trees didn't move, at least not in that way. They grew, they got thicker, their roots extended even, but they didn't move. That's not the way nature worked.

Joshua found a stick on the ground. He held it tentatively in his hand as he looked at the Widow's Hand, the name he now called that lone limb protruding over the driveway. It bobbed at him ever so gently, as if… as if…

They were beckoning Joshua to come just a bit closer.

Fear just didn't start in the stomach or run like spiders up and down your spine. Sometimes it just rammed itself down the throat and lodged there to obstruct a person's ability to breathe or scream. It paralyzed and it debilitated.

Joshua stepped cautiously toward the birches that taunted him.

Forests don't move, he told himself over and over. That was just stupid.

But still.

When he thought he was close enough, he studied the ground and found a good spot for the stick. He jammed it into the grass. At first, the dense soil fought him, but Joshua persisted thrusting the full extent of his weight and strength against it until it sunk three solid inches into the ground.

He was going to be sure that the forest moved before he said anything to his parents. He wanted them to believe him, needed him to do so. Joshua had heard their talk lately. They knew he was afraid, and that kids who were perpetually afraid usually had active imaginations. If he was going to get their trust and confidence, he wanted to be able to show them proof.

The trees rustled. A challenge?

*Joshua...*

The Voice again. The child. The boy.

*When are we going to play....?* It cooed.

The bushes shook and branches separated. Joshua could make out a form behind the dark green foliate of the shrubs. It was the size and shape of a boy, but the details weren't clear. It was a shadow even though no sunlight penetrated the thick foliage. And then as sure as it was there one moment, it quickly disappeared into the thick green surrounding natural concealment.

*Why did you leave me alone, Joshua? I thought we were going to be friends.*

Joshua's fear spiked, but unlike other times, he found his voice. It came out broken and shook.

"I-I-I don't know you," he finally managed to croak out.

The Ripple returned. It playfully slid up and down the tree line like a dog trying to entice another dog to frolic.

Joshua's eyes went wide, and his breathing quickened. The Ripple stopped and suddenly Joshua heard the boy's laughter behind the tree line. It was high-pitched and unforced.

A cold sweat dripped down Joshua's back.

*All kids like to play, Joshua. The woods are great for playing. You can get lost in the woods.*

This time Joshua saw the boy for a moment. And not just a shadow or the form, but his face. It was there and gone in a blink of an eye. It was a game; Joshua was sure of it. The boy tagged Joshua, and now it was his turn to be "it."

Joshua took a couple of steps back until he felt the gravel under the soles of his sneakers.

The driveway felt safer, somehow, like there was an unseen wall blocking the forest from getting any closer to him than what the terrain would allow.

The frivolous laughter again.

Joshua steadily backed away, but his eyes never left the tree line, searching for the boy who wanted nothing better than to take him into the woods and play a game.

***

Anne drove back from town with a handful of apologies from Henry who blamed Gus Winston in Larson for giving away the tanks he was supposed to deliver to him. Henry was miffed; well, as much as she could imagine such a nice old man could get miffed, and although he didn't curse in front of her, Anne had a feeling that if it had been Jack standing in front of him instead of her, Henry would have let a slew of few choice expletives fly.

While she couldn't pick up the propane, Anne did pick up a pack of cigarettes and took her time smoking six of them over two cups of coffee while sitting in the town gazebo near the bank. Since "quitting" the filthy habit, Anne only missed smoking two times during the day – morning during her first cup of coffee, and anytime she had one too many drinks. Other than that, smoking had been something that she did to pass time, whether that was taking breaks at work (every two hours), or in between chores at home when she didn't have it in her to start yet another load of laundry.

She always envied Jack's ability to go cold turkey. When they agreed to stop smoking, he was able to toss them out, just like that. He didn't need gum or patches or medication. He didn't need a "lucky cigarette" or any other hocus-pocus bullshit to convince him to stop. Jack made up his mind about something and he followed through without fanfare or circumstance. He just stopped, period. She didn't think he lorded this ability over her, but sometimes she did detect a subtle hint of superiority when she didn't do something right.

Anne was going to head back to the car when Dave called. Throughout the affair the one thing they had strictly adhered to was not to communicate over the phone. Now that the cat was out of the bag, Dave ignored their previous understanding and had texted her like a crushing high school boy.

"What do you want, Dave?" she said, lighting up her seventh cigarette of the day.

"That wasn't quite the greeting I was expecting," the familiar voice said.

"What did you expect?"

"I didn't call to pick a fight. I just want to know how you're doing," he said. "Is that a crime?"

"Adultery is not a crime," she said.

"Don't be acerbic. You know what I mean."

Anne cringed when she heard the word "acerbic." While Dave's body was sculpted out of marble, his brain was cupped Play Dough. Self-conscious about his lack of any formal education past high school, when they first started fooling around, he bought a word-a-day calendar to improve his poor vocabulary. Now, even when he used a word correctly, it sounded completely foreign coming out of his mouth, like watching a poorly dubbed movie.

"Look, I appreciate you checking in on me, but there's nothing to say. There's nothing I want to say," she said. "I love my family. I want to save my marriage if possible."

"And if not possible?" There it was again, the hope. Dave was nothing if not an eternal dreamer.

She was having none of it. "Is there anything else?"

"He hasn't hit you, has he?"

"What? God, no. Why would he hit me?"

"Gee, I don't know, why do you think?"

She sighed. Times like this made her wonder why she let the affair go longer than a one-night fuck-fest.

"We're working through things. It's going slow."

He shifted his approach. "I miss you."

"I don't have time for this, Dave."

"You can't tell me you don't miss me. You can't tell me you don't miss what we do."

"I can't do this," she said. "I can't do this right now."

"Betty Grace knows," he said. "She wants a divorce."

"I'm sorry to hear that."

"I'm not. It wasn't really working for a while now. You know how it is."

"I don't.  I still love my husband," she said.

He ignored her response. "She wants Stanley. It's probably better that way. I want to see you."

"It's over, Dave. That ship has sailed."

"What if Jack wants out? What if he wants a divorce? What are you going to do then?"

"I can't say I'd blame him if he did," she said. "I hope he doesn't. I'm trying to convince him not to."

"Damn you, Anne! I think I love you."

"We talked about this, Dave. Sex only. We had it. Lots of it. But it's over. Things go on. I'm moving on."

"It's not fair," he said glumly. Anne could picture his face legitimately pouting like it did when he didn't get his way. It wasn't an act; he literally resorted to a childlike response to an adult conse-quence.

"You'll be okay, Dave."

"What makes you think so?"

"What are your options?"

"Please, just one more time, okay? I don't want it to end like this. Come on. Just one more time. It's not like you are going to get in any more trouble."

Anne let those words sit as she exhaled smoke. She watched it billow in the air a moment before the wind carried and dispersed it.

"Look, right now I have to think about my future, and right now you're not in it. Goodbye, Dave. Don't call me again."

***

The call still lingered on Anne's mind as she made her way back from town. She fumbled to light one last cigarette, anxious to get that last jolt of nicotine before she tossed the cigarettes out the window. Driving through large, shaded patches, she never noticed before how the immense forest swallowed up the lone road that connected these rentals to town. It was like someone had carved this little twist of asphalt and concrete into the landscape. As a result, since trees and brush couldn't grow out of the road, they seemed content to swell around it, threatening to take back what was once theirs.

Anne shivered when she thought how much the road reminded her of a throat, the throat of the forest, which would make their cabin and the space around it, the stomach.

"Shit!" Anne hissed, when the cigarette dropped from her mouth. The burnt end landed on her exposed legs, stinging her flesh.

She leaned down to retrieve it as she turned around the bend, the car tires crunching over the gravel that signaled approach to the cabin. Her fingers fumbled for the cigarette, almost catching it with the nails of her fingers. She took her eyes off the road a second to find the filter. When she looked up, her eyes flew open and her mouth formed a terrified "O."

Joshua stood in the middle of driveway. He either didn't hear the car coming or was distracted. Either way, his slight ten-year-old frame was in the car's bull's eye and Anne saw the panic in her son's face. It cut her to the bone.

Her foot crushed the brakes, and the car squealed to an abrupt halt, spraying gravel everywhere. She slammed her head into the steering wheel. The shock of the impact was like a sap strike, making everything distorted and blurry.

Anne struggled to put the car in park. She groped for the door handle, opening it, and stumbling out of the car to her son. She searched the trembling boy for any obvious signs of injuries. Finding none, she wrapped her arms around him tightly.

"I'm so sorry, I'm so sorry," she said, clutching Joshua tightly.

Jack came running out of the cabin. He ran down the steps.

"Jesus, Anne, what the hell happened?"

"I didn't see him, Jack," she said, her voice panged with guilt. "I didn't see him."

Jack pulled out a handkerchief and gestured to her forehead.

"You got a cut."

Anne still hugged Joshua but accepted the handkerchief with a free hand. She dabbed her forehead and saw small blood blots. Jack looked around. The driveway was empty save for Joshua.

"How did you not see him? What were you doing?" he asked her.

Still shaken, Anne could only shake her head. Jack went over to the car and turned it off. He saw the pack of cigarettes Anne had failed to throw away. When he looked at her, she avoided his gaze.

"I needed to calm my nerves," she said.

He went over to them and scooped up Joshua into his arms. The boy wrapped his legs around him and held his father tightly.

"Yeah, this is real calming," he told her, before carrying his son back into the cabin.

Anne stood up slowly. Another mistake in a long list of them. She didn't know how many chances that were left in their marriage, but she was going through them rather quickly.

She didn't know what prompted her to turn around. She didn't hear anything per se, but something was there – a smell? There was the odor of decaying leaves, sure, but why would that be unusual around a forest?

Still, she looked uneasily at the birches that stood proudly at the front of the tree line. They lazily swayed side-to-side in a way that made Anne think they were waving goodbye to her, which struck her odd because where would trees be going?

***

Henry dug into his pants and found his keys. He locked the front door of the store, jiggling the handle to make sure the lock was firmly in place, a routine his father had taught him and one that he practiced every day for fifty years. He always closed promptly at five-thirty, six days a week. Sundays were for God and football.

Taking out a small notebook from his shirt pocket, Henry made a note to give Gus Winston hell for failing to deliver the propane he had promised. He owed that nice lady a tank of propane, and if he had to put his boot up Winston's ass, then by Hell or highwater, Gus would find size eleven Timberlands up where "the sun don't shine."

The walk to his pickup wasn't far. The white Ford in need of a serious wash was right in front of him. Truth was, he didn't live far from his place of employment. No one did around here. Still, he preferred to drive. He found it difficult to rectify not driving when he had a prime parking spot right in front of the shop. Like buying a foreign car, it just seemed downright un-American if he didn't.

He wondered how the folks in the Daniels place were getting along. That place had a peculiar history, one that everyone in the community knew about but rarely mentioned to each other and never with outsiders. It wasn't their business and the towns folk kept it that way. You'd be hard pressed to find someone in the area that liked the tourists that made their way up from states like Connecticut and Massachusetts and New Jersey. They talked funny, were pushy, and spoke loudly. But there was no denying it; they injected a boatload of money into the town's tiny economy and people were able to purchase some luxuries they wouldn't have been able to buy without it.

Later that night, Henry's wife Margie made pork chops for dinner, mashed potatoes, and spinach. He didn't eat much, something that his wife immediately noticed since Henry took relish in putting away his wife's cooking.

"You feeling alright?" she asked him. They had been married for forty years come September and were no strangers to each other's habits.

Henry looked up from his plate, distracted.

"What? Oh, no, nothing. I'm fine," he said.

"You barely touched your pork chops. You're either sick or they don't taste good, and I know for a fact that they taste just fine."

He chuckled softly and offered her a weak smile.

"Guess, I'm not that hungry," he said.

"Which is why I asked how you were feeling."

"Got things on my mind."

Margie pushed her plate aside and leaned forward. "Like what? Maybe I can help."

He got up from the table. "Hold that thought. You be okay with the dishes?"

"Henry Wilmer Clay, I've been doing the dishes since I made you your first plate of fried chicken. I know my way around the kitchen sink."

Henry headed to the window and looked outside. The sky had made its transition from midnight blue to charcoal gray instead of black. The past few days had been uncharacteristically overcast, blanketing the stars with and endless tapestry of dirty clouds, making everything dark.

He worked over something in his mind. When he finally had a hold of it, he turned around and went to the door that led to the basement.

"I'm going to check something out," he told Margie.

She made a sound telling him she heard him and then went back to humming a song.

Henry descended the stairs, careful to bow his head to avoid hitting the wooden beam of the low ceiling. The basement was a mess, and he suddenly remembered how his wife had put CLEAN THE BASEMENT in large block letters on his "to do" list beneath the cookie magnet on the refrigerator. The list had subsequently been buried under photos of their grandkids and their homemade cards.

He moved boxes around, cursing to himself for keeping putting off this task. He must have made a ruckus because his wife called from upstairs.

"Henry! What on earth are you doing down there?"

"Visiting my girlfriend!"

"Good! Maybe she'll take out the trash!"

Henry chuckled. Margie hadn't lost her piss and vinegar as they had gotten older. He kept rearranging things until he found what he was searching for: a small trunk under two rolled-up rugs.

He opened it and rummaged until he found a binder that had newspaper clippings in it. The earliest one was from 1949 the latest one was last year. But they all detailed stories about missing kids and the cursed Raymond property and ultimately its sale to Les Daniels.

Les Daniels wasn't a local. He bought the property from Bob Raymond whose family went back more than a few generations. The Raymonds worked in sap collection, siphoning the nectar from the trees in the area, and selling it to a few local syrup merchants. They had been doing it for years, the region being perfect to cultivate the sap due to the sunny days and cold nights that gave the final product its uncanny sweetness. The Raymonds were hard working, God-fearing, and the perfect neighbors in that you rarely saw or heard them.

They were also troubled.

There had been a couple of accidents during their stay in the area. Shortly after the Second World War, a twelve-year-old boy wandered off in the woods one night during a blizzard. No one could figure out why. Some thought he was collecting wood for the fire. Others thought he got into a bottle of corn liquor and got drunk. Whatever it was, they found the boy two days later frozen solid next to a birch tree twenty yards from the cabin. The whipping wind and falling snow probably blinded him, and instead of staying in the fight, he surrendered to the elements.

Another boy, the brother of Bob Raymond's grandfather went missing. Back then, the cabin didn't have plumbing, so water had to be collected at a nearby spring whose source ran down from the nearby mountain. He went out one morning and never came back. They searched for him for nearly a week before the sheriff concluded that the boy must have ran away from home. Kidnapping was considered a possible explanation for a while, but lack of a ransom note made it an unlikely option. No body was found, so murder or accidental death was also ruled out. The boy just up and took off. How a nine-year-old boy would run away from home and survive was never further examined or explained.

After Bob Raymond's newborn died, the Raymonds had had enough of the "Raymond Curse," blaming the environment for the series of bad luck that family never seemed to be able to shake. And then Les Daniels waltzed into the area. Les Daniels was from the south side of the state looking for an investment opportunity. The price of the Raymond place fit the bill. For a lakefront property set on an acre and change of land, Les was prepared to go significantly higher than the asking price. Imagine his surprise when he found out it was considerably lower than expected. He was more than happy to use that extra money to refurbish the cabin, "Raymond Curse" be damned. After all, his last name was Daniels, and that carried with it more luck based on his previous successful business ventures.

And he was partly correct. He didn't have a problem because he never lived there.

Unfortunately, his renters couldn't boast the same.

In the eight years since Daniels got the property up and running, there had been three incidents with children gone missing, two boys and a girl, all between the ages of seven and ten. The incidents were horrible and regrettable but categorized by local law enforcement as unfortunate circumstances. Strange yes, but circumstances, nonetheless. The first boy's disappearance summoned up memories of the "Raymond Curse." The father was an experienced hunter teaching his son how to hunt using a bow. They went off before dawn, trekking into the woods to find a good place to set up. An hour into the hunt, a buck burst onto the scene and the two gave chase. Woods you didn't know well could be confusing even for the most experienced of hunters. Everything shifts with the light and the temperature. The father got turned around. The boy pursued the buck, getting deeper and deeper until he melted into the growth and thicket. He was never seen again.

The next victim was a girl, the youngest of the three. She was last seen playing by the lake near the forest. Her mother found her coloring book and crayons. She was hysterical. The entire town mobilized to find the little girl. The idea of someone so young and vulnerable missing was unsettling to anybody, and something everyone could get behind. Many people had kids. Many had daughters. They all could put themselves in this woman's place. Volunteers coursed through the woods. Divers from the state police searched the lake. But they didn't find her. She had up and disappeared, just like the boy.

The final one was the Rothman boy. That poor kid, Henry thought. That poor family. What happened to the son was nothing less than a tragedy. But at least in that case, they knew what happened to the kid. The father went plumb crazy, or so the story went. Pure evil crazy if that man did those depraved things to his family. Whatever happened to Peter Rothman, Henry blamed the self-isolation. People always said how much they wanted quiet, but the truth was, they had no idea of what they were in for. There was a difference between a weekend away, and three months in the middle of nowhere. If you weren't careful, too much solitude could have a decaying effect, screwing with a person's mind, twisting it around. Henry sized him up the first day he rolled into town. He was going to hole up and write the great American novel, that's what he told Henry when he picked up supplies at the store. He didn't say the novel was a horror story. Henry immediately noticed the soft hands when he gave the man his change. Rustic life wasn't for everyone, no matter how much the grass might have seemed greener. Henry didn't know he had a son until later.

By the second week of May, Peter Rothman started to fail to pick up his weekly groceries, forcing Henry to drop them off at the cabin. Peter never answered the door, no matter how hard or long he knocked. He'd end up leaving the box at the front door. One time he looked back, and he thought he saw a curtain move on the second-floor window, but he wasn't sure. He dropped off the groceries the following two weeks. Each time, the cabin seemed, different. It looked less like someone lived there and more that someone was holed up inside. The last time he made a run, he dropped off a case of floodlights and noticed that the exterior lights were on, even thought it was only four o'clock in the afternoon.

A week or so later, Peter Rothman's wife Karen made it to town and found the sheriff. The sheriff found Peter Rothman on the front porch. He sat with his arms on his knees, staring at the woods. His shirt was soaked in blood, and his eyes were wild and flickering. Although Henry wasn't there himself, he had heard that Peter Rothman's face was pale as a ghost and that he was a rambling mess, saying something about dark, or it was dark, or someone was dark. Hell, he didn't make much sense.

Self-isolation drove Peter Rothman to do unspeakable things. Again, if the story was true. But

Henry knew that stories weren't always what they seemed. He had heard the stories about that cabin and those woods just like everyone else in the area. And just because the sheriff said the obvious answer was usually the right one, didn't always make it so. It just made it the easiest.

"Henry! You want a sandwich?" Margie called out.

But Henry wasn't thinking about food. He was thinking about the other incidents that weren't documented at the time that they happened, stories his grandfather told him when it was just the two of them alone chopping firewood or hunting deer. Henry wondered how many other things that people had seen or had heard of from others and never told anyone, preferring to ignore the problem, hoping that it would pass them by.

Most of all though, he wondered about the nice family with the young boy who had rented the place. The realtor probably didn't tell them about the Raymonds or the missing children or what happened to poor Mark Rothman. The dollar signs from a month's rental probably got in the way.

*****

Jack poured himself a healthy glass of bourbon. Anne sat on the sofa in the living room, working on her own glass of Cabernet. He walked in with his drink and avoided sitting next to her, choosing the recliner to the right of the couch. Anne waited for him to have a sip of his drink before asking him a question.

"How is he?" she asked him.

"You shook him up pretty bad," he said. "He's asleep for now. Had to keep the lamp on until he fell asleep. I don't know how he can sleep with a small sun blaring in his face like that. It's become quite a routine now – night light in, door open, and hallway light on. The new normal." Jack took a long pull from his drink. The burn down his throat gave him courage to say something on his mind. "You almost killed him, Anne."

"He shouldn't have been playing in the driveway."

"Can't play in the driveway, can't play on the dock... where is the kid supposed to play? The woods?"

Anne looked at him sharply. "Not funny, Jack."

"I'm just saying."

"Did you know a boy got lost in those woods? They never found him, Jack. They never found the small boy."

"Jesus, after today, I don't think he'll stray from his room."

"I'm worried about him."

He softened. "So am I, Anne. So am I."

"The dark," she said. "Always the dark."

"It's different out here. In the city, light burns 24-7, and even in suburbia it's never completely pitch-black… but here… here's everything's so…"

"Creepy?"

"I was going to say 'quiet.'"

"Quiet and creepy. Vincent Price must have grown up here."

Jack didn't laugh, but then again, she wasn't exactly trying to be funny with the remark.

***

Joshua lay very still in bed. His eyes darted back and forth scrutinizing the shadows in the room, the dark wells and pockets the light didn't touch, couldn't touch. They seemed entrenched in these hard-to-reach places, looking to emerge and expand the first time a switch wasn't flipped on or the door not left ajar enough to let hall light creep inside. He had fooled his father. Joshua was getting good at it, knowing the amount of time his father expected him to need before his breath regulated and he fell asleep.

Once his father left, Joshua turned on the lamp, supplementing the night light to beat back the shadows even further. Only when it was on did Joshua feel comfortable enough to quietly close the bedroom door so as not to attract his parents' attention that he was in fact not asleep and have them come upstairs and investigate the reason why.

Joshua stared at the sneaker he found in the woods. He didn't know why he hadn't thrown it out. It was just a worn shoe that had been exposed to the elements. What's more, even if it had been cool in some found-object kind of way, it was missing its partner which made keeping it useless. Yet, for some reason, getting rid of it didn't feel like the right thing to do. And so, it sat on the small desk in the corner near the window.

Joshua did not hear the boy come in. No sound was made and if he looked, the window was only open six inches, so even if he somehow had climbed on the porch roof and hoisted himself up to and through the window with the deftness of an alley cat, there was no way he could have gotten inside the room without attracting Joshua's attention.

Yet there he was just the same. The boy was Joshua's age, with straight blonde hair with bangs that looked like they were trimmed by having a bowl placed over the head. He was dressed in a grass-stained white t-shirt. One foot was in a shoe, the other only in a white sock covered in dirt and grime. Everything was normal except for the eyes. They were an indescribable color that seemed to be in a constant state of flux, flashing from amber to brown and back again.

But it was the voice that chilled Joshua the most.

The Voice.

Not necessarily what the boy said, but how the words came out of his mouth. They were cold the way Joshua imagined a serpent's tongue to be as it flickered back and forth, smelling the air. Its timbre was one that Joshua hadn't heard before. It was toneless, with no noticeable inflection that gave depth and personality to conversation. What's more, when the boy spoke, Joshua grew very cold.

*You found my shoe*, the boy said, smiling, revealing a set of dark, rotting teeth.

Joshua recoiled in horror. He moved back on the bed until his back hit the wall.

"You're not real," Joshua managed, when he finally found his breath. "You're not real."

The boy walked over to the bed and sat on its edge. He looked at Joshua with the curious look of a scientist plodding through an experiment. Joshua wrinkled his nose. The smell of wet decaying leaves was very prevalent.

*Not anymore*, the boy conceded. *But I was.*

"What do you want?"

Another smile. Another reveal of those mud-coated teeth.

*To play*, the boy said simply. *I want to play.*

Joshua bluffed up some courage. "Go away," he said. "I mean it."

The boy ignored him. *When you come, we'll play together. It's fun to play in the woods, Joshua. So many trees. So many places to hide. No one will find you.*

Courage gone, Joshua retreated under the sheets, burying his head, and counting to twenty like his dad taught him to do. Fear only worked if you allowed it to, he reminded himself. Count to twenty and more often than not, all your troubles will disappear. So, Joshua listened to his father's words, and shut his eyes tightly and counted slowly. When he reached twenty, he pulled down the sheets in increments.

The boy was gone.

Joshua searched for some sign of his presence but could find none. He expected to see dirt or leaves or some evidence that this boy, this thing, visited him. But there was none, not even the place where he had sat on the bed. The nightlight burned in its socket like the end of a cigarette. Joshua made a face at the Bugs Bunny icon.

You let me down Bugs, Joshua thought. You owe me one.

Joshua settled back into bed. He wasn't going to fall asleep anytime soon. He knew that. But he didn't know what else to do.

Outside the window, the trees rustled as black clouds moved in. Darkness pushed in from the woods like a mist of pollen, and the gray night suddenly grew bleaker. Again, there would be no stars shining through that gauzy veil.

The curtains billowed slightly, rippling in an unfelt breeze. The darkness swirled in front of the open window, furling and unfurling in swells.

Joshua's eyes widened as he watched the outside shadows steadily consume the limited light that had shone through the window and on the floor. The more it ate, the more the night light flickered in warning. Or panic.

His head snapped to the window where blackness oozed in through the crack. It seeped in, running down the wall and pooling on the floor in front of the bed.

*We'll play in the dark, we'll play in the dark...,* the boy's voice said.

Panic-stricken, Joshua's hand fumbled for the lamp on the night table.

The black pool in front of him seeped over to the bed. It was moving, Joshua was sure of it. This wasn't his imagination. And his eyes certainly weren't playing tricks on him.

The pool, the dark, was coming for him.

Joshua's fingers found the pull-string and clicked the light on. The new bulb, the brighter wattage, should have made a difference, especially in a near-saturated black room.

But it didn't. It should have burned a hole in the darkness. The bulb glowed dully, almost timidly.

As the black pool oozed closer, Joshua did the only thing he could think of –

He screamed. He shrieked. He flat-out emptied his lungs.

And his parents responded.

They barreled into his room after the third ungodly wail. His mom turned on the main overhead light and Jack barreled in. He raced over to him, where he had pressed himself into the corner of the bed. Once his dad got his arms around him, Joshua clung onto him, squeezing him desperately.

"It's okay, sport," he whispered into his son's ears. "It's just a dream."

Joshua's voice trembled.

"Brighter light, Dad," he said, his voice a breathless whisper. "I need brighter light."

Anne made a face.

"What's this?" she said. She bent down and picked up a young tree branch with a cluster of leaves. "Did you bring this inside?"

Joshua shook his head.

"The boy did," he said. "It was the boy."

# Chapter 11

The next day, Jack brought up a couple of cases of the lightbulbs from the basement to Joshua's room. One by one, he tested the bulbs seeking his son's reaction. Each time the boy solemnly shook his head. The last option was the charm, and coincidence or not, it was the largest wattage.

"There you go, sport," Jack said. "Bright enough to put Las Vegas to shame."

"I'm sorry, Dad," Joshua said. He didn't meet his dad's gaze when he apologized.

Jack felt the pain in his son's voice. He scooped the boy up and sat down on the bed, setting his son on his lap.

"There's nothing to be sorry about," he said. "You want more light, you got more light. I think this should take care of it. Heck, I should probably change others in the house while I'm at it."

Joshua nodded enthusiastically.

"Good," Jack said. His son seemed better, but something gnawed on Jack's mind. "Hey, can I ask you something?"

His son nodded again.

"You mentioned 'the boy' last night. Who were you talking about?"

Jack followed his son's gaze as it fell on the shoe on the desk.

"Him," Joshua said.

"Who?"

"The kid whose sneaker that is."

Jack kept his face expressionless. He didn't want to show any preconceived judgment and let his son speak. "Oh, and you saw him last night? He was in your dream?"

Joshua shook his head. "No. He was here." He pointed to a spot near the window

Jack looked. "Here? In your room?"

"Yeah."

Jack maintained his poker face. Having your parents trust and confidence was pivotal at Joshua's age.

"I see. What did he say?"

"He wants to play with me," Joshua said. "He wants to play with me in the woods."

"The woods. He used that word specifically?"

"Yeah."

"That's all? He didn't say anything else?"

"No."

"Okay, sport. Just curious."

He stood up and set Joshua on his feet. Jack grabbed the boxes of lightbulbs and started for the door.

"Dad?"

"Yeah?"

"Can you leave a few of them here?"

Jack could feel his son's fear. He set the boxes down on the floor near the closet.

"Sure, sport."

"And Dad? I don't want to play with him," Joshua said. "The boy. I don't want to be in the woods with him alone."

Jack didn't know how to respond, so he didn't say anything. He offered his son an understanding smile and then walked out the door.

***

Anne waited in her car until she saw Henry's pick-up park in his customary spot in front of the store. She glanced at her watch; it was nine o'clock on the nose. He was the type of man whose habits you could set a clock to. She got out and intercepted him just as he put his key into the lock.

"Jesus, missus," he said, nearly jumping two feet in the air when she put a hand on his shoulder. "You sure give a bigger jolt than my wife's coffee."

"I'm sorry. I just had to see you."

"I know I promised you the propane. I'm headed there this afternoon to pick a tank up for you myself. I promise."

"It's not that," Anne said, biting her lip. She didn't know how to explain what she wanted to ask him.

"Everything alright?" he asked. "Your little one okay?"

"Yes. No. I don't know," she said and released an exasperated sigh that threatened the emergence of tears.

Henry's face softened. "What can I do for you?"

"I need to know about our place."

"The cabin."

"Please. It's important."

Henry nodded. He removed the keys from the lock. "You had your coffee yet?"

They went to Mae's, the only place in town to get breakfast all day long. The waitress set them up in a booth in back and set them up with two large mugs of coffee. Then she told him everything – about Joshua getting lost in the woods, the nightmares, and the unnamed boy that her son told them about. The whole time, Henry's face remained impassive, the heavy soulful eyes betraying no internal emotion or judgment. He quietly drank his coffee, folding his hands on the table when they weren't hoisting the mug to his lips.

"I know this must sound silly, but I figured if anyone knew anything, it'd be you. At least I'd know if there was something legitimate or if I was just going crazy."

"You're not crazy," Henry said, after a moment of thought. "That place has had a history of… problems."

"Problems?" she asked.

"For as long as I can remember, there have been incidents, little things that didn't quite square, if you know what I mean. The property has had only two owners but neither one had much luck. Since Daniels bought the property and made it a rental, families would move in and things would happen."

Anne looked up from her coffee. "What kinds of things?"

Henry sighed. "The bad kind. The ones where people get hurt. No one around here talks about it much, but we all know about the stories."

Anne shrunk in her seat. "What kind of stories?" Her voice was barely above a whisper.

Henry set down his mug and looked her in the eyes.

"You want to know about the boy?"

"Yes."

"You remind me of the family that was there before you," he said. "A small family. Mom and Pop. A ten-year-old son. They were looking for a good summer away. I think the father was a writer or wanted to be a writer or was writing something or another. Anyway, they were here about a week before the same old problems surfaced again."

"Same old problems?" Anne asked.

Henry lifted the mug to his lips. Anne noticed that his hand trembled now.

"What about the boy?" she said.

"Thing about kids? They aren't tainted like adults. They aren't jaded, or prejudiced, or biased. They got no preconceived notions about what is and what's supposed to be. They accept everything at face value. No better conduit than that."

"Conduit to what?"

"See, the boy felt it first. Whatever it was, something didn't quite sit right with him. Kids are young, but they aren't stupid. So, he did what any good child does when he's concerned about something. He told his parents. And they did what parents typically do – they didn't believe what he told them."

Henry spilled some coffee on the table. He retrieved a napkin from a dispenser and mopped it up.

"I'm not knocking parents, mind you," Henry continued. "Any adult would have done the same thing. Why would any of us believe something so outrageous, and well, impossible? Kids are known to have active imaginations. But what we forget is that they're also known for telling the truth without varnish in a way that only children can. They'll ask a cripple why he's in a chair, or a guy with an eye patch what happened to his peeper. It's not about the insult with kids; it's about their curiosity."

Anne knew this to be the truth. It struck too close to the mark and the insecurity that it caused her confirmed its veracity.

"Then something happened," he said. "Something made that boy more scared than he had ever been before in his life. They disappeared shortly after. Well, the mother and son did. The father was found after sitting on the porch with blood all over his shirt."

"He killed them?"

"That's what the law believes. But no bodies were found. There were no signs of struggle, nothing that would point to foul play by another human being in or around the cabin."

"But they arrested him. They couldn't get a confession?"

"He went crazy. A doctor diagnosed him with a mental illness. So, even if he did confess, it wouldn't stand up in court. Besides, aside from the blood, there was no evidence that he did anything. Those woods were searched with cadaver dogs and they found nothing. One thing is to kill a person and burying 'em. But not to find a body? Well, that dog don't hunt, as we say."

"But the police?"

"Case closed. No one wanted to press further."

"How do you know all this?"

"The man's wife came to me, like you have, wanting to know the same things you're asking me now. Before she and her son went missing."

"That's incredible," Anne said breathlessly.

"No, what's incredible is that things like this happened over and over and over again. They all weren't deaths or missing families, but similar types of unexplained stuff. Who knows how long this has really been going on?"

"What do you mean?"

"For years, this area has withstood the encroachment of transformation. Look around you – not much has changed since the first settlers stumbled into here. Why is that you think? Developers have come, plans have been made by smart rich men down at the state capitol to turn this community into a vacation paradise. Every time they get something going and start to clear out tracts for development, the jobs ultimately end up being abandoned. No muss, no fuss."

"Land development funds dry up all the time," Anne said. Her throat was suddenly very dry. She drank down the small glass of water the waitress had set beside her coffee.

"It wasn't a money issue. The money was there. The conviction to do something was not. See, the way I figure it is that there are two natural states – light and dark, nature and civilization. When they are kept in balance, all seems fine. When not, nature has a way of setting things straight the way that only it can."

"Are you saying that the woods are alive?"

Henry looked around nervously in an attempt to see if anyone was in ear shot. When he seemed satisfied that none were, he continued. "I'm saying when the town grew, people pushed deeper into the woods. And finally, the woods started pushing back."

Anne's face drained of color. She looked like she lost two pints of bloods as she listened to the story.

"Can I – can I ask you one more question."

"Go on." Henry ran a hand across his unshaven chin. "I'm not holding back."

"What was the boy's name?"

Henry picked up the teaspoon and stirred his coffee a few times. "Mark," he said finally. "Mark Rothman."

***

Outside, Anne barely made it to the car when she bent over and emptied her stomach on the ground. She quickly looked around to see if anyone noticed. Foot traffic was scarce, but you never knew who was glancing out a window. The more she tried to tell herself these were just coincidences, the more she wasn't reassured. There were just too many parallels that warranted further and deeper investigation, but who was she going to ask? Besides, technically nothing bad had happened. Sure, Joshua got mixed-up in the woods but other than giving her a mild heart attack, he was healthy. There was that issue with the dark, and in retrospect, renting a condo at the beach may have been the smarter decision for her and Jack to hash out the things with Selznick. A condo at least gave off the perception of being among people, and there was always the strip of sand in front or the community pool to know that you weren't totally alone.

The cabin was more austere, but the remote monastic environment was what she had thought they both wanted, that they both needed.

Now she just wanted to leave.

Anne found an old water bottle in the car and rinsed her mouth, spitting out the sour taste of her bile. She contemplated on the best way to approach Jack about leaving. It would be a waste of two thousand dollars, but finances were not what weighed on her mind. There were other things to consider, their son for one. Their sanity, another.

She leaned against her car and watched some of the locals emerge and disappear into storefronts. Their faces were hard-planed, their eyes always set forward, never distracted with side glances. Smiles were reserved for the familiar. Everything else, strangers mostly, got a cold scrutiny and a formal polite nod of acknowledgement.

Anne paused before she opened the car door. She didn't feel like rushing back just yet. The town might not exactly be her cup of tea, but it seemed like neutral ground, and gave enough time for her to catch her breath and sort through the information Henry told her.

***

Joshua found his father in the living room. He was staring out the window, but with a look that told Joshua that he was "zoning" and not really looking at anything in particular. The boy noticed the glass of what he knew was his father's "special drink" and looked at the clock on the wall above the fireplace. It was earlier than he usually started with what his dad called, "the hard stuff." A black ledger book he hadn't seen before was beside him. His mother still had not returned from town. He hadn't felt like going fishing that morning. The allure of the outside and its unexplored possibilities had no appeal for Joshua. He didn't want to leave the cabin, but he didn't necessarily want to remain inside either.

He thought about the boy. His father insisted that it had been a dream, a fabrication his mind created because of his experience being lost in an unfamiliar place; of being lost in the woods. In the antiseptic light of morning, that explanation seemed reasonable. Fear was a powerful influence that made people see things, do things, that they normally wouldn't see or do. Joshua found a shoe in the forest and immediately his mind sought to come up with an explanation of why a lone sneaker would be so deep in the woods. There was a child's shoe, so naturally there had been a boy out there at one time or another. He could have been camping or searching the area with friends or family. He could have been playing a made-up game or imitating a TV show he had watched.

But why did the shoe come off?

That was the nagging question Joshua kept coming around to when all of the other possibilities filled in the blanks.

The shoe was the key. If he could solve the mystery of the shoe, then he could put unanswered questions to rest.

Joshua carried the sneaker in his hand and set it on the coffee table. His father looked up from his book, then at the shoe, then Joshua.

"What's going on, sport? Change your mind about netting some fish?"

The boy shook his head. He had something else on his mind. He gestured to the small dirty shoe.

"The sneaker," Joshua said. "How did he lose his sneaker?'"

Jack sighed. He closed his book and set it aside. "I don't know, Joshua. He was a careless child obviously. Kids aren't very responsible in the first place. How do you lose a shoe?"

"I haven't lost any shoes," Joshua said.

"How would you, you think? Playing comes to mind to me. Running around, his foot gets snagged in an upturned root, his shoe pops off."

Joshua considered the scenario, then shook his head.

"No," he said. "You would know your shoe is off. Running around without a shoe would hurt your foot. He wasn't playing."

"Okay," Jack said. "Who said he was wearing the shoe in the first place? You assume he was but what if he and his dad were just hiking through the forest and it dropped out of a bag or something. If they were hiking, sneakers wouldn't be the best attire to traverse across uneven ground and through streams."

That thought had not occurred to Joshua. The boy's face registered the legitimacy of that prospect.

But his contentment was short lived, and the furrowed brow returned on his forehead.

"Maybe," he said. "But I don't think so. I didn't see anything else that might've fallen out of an unzipped bag."

"It's a big forest," Jack countered. "Things could be dropped anywhere.  Animals pick up them up."

That answer was less than satisfactory. Joshua wasn't convinced. Jack sighed.

"So, how do you think it happened?"

"I think the boy was running," he said matter of fact.

"Like I said. He was having fun. Running, playing, and then pop! It's off."

Joshua shook his head. "Fear," he said.

"What?"

"Fear. That will keep you running out of your shoes. That will keep your feet from hurting when you step over jagged rocks or sprint past thorns and prickles. That will keep you moving when it's hard to breathe and your lungs hurt. It was fear."

His father's face was frozen with the simplicity of his explanation.  He opened his mouth to respond but the words had not formulated in his mind yet. When they did, what came out was meaningless.

"I don't know what to say," he said. "It's possible."

Joshua nodded in silent agreement. Then he looked at the shoe and at the trees through the front window. He started for the front door.

"Where you going?" Jack asked.

"I want to check on something," he said

"Don't stray too far. Your mother will be home soon."

"I'll be right out front."

***

Joshua stood at the edge of the gravel driveway looking at the tree line marking the beginning of the woods. He took his time with his examination. He trained his eyes at the far end of the line and slowly tracked the clear demarcation between forest and grass, taking in every branch, every base, every tuft of weed, and every leaf before moving to the next set. It was a painstaking process but a necessary one for his own well-being.

Every time he inspected the trees, they seemed different; changed somehow. There was nothing specific he could point to, nothing so obvious as a blatant change of color or tree genus. It was not like the white birches suddenly turned red or the thick clumps of pine suddenly sprung up where none had been before. Still, they just didn't look right.

Even the Widow's Hand seemed to have altered slightly. He borrowed the name from a horror book he had read but the moniker seemed well suited to describe the one limb that protruded into the space above the driveway. The naked branches gave them a bony appearance reminiscent of the gnarled fingers of a skeleton. Only the limb seemed to hang lower now, the ends of the bough tantalizingly closer.

Joshua started to walk along the line. The Ripple returned. It was subtle, but he noticed it immediately, and to confirm his suspicions, he'd pick up his pace and then slow to a crawl seeing if the change of tempo altered how the Ripple reacted. Whatever he did, the Ripple kept pace with him, just a step behind like a predator.

"You are alive," Joshua said to the Widow's Hand that swayed when the Ripple stopped with him. He could almost touch the lowest gnarled branch and was considering doing so until he thought better of it. While he couldn't see any overt danger in doing so, there was also no tangible benefit, and the unknown was never a comforting choice to make.

Joshua walked back to the driveway. He didn't need to turn back to know that the Ripple followed him lock step. But he did so anyway, as he needed to check on something. His eyes unsuccessfully searched for his target, scanning the area in which he thought he had left it. Yet, there was no sign of the marker, which perplexed Joshua. Only when he saw the long grass and the brown dead pine needles did he understand what had happened, and that realization chilled him.

The twelve-inch distance he had marked with a stick had shrunk considerably, by almost half as far as Joshua could estimate.

Either the forest shifted closer, or one of his parents had moved the stick.

One explanation was entirely plausible, the other anything but. Still, if Joshua had to bet, he would put whatever he had in his savings account on the former and not the latter.

The branches rustled and swayed in front of him, as if to confirm his suspicions, and as a reward for his understanding, was making a distinct overture.

An invitation.

For what? To enter the forest? To play?

Joshua got an idea. He saw the soccer ball near the front porch and ran over to retrieve it. He dribbled it across the gravel to the start of the grass near the tree line. He teed the ball up on a good clump of grass. He picked his spot, a clear space between two birches and above a tangle of Arrowwood, whose creamy white flower clusters covered the ends of the multi-branched shrub.

His soccer instincts kicked in. He studied the target like his coaches had taught him and then gauged the distance between him and the ball like he did when he practiced penalty kicks. When he was ready, he strode confidently and kicked the ball hard with the instep of his right foot. The ball quickly travelled the distance sailing over the top of the Arrowwood. Joshua lost it in the thick folds of vegetation, hearing the ball crash through branches and foliage before coming to a stop.

Joshua waited, his eyes flickering back and forth to see the tree line's reaction.

When he had just about given up, the trees answered his call. The leaves shook fervently, and bushes rustled as if thousands of unseen creatures coursed through the underbrush. The tip of the Arrowwood bush trembled, ejecting the soccer ball. It landed on the ground, bouncing twice before rolling to a stop a foot away from Joshua.

"Holy crap," Joshua said.

The Ripple moved back and forth like a dog's tail wagging happily.

Joshua stood transfixed. He didn't hear it when his father called him for some lunch. He just stared at the tree line that wanted him to play so badly that it hurt.

"Josh!"

The angry call from his father snapped Joshua from his spell.

"Coming!"

He grabbed the ball from the ground and hustled back to the front porch. He looked up at the pewter-gray sky as he walked up the steps. It had been overcast for so many days, Joshua had almost forgot how hot and humid it was when his family first arrived. The gray had become part of the landscape the past few days, and was a constant reminder that night was only hours away. And so was the dark.

He would be better prepared tonight. The brighter bulb in the lamp on the bedside table would drive anything spooky back into the corners from which it came.

No more surprises, that's for sure.

Joshua would be ready.

***

Children's fears of the dark had origins that likely stretched back to the fires of civilization when humans first understood there to be a difference between light and black. Dark was the absence of light, and anytime a person couldn't see, there was immediate alarm of the unknown. Fear was deeply rooted in uncertainty. It fed on imagination and failure to conceptualize. That's why children were prone to being afraid of the dark – it first took hold when their imaginations were developing, when they lacked the ability to differentiate fantasy from reality. Things were scary because there was no reason for them not to be. If it wasn't familiar, then it was something to shy away from. Better to keep a low profile than be eaten by something that lurked beneath the bed.

This happened naturally and to everyone, and as children grew into adults, these concerns were typically shed like an old skin.

Well, most of the time. Some kept it up to and through adulthood. They didn't speak about it much and never to anyone, but they were the ones that would make sure doors were closed and LED displays were raised to the highest levels of illumination.

In some instances, there was an inciting event that led to children's and even adults' fears of the dark. For example, being stuffed into lockers or shut into a closet for long periods of time could serve as catalysts for this anxiety. Unfortunate victims of school bullies often found themselves in this category. Not that everyone who was bullied became scared of the dark. But adults who still carried that fear, and were honest with themselves, usually could trace it to a specific occurrence that transpired during their elementary school years. These afflictions generally lasted longer, requiring substantial time with a therapist or psychiatrist to determine the sources of these issues and to develop appropriate treatment strategies to manage them.

Joshua's fear was not borne of any school transgression. He wasn't the target for ridicule or harassment and was generally well-liked by his peers. When it came to playground games, he was usually among the first picks when teams were chosen. The older kids left him alone, seeking more attractive children on which to inflict their self-inflated superiority.

No, Josh's fear came much earlier. He had no recollection of the event that started it. He couldn't have had. Not at six months of age. But that was ground zero. That's when the fear imprinted itself on his mind.

He never knew this. How could he know?

One Saturday night, Anne brought Joshua to his crib. She read him some books and played with the spongy plane mobile hanging over him. Joshua smiled. Up until that night, he always smiled a lot, a happy baby that gave her no more fuss than any other healthy baby.

Jack was working late at school. He was still on his probationary period at the community college and he wanted to demonstrate his commitment by putting in extra hours, seeing students longer than his established office hours, tutoring, and otherwise giving the dean a glimpse of what he could expect from Jack if given a full professorship.

Once asleep, Anne went down the hall to the living room. She opened another bottle of wine (the previous one only had a glass and a half left, all of which she consumed as she fed Joshua) and settled in to watching bad TV. This one was red, but it was still wine and tasted far better than beer, which would have been her only alternative.

Had she not been tipsy already, she would have remembered to turn on the baby monitor in Joshua's room. She did not and even the receiver on the coffee table did not help remind her to do so. After her second glass of the red, she thought it went down pretty well, all things considered. Malbecs tended to be a little "meatier" than what she customarily drank; whites were crisp and light and therefore easily consumable.

She didn't hear Joshua's first cries, mostly because the television's volume was too high. The movie was a favorite, one that Anne had seen a thousand times before and that she would watch anytime it aired regardless of where she picked it up. Once she found it, she topped off her glass, curling her feet underneath her on the couch. Her buzz settled in nicely, making her cheeks warm and softly blurring the edges of her vision.

Her mind drifted a bit like it did when she drank too much. A scene between the main couple in the movie made her think of times in college. The actor bore a resemblance to one of her college boyfriends and the association made Anne think of him and their brief three-month fling.

Fooling around in the basement of the college library? Hello!

Joshua cried again, louder this time, but Anne did not hear her son for a second time. She was back in college with the most handsome of the men with whom she ever had relations. What happened to him? she thought, making a mental note to Google him sometime. She closed her eyes to focus on his face, imagining his sloppy hair and the horned-rim glasses that he always wore…

Anne bolted upright. She looked around to gain her bearings. The movie she was watching had finished and another one was in progress. She looked at the clock – forty minutes had passed.

The screaming was unlike anything she had heard before.

It sounded like… anguish. Pure anguish.

And pain. The type of pain that only fear can instill. It wasn't corporeal. It was deeper than that.

Anne got up too quickly and almost tripped over the ottoman. She caught the bookcase and was immediately thankful it was bolted to the wall. She steadied herself and hurried down the hallway to Joshua's room.

She froze when she turned on the light.

She wanted to vomit.

Her son lay on his back, screaming bloody murder. The boy's small hands clawed frantically at the space above him. For a split second, it appeared to Anne that Joshua was fighting something that only he could see.

She rushed to the crib and scooped the boy up and held him close to her. The little body trembled, and she cooed as best as she could to soothe the frightened boy.

Anne and Jack chalked it up to babies being babies. They cried. They screamed. That's just what they did. They were experiencing the world in which they entered. There was nothing more to it than that.

But the boy refused to sleep in a dark room after that. Anne and Jack moved the crib to their bedroom, and if they wanted to get any sleep, they learned to keep the light in the hallway on and the bedroom door open. Jack was certain that the boy would outgrow the issue.

He was wrong.

The move into a big bed seemed to ameliorate the situation at first. The space was less confining than a crib, which suited Joshua's tendency to move around in different positions when he slept. The reprieve ultimately proved temporary.

When Joshua was six the night terrors returned. They were infrequent at first. A night or two a month, nothing more. But the older Joshua got, the more frequent they became.

Anne and Jack's marriage wasn't in the best position, and this development didn't help matters any. Their pediatrician conducted physical exams but did not see any adverse malady that would contribute to the terrors. The doctor talked with Joshua in private, seeing if there was something in the descriptions of them that might provide a clue to whether this issue was physical or emotional. Concluding the latter, he recommended that Anne and Jack take Joshua to a Dr. Valerie Larson, a specialist that operated a practice from her home.

After a few meetings, Dr. Larson recommended Joshua undergo polysomnography – a sleep study to try to determine what may be triggering the night terrors. The study provided little useful insight aside from informing them that Joshua's night terrors occurred during the deepest stage of non-rapid eye movement sleep, and occurred during midnight and 2 a.m.

Joshua had five more sessions with Dr. Larson before the doctor told them that there was little that could be done. Her professional opinion was that the night terrors would pass in time and the best thing that they could do is to reassure their child, speak in soft and calm tones. The terrors would pass, she told them. He was fine.

The doctor was right. The terrors did pass but Joshua's fear of the dark did not. He would not go to sleep without some light source nearby and visible. That made Jack rummage through the attic for boxes his mother kept from his childhood to find the Bugs Bunny night light. A year and a half later, his son still used the light.

# Chapter 12

That night, Joshua's bedtime routine did not skip a beat. His father read him a story, and then they talked a bit about how he was doing. He even let Joshua ask him about what was going on between him and his mother, and what would happen to Joshua if things went one way or the other. Jack did not rush the boy, letting him work through the situation in his mind. He also didn't sugarcoat anything either. Jack was giving him, as he said in his own words, the straight-dope, no malarkey. Nothing was decided, largely because he wasn't sure what to do. What he was sure about, his father stressed, was that he wanted to return to the way they were before the indiscretion. Back when they told jokes, and all made bad meals together. When they were a family.

In the end, Jack tucked the boy in, checking the night light before walking out, and leaving the door half-way open. Once he heard his father go down the steps, Joshua got out of bed, giving the room a thorough investigation to ensure that nothing was under the bed or tucked secretly away in the closet. Only after he double-checked his satisfaction did Joshua return to his bed, sitting up with his back against the wall. That was the way he began his night, that he would begin all of his nights from then on –

watchful and waiting – like a soldier waiting for an unseen enemy to come into view.

Outside, darkness billowed. If Joshua didn't know better, he would have said that it appeared to be sizing him up.

***

Anne wanted to talk to Jack. She waited in the living room for him to come down after putting their son to bed. She had opened a bottle of red and drank two glasses before Jack emerged from their son's room. She had a glass ready for him when he sat down before telling him about her meeting with Henry. Anne studied his face, looking for a reaction, as she relayed everything she had been told about the cabin, the area, the troubled past, and the last family that occupied the space in which they now sat.

She appreciated that he didn't interrupt her the entire time, letting her get it all out. She needed to free herself of the burden of the truth. It was all too fantastical to be broken up in pieces. Then it would seem less real, more musings than fact. When Anne finished, she downed the rest of the wine in her glass, which happened to be her third. She had finished three-quarters of the bottle on her own.

"It sounds like a ghost story, Anne. The more rural the place, the better the story."

Jack's response was not what she expected, but she was prepared to respond to it.

"He wasn't telling a ghost story, Jack. He didn't even want to say anything. I had to practically wrestle it out of him. It's like it's a private thing with the people that live here. They ignore it as long as it doesn't touch them. It's like they know if they just leave it alone, that the bad things won't feel threatened and go after them."

Jack finished the wine in his own glass. "You know how that sounds, don't you?"

She nodded her head, emptying the bottle of the last drops of the red liquid. Jack wasn't convinced fully, she knew that, but was coming around.

"What do the authorities say about this?" he asked, handing her his glass to drink. "What was their take of events?"

"What do you think? They are all open, unsolved cases. Well, except for the latest one."

"What do you mean?"

"The family here before us? They found the father sitting on the porch, his shirt soaked in blood. He lost his mind, mumbling incoherently. And the wife and son? They searched the cabin and the surrounding area but couldn't find them."

"He killed them?"

"That's what they believe. But they didn't find the bodies. Not a trace. There were no signs of dismemberment or corporal decomposition. They just disappeared. All except for a crazy man, who's now a resident of the looney bin in Larson."

"I don't know, Anne. Sounds pretty much open and shut."

"I'm not so sure, and if you gave it any thought, you wouldn't either."

"Just because they can't find bodies, doesn't mean he didn't do it," Jack offered. Even his face betrayed belief in the words coming out of his mouth.

"Cadaver dogs cased the area, Jack. Divers searched the lake. They came up with nothing. Where does a person hide two bodies here?"

"Yeah, I know, but still..."

"Come on, Jack. Take a look around you. The sheriff doesn't look like he exerts too much effort for tourists. But in this case, he did."

"They could have left," Jack offered. "They could have picked up and gotten out of there. Maybe he was abusive? Maybe they were having problems?" He took back the glass of wine for the final gulp.

"Lots of maybes. But why stay hidden? And who can fall off the grid like that? I don't think so. There's something else to the story."

"What are you trying to say, Anne?" he continued. "The woods are cursed? There is a boogeyman that comes in the night?"

Anne reached out and touched his hand. "Jack, I'm scared."

Jack regarded her hand. He set the glass down and held it for a moment. Anne liked the familiarity of his touch.

"I don't know, Anne. Why didn't we hear about this before? I mean, you'd think that something like what you're telling me would have made the bigger news cycles at some point."

"I've been thinking about that. The nearest thing I can figure is that the volume isn't there. It's not like this is a serial crime in the sense that we have come to understand them. A killer like that may take a month or two off, but the numbers start piling up in a noticeable way. Even Ted Bundy couldn't escape that. This is different. It's a small town in a small area and people, if you haven't noticed, stick to themselves and don't offer too much to visitors in the way of pleasantries."

"You want to leave?"

"Very much."

She didn't hesitate with her response. Her husband looked into her eyes, searching for something. He released her hand and stood up and went to the kitchen to get another bottle of wine. He popped the cork and walked back to his wife.

"We can go, sure. But what does that really accomplish? I can't help but think that on some level these stories are more about concealing the bigger problem between us."

"We can hash that out back home, Jack."

"But we didn't, did we? Isn't that what prompted us to come here? To avoid distraction, to be able to address the problems at the root and see what can be done?"

"Yes, but this is different. This is – "

"Serious? Look, I hear what you're saying. Am I spooked a little by what you told me? Yes. And God knows don't let Joshua hear that talk. He'll never get to sleep again. But I guess what I'm asking is, if we leave before we settle things, aren't we just kicking the bigger problem down the road?"

Anne's eyes flared, but then she got control of her emotion. She breathed deeply and looked him squarely in the eyes.

"I own that, Jack, okay? I own it. But I'm not talking about an affair that means nothing to me. I'm talking about things that scare the shit out of me. I'm about twenty years too old to be this scared about things that go bump in the night. And the fact that I am tells me everything I need to know about whether this is about trying to dodge the truth or making sure my family is safe."

***

Henry sat on a folding chair in the basement, hunched over the trunk he jokingly referred to as the "Time Capsule" because of all the newspaper clippings and articles that he kept and preserved inside. He performed a necessary service, curating all of the newspaper clippings and articles that documented the activities in the area. Some of the early newspapers were so brittle that Henry had to buy plastic covers to preserve the integrity of the pages. His grandfather had started keeping these mementos the moment the first incidents happened. There may have been others. If there were, Henry certainly didn't know about them. As long as things stayed the way it should, the town didn't care. This gave Henry the unceremonious title of area de-facto historian, documenting the incidents people wanted to forget, keeping them tucked away for a rainy day.

Small clippings with titles like "Missing Boy" and "Family Disappears" and "Accident by Crescent Lake" filled the trunk, the last record of the people's lives detailed in a 120-word column on page three of the local rag. There were more headlines like those, because there had been more questionable incidents than he had told that nice lady. He decided not to give her full disclosure; he didn't think he had to; the point having already been made. Still.

He dug out the most recent story that featured the Rothmans. Even the author – Mitch Applebaum a sanctimonious S.O.B as far as Henry was concerned – succumbed to the Council, softening the story's rougher edges, painting poor Peter Rothman as a disturbed and unhappy individual. The slanted article bordered on character assassination using an unidentified source that "let it slip" that Peter Rothman was an unfit father and husband. The article wrapped around one of the last photos of Mark Rothman, smiling, a child of possibilities that were suddenly ripped from him by the person who should have most protected him.

Well, it was pouring now.

His pudgy wife padded down the steps and walked over to him. He heard her approach but was too transfixed by the sheer volume of questionable occurrences to acknowledge her presence, even when she put a hand on his shoulder.

"It wasn't your fault, Henry," she said softly. "You talked to them. You tried to tell them. What else were you supposed to do?"

"Get them to listen," he said gruffly.

"And what? Have Les Daniels get a whiff of that and sue you for slander? No, thank you. You did your part. More than your part, as far as I'm concerned."

"You keep saying that and I keep feeling different."

"You warned them about the woods. You warn all of them that come by. You've done what you can."

"Words, Margie. There are words and there are actions. I needed to get my fingers dirty, and I didn't. I got to live with that."

Margie bit her lip. She wasn't prone to anger, but Henry could see her cheeks reddening.

"I swear, if people just learned to stay home, focus on themselves and theirs, that cursed cabin would starve and die."

"Good way to put it," Henry said.

"Good way to put what?"

"Starving that place out. Letting it die."

She knelt beside her husband and forced him to look into her eyes.

"It's always been what it's always been," she said. "The natural order, so to speak."

"The natural order," Henry muttered.

"Someone ought to burn that place down to the ground. End the cycle or whatever it is that makes it do all of those horrible things."

An idea leapt to Henry's mind. "Or woods," he said.

"What?"

Henry sighed. It wasn't as crazy as it sounded. After all, the cabin was just that – a structure made of wood, and plumbing, and dry wall, and well, things. Blaming the cabin for the craziness was just about as absurd as blaming it on the weather or the spring that rain from the mountains.

The woods were different. Henry knew that. Hell, they all knew that.

The crammed woods with their high canopies and thick leaves that blotted out the sky and made everything so…

Dark.

Henry got up off the chair and helped his wife to her feet. Her expression was one of concern. They had been married long enough for her to understand when he had reached a decision.

"Where are you going at this hour?" she asked.

"Out," he said.

"Henry…"

He turned to the only woman he had loved his entire life. His eyes softened just a bit and he touched her cheek delicately. They never said they loved each other. Words like that didn't need to be said between them. They preferred to show it in the little things that they did for one another. A sandwich that was never asked for but ready for him at the table. Or a bolt of fabric that he automatically picked up at Henson's when he knew she was looking to make a dress for herself for the summer festival. Love that had to be articulated wasn't true love; it was something to be marked off a checklist. Those that had to say it had to be reminded of it. For people like Henry and Margie, it simply was.

"I'll be back in a while," he said. "Don't wait up."

Margie feigned indignation to cover her obvious fear. "Henry Wilmer Clay, I haven't gone to bed without your smelly feet by my side since you put this ring on my finger, and I'm certainly not going to start now. I'll be up. And I'll be waiting."

"It's a deal."

He smiled one more time, and then headed up the stairs.

***

The windless breeze stirred, and the birches and pines at the front of forest's edge that faced the cabin rustled fervently. The trees on the other side remained eerily still, as if standing in quiet witness to the events unfolding. The evening's overcast sky deepened with hues of opacity as if some painter mixed various hues of black and white and spread them in a series of dabs and strokes. Even to an untrained eye, it was apparent that something was building.

Darkness continued to pool in from the woods, gathering and billowing into a formidable presence. It was a truly magnificent sight, something that few could imagine and even fewer could pre-sume was naturally possible. There weren't that many things in nature commanded this type of awe – a tsunami for sure, earthquakes registering eight or higher on the Richter scale, and tornados with 300 mile-an-hour winds were in a singular, near-peerless category. But darkness that shifted and realigned on its own, independent of any outside influence, well, that was just something special.

That was just straight-up Old Testament.

Once it collected itself, the darkness oozed across the gravel driveway, swallowing up the stones over which it passed. It creeped soundlessly, leaving no trace of its progression, stopping only to recali-brate and reformulate its entirety. Then, the darkness stretched itself upward in a great unfurling. An amor-phous mass, tentacles of black curled and uncurled as it rose to the second-floor window, the one above the porch that faced the great forest face. It paused as it settled hovering in the space, looking inside, wait-ing for its moment to strike.

***

The boy's voice came in clear. It was looking for Joshua. It wanted him.

Joshua, come out and play…

Joshua sat up in bed, sheets drawn tightly around his neck. It was a trick he learned from his friend about vampires. They couldn't bite your neck if you had it protected. At least, that was the idea. So, Joshua brought them up tightly under his chin. If it worked to dissuade vampires from creeping in on him and sneaking a bite, it might accomplish the same objective with this – whatever this – was.

*We will have fun together forever and ever and ever...*

Outside, the Darkness blotted out whatever minimal light that came through the window. Like a solar eclipse, everything quickly became squid-ink black, only instead of passing like an eclipse, it remained in place, blocking out any and all exterior light that penetrated through the overcast sky. Worse, the Dark seeped through cracks in the window seal, running down the wall onto the uneven wood floorboards.

Joshua's hand trembled as he reached over to the lamp. His fingers fumbled to find the dangling metal pull-string. He clicked on the light and the bright wattage lit up the room like a super nova. The light was pure white, a stark contrast to the blackness that was trying to encroach. The intensity beat back the shadows, stalling the movement of the night.

The victory proved unsatisfying and short lived. The fierce starkness of the bulb suddenly and steadily dimmed, succumbing to the Darkness pressing in through the crack in window. It was impossible; Joshua had tested it twice that day. The socket was good. The electricity, plentiful.

But the bulb went out.

It didn't pop or crackle. It was as if the Darkness wrapped its slender jawed fingers around the base of the bulb and squeezed the very life out of it.

Panicked, Joshua slipped quickly out of bed, his bare feet touching the floor. It was remarkably cool to the touch, almost as cold as those early January mornings during the wintertime when his parents kept the heat down to save a few nickels and dimes. He glanced out his window and suddenly froze in his tracks. He couldn't see a thing. It was a black square without any indication that something existed beyond its thick curtain.

*Come play...*

Joshua scrambled over to the night light in the wall crouching down next to it, trying desperately to tuck his feet underneath him so that his entire body was contained within the glow of the orange sphere.

Trembling, white-faced, he watched in horror as the murky ink spread across the floor toward him. A child's giggle bubbled through the tension, although there was no indication that the boy who had visited him before was anywhere to be seen.

Joshua shut his eyes tightly and whispered over and over the mantra his father had taught him.

"Nothing will ever dim this light, nothing will ever dim this light…"

***

Henry parked the truck in front of his store. The streets were deserted at this hour, though the clock would show that the time was well on the left side of midnight. People worked and then went home. There was little reason not to. The town was architected so that people went to their jobs and then left them behind at the end of the day. Even Mae's Café, the town's primary eating establishment that doubled as a place to get a cold beer and watch the ball game on the television, was closed, its neon sign that simply advertised "Eats" was off for the night.

He flipped on the lights and walked instinctively to the aisles to collect the material he needed. He grabbed a red five-gallon gasoline jug and a couple of axe handles. Then he rummaged the shelves until he found a box of Blue Tip matches, the kind that you could strike anywhere and get a spark. He then went in back and retrieved three aprons off the peg on the wall. Henry brought them to the counter where the paper cutter was. One by one he lined up each apron, bringing down the razor-sharp scimitar-like blade down, cutting the cotton fabric into three-inch strips. When he had everything that he had come for, he headed to the front door, looking back at his shop – the product of generations of hard work and an ethic that made you show up each day to do your job because that was just the right thing to do.

With a wry smirk, Henry shut off the light and closed the door. He was in the cab of his pick-up before he realized he hadn't locked the store's door. He was about to climb out of the cab but stopped himself. In a town this small, secrets were minimal. Everyone knew one another. Everyone knew the Bible thumpers and the petty thieves, the ones that drank too much, and the ones whose appetites took other illegal forms. Everyone knew who said and did what about and to whom. In this way, the town was a comfort for those that lived there. The town knew itself. It took care of itself. It policed itself.

To a point.

It was that point that Henry was going to take upon himself. The collective mentality that had protected the town throughout its history was a durable solution for only so long. Then it became self-enabling, justifying lapses of judgment and accountability. If everyone messed up, then no one messed up. A finger pointed at one was pointed at all. Who in their right mind was going to spit in the wind knowing that it would ultimately come back on them?

Henry had two more stops to make before his night was over. The gas station to fill up the kerosene tank, and then the woods. He drove down the road, the dirty white pick-up truck visible only as long as the streetlamps were lit, before the night swallowed up the old Ford into its hungry mouth.

***

Joshua watched the indigo ink shadow ooze toward where he took refuge by the night light. It moved slowly but with purpose, not seeking to consume as much as seeking to get to a specific place. There wasn't a doubt about where that destination was.

As the pool rippled toward Joshua, it unexpectedly stopped its progression at the edge of the orange halo emitted by the light on the floor. Joshua watched as it moved laterally around it, searching for a way inside the bright perimeter but funding none.

It couldn't cross the threshold.

The Dark had been stopped.

But it was waiting.

For now.

Joshua felt an immediate sense of relief that was quickly squashed with the sound of two words.

*Hello, Joshua.*

The boy stood by the window, dressed in the same white t-shirt, wearing the same one sneaker. The smile he gave him was less than friendly. It was sterile, not forced per se, but not genuine and warm. It was paralyzing in its directness.

*It gets so lonely playing by yourself. Do you like playing by yourself?*

Joshua couldn't formulate any words. His heart rate increased, and his head hurt. When he opened his mouth, a strained wheeze emerged. This is what it must feel like to have a heart attack, he thought. This is what it feels like to die.

There was nothing intimidating or frightening about the boy at face value. He was normal every way a ten-year-old boy should be. But that's what made him so scary. If he showed up looking like a blonde-haired rotting corpse without eyes in their sockets and slime dripping down his mouth, that would be one thing. It would be horrible and hard to look at, yes, but it would be manageable because that's what monsters are supposed to look like. Joshua could avoid or outrun something that he could see. But it was the unknown that made him want to piss his pants. You don't know how strong, how fast, or how evil something was if you couldn't see and put a tangible value on it.

No, this boy could have been any one of Joshua's friends at schools, save for the fact that the boy wasn't real. At least, he wasn't alive.

The boy glanced down at the shadow pool, following the trail from the window to the perimeter where the inky mass agitated back and forth.

*Why so much light, Joshua? The dark is better. There are so many more games to play in the dark. Better games.*

"Go away," Joshua said. It wasn't a firm command, lacking firmness and conviction.

*I can't go. I need my shoe.*

The boy approached him. Joshua tried to scream, but only an anemic squeak emerged. His lungs felt heavy and difficult to breathe. He knelt outside the orange sphere on the floor, dipping his pale-yellow fingers into the murky pool.

*Don't worry,* the boy said. *It only hurts at first. Then you don't feel anything. Then it's all over and then we can play.*

"Leave me alone," Joshua said. He meant to sound firm and threatening, but he only managed a hoarse whisper.

Joshua watched in terror as the boy removed his fingers from the ink-black puddle. The Dark ran down his fingers like chocolate sauce, along his palms and to his wrists. It wasn't an uncontrolled consummation; it covered him neatly, like a form-fitting black suede glove.

*It's beautiful, isn't it? Like a dream, Joshua. A never-ending dream. You like dreams? We can do whatever we want in our dreams. We can play without ever having to stop. We can play forever in the woods.*

Joshua couldn't move and he couldn't stop looking at the Dark travelling across the boy's arm spreading down toward his chest and up to his neck. It wasn't so much that the Dark was swallowing up his body as transforming it. They weren't separate entities; they were one.

*How come you didn't ask my name, Joshua? I know yours. You don't know mine.*

The boy was full shadow now, a photo negative of a ghost. Full Dark. The form was there but it was more fluid, able to break out of that configuration into something better and more useful.

More powerful.

The night light stuttered, the orange glow flickering like heat lightning. The Dark was trying to extinguish Bugs Bunny, to douse the brightness and open up an avenue for the shadows.

But the night light held. At least for now. The boy looked curiously at the flicker.

*Turn off the light,* the boy-shadow commanded.

"No." Joshua didn't even recognize his own voice.

*Turn off the light.*

"No."

The Dark was perturbed. It rippled on the floor and bubbled as if trying to spatter, sending even a small bit over the line. If a little got over, then everything would change. If it touched Joshua just a little bit, it could take Joshua.

*What's my name?* the shadow prodded.

Joshua shook his head.

*Come on, Joshua. You know. Deep down you know. You saw my shoe. You found it when no one else did. What's my name?*

Helpless and broken, Joshua curled himself into a tight ball.

*My name…*

"Mark," Joshua said quietly. He shut out the outside world by shutting his eyes and tightly holding the lids down. "Your name is Mark."

And with that admission, Joshua found the fire of his voice and screamed like he never screamed before.

*** 

Henry had pulled off at the edge of the road about a half-mile away from the Daniels place. He shut off the engine but kept the headlights on and turned on his hazards. There were no streetlamps, and the looming trees made a sea of black even blacker. The truck's headlights did a poor job illuminating the thick forest in front of him.

He opened the glove compartment and took out a pack of unfiltered Camels and a silver Zippo lighter. He had given up the habit nearly twenty years ago, but he snuck one every now and then when he needed a puff or two to calm his nerves. For what he was about to do, a Camel wasn't going to kill him at this point.

Henry got out of the pickup and walked to the back bed to get his supplies in order. He wrapped the aprons' torn strips and fastened them securely around the ends of his axe handles, making sure each had enough fabric and looked like a giant Q-tip. Then he proceeded to soak them in the kerosene. The oily smell filled his nostrils quickly, and he had to exhale through them, shaking his head to clear that odor from his nose. Henry made sure the Zippo lighter worked sufficiently and tucked it into his shirt breast pocket. Finally, he picked up the yellow industrial hand-held lantern light and turned on its powerful beam.

It might have been the night and the way shadows played across the ground, but the forest seemed fuller than it had a short five minutes ago. Like an animal feeling threatened, everything tried to make itself look bigger: bushes swelled fuller, the trees got thicker, and undergrowth somehow stretched out farther. The woods were intimidating this way; they always grew more expansive, darker, meaner.

Henry let out a snort and started up the incline with the cigarette clenched in his teeth. He contemplated his service in the Marine Corps, silently chastising himself for seeing any action. That would have prepared him for what he was about to do.  Still, trudging up the hill made him feel like he was going into combat, no less a live-or-die reality as storming a beach, clearing a village, or surviving an ambush.

After studying the terrain, he determined that there was no good entry point, so he just pushed his way through the first line of the forest's defense. Branches scraped his face and thorns tugged at his flannel shirt. A limb de-hatted him, sending his green John Deere cap  onto the bank. He decided not to pause from his goal. If he stopped, he might think, and if he thought, he may talk himself out of what he had to do. Instead, like a bear, Henry moved forward despite the resistance. There was a bigger goal in mind, and it lay about a mile walk ahead.

Thirty yards in, Henry could barely see the road. The halogen bulb of the lantern provided limited visibility. Despite boasting nearly 100,000 lumens, the bright light did little to reveal the forest through the darkness.

He moved purposefully across the uneven ground, the tip of his work boot snagging gnarly roots and unforgiving tangles of weeds and twists of bush. Henry stumbled a few times, nearly losing the axe handles.

The farther he got, the colder the air became. Cold air could be sharp on the lungs. Quick breathing was like sucking in shards of glass. It cut the throat.

And it was quiet. Crypt-quiet.

Henry paused to gather his bearings. He had hunted these woods when he was younger but stopped going when the incidents with children started becoming more commonplace. At one time he would bet his house that he could be dropped blind-folded anywhere in these woods and he would find his way out in an hour. As he surveilled the area, every tree was a hostile face that lacked any sort of familiarity.

And Henry started to feel something that he hadn't felt since he went to boot camp all those years ago.

Fear.

"Come on, you old goat," Henry said to him-self as he trained his light on the destination in front of him. "It's nothing. Get going."

But the pep talk wasn't convincing, and he didn't immediately move. He needed a few deep breaths first. The exact amount of time it would take someone to silently say the Lord's Prayer.

***

They had gone to bed together that night, the first time since they arrived at the lake, though they lay with their backs facing one another. Still, it was a step in the right direction, something that could be built upon and developed. Jack had told her that it was better that if he stayed upstairs, in case Joshua had another nightmare. While that may have been true, she also knew that was Jack's way of telling her that he wanted to be closer to her as well. Anne knew that he had still harbored misgivings over the stories that Henry had told her but the questionable events that had been happening had chipped away at his skepticism. The fact that he was ready to share a bed with her again showed Anne that Jack was softening and that he loved his family – all of them.

She heard Joshua's screaming first. Anne was never a sound sleeper without the assistance of a half of a bottle of wine. She slept in two-hour clips, waking up for a period before turning over, adjusting her pillow, and drifting off again.

Anne never got used to her son's screams. She would have thought that as a parent, she would grow attuned to her son's crying and tears – what was motivated by fear, pain, anger, or any other emotional catalyst.

The primal caterwaul shrieking through the cabin wasn't just fear; it was terror.

Anne was out of bed with Jack a few steps behind her.

"What is it? What's wrong?" Jack said. He had been in full REM cycle and looked lost as he followed her down the hall.

She opened the door to find an empty bed. Panic spiked in Anne as she frantically looked around the room. He was nowhere to be seen.

"Joshua!" she screamed.

His wits about him, Jack checked the closet and then went to the double hung storm window. He frowned when he saw that the bottom half had been fully raised with only the screen separating the room from the outside.

"What is it?" she asked him.

"I closed this before I left. I'm sure of it."

The statement was left hanging when a whimpering from beneath the bed drew their attention. Both Anne and Jack fell to their knees and found Joshua underneath, his legs tucked up close to his body. The boy was mumbling to himself, his voice trembling, saying the same thing over and over.

"Nothing… will dim this light. Nothing… will dim this light…"

Jack reached and got a hold of his son. He gently pulled the terrified boy out. Once exposed, Joshua desperately clung to his father.

"Jack…?" Anne gently asked.

Her husband shot her an "I don't know" expression. She went over and stroked the boy's hair and could feel the boy's body shaking.

"It's okay," she cooed into her son's ear. "Everything is fine. Everything's going to be okay."

None of them made a move. They held each other tightly, Anne squeezing Jack and Jack squeezing her, and Joshua surrounded and protected with that love.

Outside the window, the trees agitated. Branches rustled intensely, whipping into an eddy of leaves. It swelled and swirled around angrily before rippling quickly away down the tree line. A casual observer might incorrectly interpret the activity as a setback and a retreat, but those who had grown up and lived in the area would not be so dismissive.

The forest never ran away from something as much as it ran to something.

Or in this case someone.

The forest protected its own.

***

Henry paused. His chest heaved as he fed his lungs with great gulps of air. He rubbed his sweaty forehead with the back of his hand that held the lantern, the halogen beam waving haphazardly above him. Henry looked up and shined the light at the canopy above. He couldn't make out the sky through the tightly interwoven foliage that blocked out the rain from hitting the woodlands floor.

The forest was quiet. The night custodians – the grasshoppers, crickets, and insects – that usually chattered at this hour were noticeably absent. It was as if they had made themselves scarce, intimidated by something more predatory.

And then that predator materialized. Not in form, but sound.

The Noise suddenly pierced the quiet. It was grating, the sound of a blade scraping against a rusty pipe. It was both primal and unnatural.

Henry's heartbeat picked up. He looked around trying to pinpoint the Noise's location but couldn't. It was omnipresent and everywhere.

"I'm getting close, aren't I, you son-of-a-bitch?" he said. "You ain't stopping me. No sir, you ain't stopping me one lick."

He pushed forward. The tangles got thicker as if being directed to get in his way and muscle him back. Henry gritted his teeth. It was getting harder to brush aside the branches intent on touching him. He swatted aside a branch and let out a grunt. Unseen briars scratched him across the throat, lacerating the skin and drawing blood.

Dumbstruck, Henry instinctively dropped the axe handles and touched his throat. He trained the light on his fingers. There was blood. A lot of blood.

If the briars had dug any deeper, they might have lacerated his jugular.

"Jesus," he muttered.

He flashed the light beam in front of him, studying the terrain. The overlapping brush and bushes made the forest seem like a seamless interlaced tapestry without any clear-cut beginning or ending.

Henry would have missed it if he wasn't accustomed to the idiosyncrasies of the forest. Rarely was there symmetry in the natural world; things grew out of a need for survival. They twisted around, rooted firmly to the ground, claiming space. Like a mother, it wrapped its collective arms around the larger whole, protecting itself from outside interference.

But if you understood the geometry of the agriculture, you understood where to look for things. If you were cutting back the landscape, for example, you knew how to identify structurally unsound or invasive vegetation, and where to prune it so that it stymied its growth.

Most people would have missed the pattern on the ground in daylight, no less at night. But Henry wasn't like most people. Things like the flow of the undergrowth and how the ground slopped away aggressively stuck out to him. It reminded him of what they taught him in the Marines. Camouflage was never perfect but was meant to deceive the lazy or untrained eye. Both of Henry's worked just fine.

The entrance to the small clearing was unremarkable at first glance. There were no stone formations or magnificent natural markers to signal the clearing's importance. It had remained unnoticed all of these years because it wasn't a destination people knew about and wanted to get to. Henry had heard about the clearing's existence, but they were just rumors. And while rumors made good stories, they didn't carry any real weight. One thing was certain though. While those unlucky few who had stumbled across the clearing were not looking for it, it was the last place they ever saw.

Another thing caught his eye – the vegetation was thick in a way that indicated it had been unnaturally fertilized. Everything was too lush, too abundant, too vibrant.

Then the Noise sounded again. Harsh and rattling. For some it might have resembled a warning, or a challenge.

Back off or else.

But an animal makes the same kind of sounds when its foot is caught in a trap. It blusters a lot, but at its core, the animal is scared.

The clearing or whatever force was behind it, was scared. He was sure of it. Henry had hunted most of his life and was familiar to the nuances of the sounds that animals made when they knew they were being hunted. He was sure of that.

He picked up the axe handles from the ground and steeled himself one final time. The woods seemed to shift around him, trying to distract him from his purpose.

"Here I come you son-of-a-bitch," he said, walking forward. This time, the low branches and thick shrubbery provided little resistance, allowing him to pass.

There were many reasons why clearings existed. Sometimes they were the result of specific environment conditions, poor soils and natural events like heavy snowfalls or drought-driven summer fires. Sometimes they were caused by years of heavy herbivorous animal traffic that fed voraciously in a particular area. And in very rare but no less impactful cases, unnatural influences of which no rational explanation existed created these small open areas.

The clearing that Henry faced now was not a pure treeless area. In fact, one large, twisted tree grew in the center, its limbs gnarled and jawed, and noticeably leafless. Henry's mouth dried up and he found it hard to swallow. The tree did not belong here. It wasn't like the surrounding birches and pines that were predominant in these parts.

No, this tree was different. It had been part of the rumors that had been circulating around town for several years. He had heard people whispering about it. Someone stumbled upon the tree when they had been hunting and found decaying animal carcasses littered around its base. Someone else had heard that was where that crazy old Rothman sacrificed his family to some pagan god.

Henry had ignored the talk, because he knew it was just that – speculation from people that relished in fiction more so than fact. But truth be told, Henry had a better idea about what that tree was all about than anyone else in town. The first time he laid eyes on it, it was merely a sapling with a filthy canvass sack covering its roots. Now nearly full grown, its familiarity was unsettling. It wasn't possible for a tree to grow to this size over such short of time, and yet, here it stood. No doubt about it; it was unnatural, an aberration.

Now, he understood.

Henry set the lantern down. With the beam pointed at the tree, the Darkness filled in any pocket not touched by the halogen's touch. The air was downright cold. Henry could see his breath expel from his mouth in a cloud of white condensation.

He removed the Zippo and struck it. The flame held briefly before a rogue wind surfaced and disappeared as soon as it extinguished it. So much for being "wind proof." Henry repeated the motion and for a second time the gust reemerged, putting out the threat.

Fear crept up his back, closing its taught ragged grip around his throat.

The Noise returned. Not Noise, Noises. All around him. That scraping metal cacophony was enveloping him, taunting him from all sides.

"Come on, dammit," Henry said.

For a second time Henry failed to get the Zippo lit, forcing him keep the lighter close to him as he hunched over, shielding it from the indiscriminate wind. He struck it again. This time, the flame burned, and he immediately touched the tip to one of the soaked rags. It immediately caught turning the padded end into an orange fireball. He held the torch high, its burning hot eye beating back the Darkness.

All around him things rustled through the brush. He heard their frenzied movements, but he knew that they weren't the frantic chaos of unnamed nocturnal critters. He hadn't seen one or heard one since he began this ordeal. No, these were shadows. Shadows that scurried around the clearing, circling him, dodging the torchlight.

The tree, Henry thought. It's got to be the tree. They are protecting the tree.

But as he took a step forward, the Darkness not kept at bay by the torch pushed in from the clearing's edges in a pool of black ink. The hair on

Henry's neck stood on end. He paused, and turned around quickly, seeing the encroaching darkness stop in its tracks.

"Oh, Lord," he whispered. In that moment, fear pulled a year's worth of life from his body.

He spun around in time to stop the Darkness from slipping up in front of him. He went back to the other two axe handles on the ground, lighting one for his other hand. Now two fisted, he again made his way toward the gnarled, wicked tree.

He waved the torches around like he was directing a plane to land, watching the Darkness recoil from the flame. The closer he got to the tree, the more these strange gusts emerged, causing the torch flames to flicker and dance in the wind. Henry's eyes widened with fear and his heart skipped, but the fire held.

Something bit at his ankles. Even through the dense coarseness of the denim, Henry felt the sharp teeth dig into his skin and draw blood. Henry let out a yelp, and the Noises increased their frenzy, feeding on the pain the Darkness had delivered.

"Oh, God," Henry said, through gritted teeth. "Give me strength."

When another bite sank deeper into his calf, he let out a deep groan. He waved one of the torches at his feet to drive the Darkness back.

He didn't see it clearly; it was exposed only for a second, maybe two. But what he was able to glimpse was too fantastic and too terrible to make his worst nightmare seem like an adolescent's wet dream. The entire black shadow was formless and yet seemed to move in concert with the other patches of Darkness around him. There wasn't a discernible mouth, per se, at least, not in the literal sense. But when it bit him, he saw the teeth – rows and rows of thin, razor-sharp teeth that had a taste for flesh and blood.

"Back off, fucker!" Henry screamed at the top of his lungs. It made little difference. The insistent cricket-chatter of the Noises grew greater and more numerous. The bites came more frequently the closer he got to the tree, sniping at him like a pool of piranhas. Waves of blackness swept by him, biting hard before scurrying to the opposing edge of the clearing to watch him before attacking again.

The assaults took their toll. Ten feet away from his target, Henry stumbled, dropping one of the torches. Once the flame hit the ground, the fire quickly burned out eliciting the happy chatter from the audience of shadows. Another bite shredded the flesh on his left hand. Blood flowed freely, dropping on the ground, absorbed into the soil.

Henry tried to stand but the Darkness stepped up its piranha-like attacks. He struggled to get to his knees, but the shadows grew bold. Henry thrust the torch forward at the blackest part of the Darkness, it resisted at first but then recoiled.

He crawled toward the tree, keeping the torch high. He was going to light this bitch up and burn it down. Burn the whole forest down if he had to.

The torch flame flickered as the last angry gust blustered. It was the strongest of the night and it blew in the space between the tree and Henry.

Crushed, Henry hung his head after he saw the fire go out.

Darkness enveloped him now and the smell of burnt kerosene filled his nostrils. The Noises became agitated, chanting, their frenzy increasing in volume. It was the sound of rebellious victory.

"No… no…," Henry said.

But his sorrowful voice was drowned out in the chaotic crescendo. Once the Noises reached their fevered pitch, the Darkness collapsed on Henry from all sides, the chattering replaced by the sound of gnashing of teeth and human bone.

# Chapter 13

After days of overcast skies, the sun's emergence was a welcome reprieve. Even the creatures of the forest buzzed with excitement, coming out of their holes and hideaways to forage for food and supplies to fatten their dens and hideaways. In the horizon, the sun rose steadily, casting a magnificent reflection on the lake. When the water's surface was still like it was now, Crescent Lake was a perfect mirror, making an everyday spectacle like a simple sunrise into a breathtaking natural choreography.

Joshua slept in the comfort between his parents in their bedroom. Jack glanced over at Anne who slept soundly. After a night with a series of ups and downs and trying to soothe a terrified child, she finally collapsed in exhaustion. She had been a trooper, summoning every innate motherhood tactic to comfort their boy through the tears.

Jack carefully slid out from between the sheets and stepped carefully to the door. He walked down the hallway to Joshua's room. He paused at the doorway, scrutinizing the room with a fresh set of eyes.

What was so terrifying about this room?

The window immediately drew his attention. He went over to it, looking out at the front view of the cabin. Jack frowned. The tree line seemed closer from this vantage point, and he wasn't sure if this was just because of the perspective or the fact that he was really seeing it for the first time.

He went down the stairs, putting on his shoes by the door and went outside. There was nothing that he could put his finger on, but something seemed, well, off. Jack walked down the steps and walked across the driveway toward the forest. He walked slowly along the line. He couldn't be certain, but the strip of grass between the forest and the driveway seemed smaller than it was before.

"Jack!"

He paused his inspection and turned to see Anne at the doorway.

"He's up!" she called out to him.

Jack nodded and walked back to the cabin.

Breakfast was quiet. They sat at the table. When Anne made pleasant conversation, much to her surprise, Jack joined in. Things were difficult enough that he didn't need to add on to the stress. Whatever happened with his wife and Dave Selznick didn't matter right now. The family was fracturing not because of an affair, but because something was happening to their son. One thing was for certain – it had to do with this place.

After breakfast, Jack helped her in the kitchen. Joshua sat on the deck looking at the lake.

When Jack had encouraged him to go down to the dock, his son shook his head too quickly. His wife put a rinsed dish into the rack and looked through the window.

"What are we going to do, Jack?" she asked him.

"I don't know. I don't know what's happening, Anne. But I don't think our panicking is going to help him any. Is something "off" around here? Hell, yeah it is. But how much of that is him trying to make sense of all of this?"

"He never had nightmares because he saw me kiss Dave Selznick," she insisted.

"His fear of the dark started before that," Jack countered. "Put the two together, and I think our son is going to be in therapy for a while."

"Bite your tongue," she scolded.

"I'm just saying," he said.

She put the last glass on the rack and turned to her husband.

"I want to go home, Jack. I want to go back to our house."

"You sure? We paid for another couple of weeks."

"I don't care. I want our routine back. I want suburban boredom and bad local pizza."

Jack cracked a smile and Anne reciprocated with one of her own. It was the first time they had smiled together in a long time.

***

Anne took the car into town one more time to see if she could come to some sort of an agreement with the realtor that leased the cabin to them. She couldn't help chuckle that the previous trips had been with the purpose of acquiring a tank of propane, one that never materialized despite Henry's repeated promises. She didn't hold it against the old timer. Grilling was meant to be a distraction, a way of getting the three of them outside together to reconnect.

In light of recent events, she didn't care if she ever saw the great outdoors again. Who gave a shit about hamburgers on a grill? Microwaved sliders and Chinese delivery suited her just fine.

When they got back, she'd make it clear that the affair was just that – a brief interlude of time when she allowed her own insecurities to take over. She would admit to everything, show her remorse, and promise penance.

Whatever it took to get them back on track. She wanted that and she thought that Jack felt the same way.

Their son was in a delicate position, teetering on a dangerous precipice. A self-implosion of their marriage could have long-term effects on Joshua. A never-ending stream of psychotherapists and psychiatrists dissecting his brain and emotions because mommy couldn't help but sleep with the father of his friend. He didn't deserve that.

No one deserved that.

Anne was twenty minutes early before the real estate office opened up. She took the time to get some coffee and sit on one of the public benches along the promenade. Some locals were out and about with stern unsmiling faces.

How much did they know? Anne wondered. If what Henry had told her was true, every one of them had a part of the activities at the cabin. Silence was not permissible when it came to missing children. They each bore a black smear of guilt on their hearts. She felt badly for Henry, who knew that their lack of activity was unacceptable but lacked the influence, power, or just sheer energy to change it.

Anne turned in time to see a pudgy lady approach the door of the Sun Lakes Real Estate office. She was smaller than Anne, older and pudgy, with hair that had been recently touched up to blot out the gray. The woman was dressed smartly in a fashion different from most of the others. Anne figured it was her way to visibly display her success at running a profitable enterprise.

Anne got up and followed her inside. The woman looked up unexpectedly when she heard the bell above the door ring. She had just set down her coffee and was in the process of removing her scone from a small paper bag.

"Oh!" she exclaimed. "You startled me. I don't get many people the first thing in the morning." Despite her practiced pleasant tone, it was difficult not to sense she was annoyed that she wasn't able to dig into her breakfast.

Anne didn't care. She took one of the seats in front of the aggravated Lillian Lebel.

"Please," she said to the realtor, gesturing to her scone and coffee. "Don't mind me."

Lillian Lebel gave a forced smile and sat down. "How can I help you today?"

"I'm Anne Bradford. My family and I rent the Daniels place off Rattlesnake Road."

"Oh, yes, of course. How are you? That view is amazing, isn't it? I'd never get tired having my coffee looking at that lake."

"Yes, the lake is beautiful, Ms. Lebel, but…"

"Please, call me Lilly."

"Lilly," Anne corrected. "We are booked through the end of July."

"Yes, you were very lucky. The Daniels place is extremely popular. What we call in the business as a 'hot property.'"

"Right. Be that as it may, I want to know the possibilities of recouping part of our rental. There are some family issues, and we have to get back home immediately."

Lilly sat back in her chair. She chewed part of her scone thoughtfully.

"I'm sorry to hear that, but I'm afraid that's just not possible," she said.

"Really? I don't see why not."

"There's more to it than that. Things have to be completely flipped, linens, professional cleaning. So many variables renters don't even think about."

"I understand, but there's nearly three weeks left. You could find somebody easily. Like you said, it's a hot property."

The fake smile grew even wider on Lillian Leber's face. "That's not the way it works," she said.

"Says who? You run the business. I think the way it works is the way you want it to work."

Lilly sat up rigidly and sipped her coffee. "That's right, and I don't want it to work that way."

Anne was aghast. "We paid up front. You can't even see it to cut us a deal?"

Lebel dropped the catch-more-flies with honey act. "Honey, if I did that for you, I'd have to do it for everyone else. If everyone else does it too, I wouldn't stay in business for very long."

Anne shook her head in disgust. "Unbelievable. You people..."

"You people?' Ha! If I had a nickel for every time one of summer renters make snide little comments, I could retire tomorrow."

Anne stood up. "Thanks for nothing."

She stormed to the door. Lilly piped up one final time.

"Tell you what. Just so there's no hard feelings. If you want, I can put you on the top of the list for next season. How does that sound? Well, think about it at least. Have a nice day!"

"We'll drop the keys off before we leave."

Anne purposefully closed the door loudly, letting the slam underscore her perturbance at Lilly's lack of compassion. She instinctively reached for cigarettes she did not have and sighed when she realized she didn't have any.

She headed to her car when she spotted a summer renter emerge from a small market with a bag of charcoal slung over his shoulder. Anne immediately thought of Henry and decided she would let him know that they would be leaving.

Although the front door of Remington Supply bore the "CLOSED" sign hanging on an angle on the inside, the door was slightly ajar. Anne cupped her eyes and leaned in close to the window. The lights were off and there was no sign of anyone inside. Per the sign advertising the store's hours of operations, it should have been open two hours ago. She tentatively opened the door further and stepped inside.

"Hello? Henry? You in here?" she called out to the empty room.

There was no reply, only the eerie silence of the shelves and racks of inanimate supplies. Anne stepped in further, moving cautiously even though she had no reason to be cautious. Still, the silence disturbed her, a foreign sentiment in a store that she knew only as warm and inviting.

"He ain't in yet, ma'am," a gravelly voice said behind her. Anne turned and met the face of an older man around Henry's age. He was dressed in jeans and a fisherman's vest. He had crisp blue eyes and an unshaven chin. The cap on his head was well faded and had a fishing hook wedged in the bill.

"I'm sorry, the door was open…"

"Yeah, it was like that when I showed up this morning to deliver the propane tanks. It doesn't close fully unless it's locked, which it usually is, if I know Henry Clay."

"I take it he's not here."

"No, ma'am. You know where he is?"

"I don't, sorry."

The man nodded and looked around the store. "It ain't like him to not be here."

"Maybe he took a day off?" Anne asked, hopefully.

The man chortled. "Henry Clay? That man works more days than a missionary. Even if he was sick, he or his wife would be here. He don't take no days off. Who can afford to this day and age? This store is always open. It has to be. Well, that is, until today. You see him, you tell him Gus Winston from Larson stopped by and delivered his order."

Anne watched the man shuffle off.

"You know where he lives?"

The man kept going without turning back. But he called out:

"We fish enough together to know it. Mile off Webbs Mill Road. Chester Lane. It's the second road on the left. You can't miss it."

***

Through the window, Jack watched his son on the front porch. The boy had not moved in at least a half-hour, the entire time staring at the forest. The boy stood almost perfectly motionless, as if any movement would attract something predatory that lurked unseen in the deep folds of green. He saw something, felt something, Jack couldn't, like a dog or cat that sensed an approaching storm that escaped human perception. The more he thought about it, the more it seemed right to leave here. So, what if Anne couldn't get back at least some of their money. More money could always be made.

He studied Joshua's face. The boy's expression was impassive. Days without sun and not going outside for any length of time had made Joshua's skin pale. His hands hung down his sides and his fingers twitched ever so slightly. He would have looked like he was sleepwalking if not for the eyes. Joshua's eyes were fixed like a cat's when it trained on something that interested it. They were wide to absorb all the visible facts available, looking for any sign of life.

Jack's own face grew concerned and a bit scared. He walked outside onto the porch and stood by his son.

"Whatcha looking at, sport?"

Joshua didn't immediately acknowledge him. His eyes darted back and forth before turning to his father.

"Nothing," he said.

"Yeah, there's a whole lot of nothing out there alright," he said, trying to make a joke. "You know," he continued, "your mom and I are working things out. I think it's important that you know that."

"Are you still mad at her?"

Jack didn't immediately respond. It never ceased to amaze him how intuitive kids were and how they could strike through to the heart of any issue.

"I don't know," Jack said truthfully. "It's complicated."

"I saw her kiss Mr. Selznick. I saw that."

"Yes, you did. You know that and I know that. And Mom knows that. And that's good that we all realize what happened. But that's only part of it."

"What's the other part?"

Jack fumbled for an answer. "It's complicated," he repeated himself.

Joshua didn't respond. His eyes still focused on something that only he could see.

"You said that already," his son when he finished his visual search.

Jack sighed. "Well, it's like that thing you have with the dark."

"I'm afraid of the Dark."

He said that word in a way that made it specific. He wasn't talking about general darkness, but a monolith, a being. Something that had an identity, and because it did, it was something with which to be reckoned.

"Right," Jack continued. "Because it's the unknown. Well, the same thing happens to adults. They can be afraid of things that they don't quite know or understand. And that preys on their subconscious. It makes them think twice about things and then they doubt themselves."

Joshua thought about this but shook his head.

"I don't have that," the boy said. "I don't doubt myself. I know what I see, Dad. I know what I see and that's what makes me afraid. Because it's not unknown. It's very known to me."

"And what's that, Joshua?"

Joshua turned to his father. The boy's lip didn't quiver. His eyes didn't mist up at the corners. His voice didn't shake. He spoke softly, directly, and from the heart.

"The Dark comes after me."

"What are you talking about?"

"The Dark wants to take me into the forest. That's why those trees move. They keep watch over us. And when night falls, the Dark seeps in from the forest and comes into my room. It tries to take me, but I won't let it."

Jack was incredulous. "Who told you this? Did your mother say something?"

His son shook his head again.

"It's Mark."

Jack kept his cool. "Who is Mark?"

"The boy before me. I found his shoe, remember? He wants to play. He wants to play with me in the Dark."

Jack couldn't hide his reaction. His brow furrowed and a grimace crossed his mouth. He didn't know what to make of this. Was his son losing his mind? Had the affair caused too much emotional damage from which to recover?

He got down on one knee next to his son.

"Look, sport," he said. "The dark's just a symbol of something deeper. You see Mom and me fighting and it's like a void you're powerless to stop. And I apologize for that. That is my fault, our fault. And I'm sorry."

The boy's crestfallen reaction said it all – his dad didn't understand.

"How do you stop the Dark?" his son asked.

The strange question stumped Jack.

"What do you mean?"

"How do you stop the Dark from coming?"

Jack shrugged. "I don't know, Joshua. Turn on the light?"

"Right," Joshua said. "But what if that doesn't work?"

"Joshua…

"What if it doesn't work," his son repeated. "What then?"

Jack brought his son into his arms and hugged him tightly.

"We'll get through this, sport. I promise."

When they separated Joshua took his father's hand.

"I want to show you something," he said.

Joshua then led his father down the steps and across the gravel driveway to the strip of grass that bordered the forest tree line. The boy seemed to be looking for something.

"What is it, Joshua? What are you looking for?"

The boy didn't respond. He walked slowly through the tall grass. If his leg hadn't scraped by it, he would have missed it.

"Here! Dad, look here!"

Jack went over and looked to where Joshua pointed. He saw a stick in the ground, surrounded by tall grass.

"It's a stick," he said, not understanding the significance.

"I put it in the ground a few days ago. I thought the forest was moving, but I wanted to be sure. I wanted to have proof before I told you guys. I swear I never moved it. And look. The forest is creeping closer. Do you see it, Dad? The forest is alive."

***

Although the directions seemed ambiguous at best, Anne quietly admitted to herself they proved to be fairly accurate. The roads around Remington may have been sparse but they were purposeful, which was a fair assessment of the town. There were no senseless turnoffs or roundabouts. Webbs Mill Road was a primary two-lane black strip that wandered through the environment in which it cut with streets forking off, much like the limbs of a tree. Everything connected to that main road making getting lost virtually impossible, despite the noticeable absence of street signs and streetlamps.

Anne turned off Chester Lane, a semi-paved road that ultimately dead-ended at a rustic cul-de-sac. In the hub of the makeshift circle stood Henry and Margie's Cape Cod-style house. The filthy white pick-up truck was noticeably absent in front. Anne parked in front and waked to the front door. The house had seen better days, not that it was falling apart as much as it looked like it needed considerable repair. Home ownership was universal regardless of geography; things fell apart at a faster rate than people had the capacity or financial means to fix.

She knocked on the door. As she waited, Anne regarded the hanging windchimes dangling from the porch roof support beam. There were four of them made of polished stones and sea glass. A new porch light was mounted above the door. It looked oddly out of place on such an old house, and judging from the size, Anne guessed that when lit, it was bright enough to light up the entire front of the property.

The door opened and Anne turned to see Margie behind the screen door.

"Can I help you?" the old woman asked. She looked suspiciously at Anne. From her reaction it was clear that she didn't appreciate seeing an unfamiliar face on her front porch.

"Hi, I'm Anne Bradford. My family rents the Daniels place. I'm a good customer of your husband's store."

Each data point seemed to fall short of their mark. Anne didn't know what else to say.

"Okay," Margie conceded. "What do you want?"

"Your husband," Anne said. "Is he home?"

The screen was dirty, but Anne saw concern wash over the old woman's face.

"No," she said, but something caught in her throat and her answer came out raspy.

"Are you okay?"

The old woman choked back a sob. Then after a prolonged sigh, she opened the screen door for Anne to come inside.

"Come inside," the woman directed.

Anne went inside and Henry's wife led her to the kitchen table. She gestured for Anne to sit down as she walked over to the stove, removing a kettle of hot water.

"I was fixing myself some tea," Margie said. "Can I pour you a cup?"

"Please."

She filled two cups and brought them to the table on a tray with sugar and milk.

"So, you're the lucky ones to rent that place," she said. There was no hint of mirth in her voice.

"Unfortunately, yes. We're leaving soon though."

"Can't say that I blame you for that. Bet that sit with Lily Lebell like a sinner in church."

"She wasn't exactly amenable to our early departure. Or willing to refund what we already spent."

"That woman squeezes a quarter so tightly the eagle screams in pain."

Anne took a sip of the strong tea. "Too many things have happened since we've been here. Strange things. I don't know. I don't mean to be disrespect-ful, but I don't like it here much. We're not used to this."

"No one is. Not really. People around here turn a blind eye as long as it doesn't crap in their lawn, 'scuse my French."

"What do you mean by "it"?"

Margie's old eyes narrowed as she blew on her cup. "I think you know what I mean."

"So, we're not crazy?"

Margie sipped her tea. "No."

"And the stories your husband told me?"

"All true."

"Jesus… Why doesn't anyone do anything about it?"

"What? The disappearances? Or the fact that the woods seem to have a mind of their own?"

Anne sighed. This was all too much to get her mind around. "I don't know. All of it?"

"Oh, they tried a long time ago, honey. But this is a small town. It barely breathes with those living here. Whenever something happens, enough time passes to make people forget. I used to blame them. Now, I can't. But you don't really forget. None of us do. You can see it in our eyes. People think we're stand-offish. We're just folk that our tied to a place and a terrible, terrible secret. No, we don't forget. We can't. Because darkness comes no matter what."

Anne watched Margie's hand tremble slightly as she brought the cup to her mouth.

"Why do you stay?"

Margie looked up from her tea. "Where are we going to go? Florida? I grew up not twenty miles from here. I don't have family left. It's just me and

Henry. If we were going to leave, we needed to do it forty years ago."

Anne nodded. "I should be going."

"Wise decision."

They both rose from the table and Margie escorted her to the front door.

"Do you know where Henry is? I'd like to say bye to him personally, and not to worry about getting us that propane," she chuckled softly.

Margie's expression changed. "Henry hasn't been home in a while."

A cold chill ran down Anne's spine. "What do you mean?"

"Last night he left, and he hasn't come home."

"My God… Aren't you worried?"

"Of course, I'm worried. I'm scared out of my mind. But I know he's not coming home. I can feel it. You been married as long as we have been, you just know things."

"I'm sorry, I don't understand."

"The woods got him.  The Dark."

"No, that can't be right," Anne said weakly. She was suddenly flushed with cold and shivered slightly.

Margie continued. "Several years ago, when Henry was a ten-year-old boy and his grandfather owned the store, Henry was expected to help out when he wasn't learning the three 'Rs' at school. Anyway, back then generations of Raymonds owned the place, and the old patriarch was a few sandwiches short of a picnic. He always got Henry's grandpa to order some special items from overseas. He had served in the military and had been stationed over in Europe for a few years. He travelled the countries. He met some farmers. He learned things. One day that fool Raymond asked for Henry's grandpa to get him something from over there. Something rare and special. It took nearly six months to get it to Remington. But this thing, this abomination, was no ordinary sapling. I don't know how to describe it 'cause I never saw it. But I heard Henry talk about it. And what it did to people. Old man Raymond went crazier if that was possible. He went to the woods and planted it there. That's when things started to go bad in the area. And people started getting hurt. And others, like the kids, just up and disappeared. But if you ask me, it all started with the root that day. A single root created the hell in which we all live."

"What happened?"

"From what I understand, one of the roots cut him."

"Cut the old man? A root? How's that even possible?"

"It wrapped around his wrist, squeezing tighter and tighter until it broke skin and drew blood.

Henry saw it that day when Mr. Raymond picked up his prized package. He took it out and the roots just came alive. That's what Henry said, word for word. And don't get me wrong. This was not like some crazy wildness mind you; it was more just stirring like they had been awoken from a deep sleep. The root grabbed the old man's finger and tasted blood. And it liked it."

Margie kept a sob that had been building in her throat in check. "So, you want to know where Henry is? I think he went out to try and kill it. And he didn't succeed."

***

Margie was right. Henry had come out to the woods. Anne nearly missed the vehicle on her way back home, but she saw the taillights and the back tailgate of the truck. The rest had been consumed in an unruly tangle of bushes. She pulled over the side of the road and walked slowly over to inspect the abandoned vehicle. The rest of the shoulder of the road remained trimmed back and clean. Only at this spot did the forest overgrowth stretch out from the forest's banks and grabbed the pick-up's bulkhead, spreading its vines, getting them into the engine block and through the dashboard. It looked like a savage attack by nature.

"Christ," she whispered. The scene was frightening. She had never seen woods be so violent.

She inspected the scene. The cab had been breached and was full of twisting vines. The windshield had been penetrated by a tree limb. If Henry had been in the driver's seat, he would have been impaled. Lack of blood or any other clues told her that Henry was not inside when this attack occurred.

Anne saw something on the ground twenty feet from the truck. It was trapped in a bush's limbs. It was Henry's ballcap.

"Oh, Henry," she said sadly.

The familiar crawl of fear crept along her skin. She tentatively walked up the embankment. The bush shifted in the breeze. She reached out to retrieve the cap and withdrew her hand quickly.

"Ouch!" she looked at her finger. A rivulet of blood formed on her forefinger. A thorn had pierced her skin. It was deeper than typical thorn-pricks. The blood ran down her finger and dripped onto the ground.

At that moment, the forest rustled, the trees in front of her swishing back and forth. It sounded just like a chuckle, a mirthless, frivolous sound.

The woods were mocking her.

The Ripple was not subtle this time. It rolled like a tsunami from deep inside the forest. If this were the times of the dinosaurs, Anne would have expected a T-Rex or some other large beast to break through the trees.

She backed away too quickly and stumbled down the embankment, falling on her ass and landing on her back with a thud. The Ripple flowed along the tree line in front of her, moving with the pent-up fury of a caged panther.

Though dazed, Anne scrambled to her feet. Her heart pounded with the flush of adrenaline, and her breath quickened. She ran back to her car, and quickly climbed inside. A cold sweat ran down her temples, stinging her eyes. She wiped them with the back of her hand as she started the car, flooring it down the road.

She did not notice the Ripple following her until it eventually tapered off when she rounded the bend.

***

Jack remembered the Rothman journal that morning but didn't get around to reading it until slightly after ten. Rothman may have been crazy, but Jack wasn't sure if that happened before or after his stay at the cabin. The early entries were certainly co-gent enough, but the musings became increasingly erratic and disturbing. Solitude wasn't for everyone, that was for sure. But driving someone to kill his family, well, he had read enough true crime books to know there usually were signs prior to that to give a heads up to friends and families that that person was a few sandwiches short of a picnic.

He waited until Joshua was out of the room before he settled in to pick up where he had left the journal.

The Rothmans had not left, despite the wife's preference to do so, that much was clear. Papa Pet had kept them there. Then the incidents started piling up. Voices. Mysterious happenings in and around the forest. Mark Rothman's gradual withdrawal from the others. He was seeing something they didn't. He had expressed his concerns. They didn't listen.

At least, Peter didn't.

And that's when the entries became brief and sporadic. The pages contained a series of childlike scratching, something a four-year old would do when he was just learning to draw pictures. Jack had no doubt that this was the product of Peter's hand. Kids Mark's age took pride in their sketches. They wanted dinosaurs to look like dinosaurs, flowers to look like flowers.

These scribblings came from internal chaos, from extreme emotions, from a furious need to express something that couldn't be captured in words.

Mark wasn't the only person that knew something was off; Peter felt it too. But how it affected him was different. Mark's reaction was fear; his father's bordered on madness.

Jack turned to the last page. There was a scrawl of heavy black marker. While he couldn't be certain, the impressionistic picture looked like a forest, or at least several trees at least surrounding one tree in what Jack could imagine was a clearing of sorts.

There were heavy black lines zig-zagging up and down, like a chaotic pulse or a strange stock market graph. Jack dismissed it as delusional caricature, a disturbed expression of the rapid deterioration of the human psyche.

Jack thought about his son's behavior, the Rothmans, and what Anne had told him about the former owners. It was too much to wrap his head around without more clarity. He needed some answers.

And there was only one person who could provide them to him.

It took Jack three phone calls to get the number to the Elmwood Psychiatric Center, which was forty miles up the road. It took two more calls and a bit of social engineering to discover that Peter Rothman was still interned there, and another three calls to find out that he could be seen if he were a family member on the list. A few more Internet searches and a 99-cent investment into a People Finder search engine provided him info on not only Peter Rothman, but his two brothers, mother, and father. One more call to the Center confirmed that his younger brother Chris was on the visit list. Speaking as Peter's brother, Jack made an appointment that afternoon.

When Anne came back, she relayed the information that Margie had told her. She spared no detail, repeating word for word everything she had heard. Jack's expression was markedly different this time than the previous time she relayed information from Henry. Instead of being unreadable, his eyes burned with interest, and he asked poignant questions where appropriate.

"Can we go now?" she said.

"We will," he said finally. "But first I need to see someone."

"Who could you possibly have to see here?"

"Peter Rothman. He's in a facility close by. Don't worry, I called ahead."

Anne fidgeted. "I don't like it, Jack. What is that supposed to accomplish?" she asked, incredulously.

"Maybe something that will help make sense of all this. Maybe something that will help Joshua overcome whatever it is that's afflicting him."

"Getting out of here will help that."

"You know what Joshua showed me today? He had put a stick in the ground a few days ago to mark where the forest ended. It took us fifteen minutes to find it because the forest had encroached nearly a foot in that time. A foot, Anne."

"That can't be right," she said nervously. "He was mistaken, or maybe an animal…?"

Jack shook his head. "I believe him."

"Even more reason why we should get out today. Get out now."

"We will. But if we're going to understand this, if we're going to have any shot of helping Joshua, then this is the guy that can tell us what's happening here. It's worth the trip."

Anne hesitated. "You really think so?"

"If this guy suffered the same things Joshua suffers, then yeah, I think it's our best chance. We can't hope to fix this if we don't know what we don't know."

Anne sighed. She flipped him the keys. "I'll get started packing."

"We'll leave first thing in the morning, okay?"

"Okay."

He smiled and held her. It was a familiar embrace, one that neither he nor Anne had experienced in what seemed like forever. His strong arms applied enough pressure to make her feel safe and she responded in turn.

***

The facility wasn't large. The main faded brick building had two stories, with short stubby wings that protruded back from the main structure. They formed the horseshoe perimeter for the exercise yard with a rusty restraining fence closing the "U." It was a structure in decay and neglect; the state was in the process of closing these smaller facilities in favor of larger brick and cement fortresses in the bigger cities in order to save money on upkeep and maintenance. When patients died or were "cured," rooms were stripped down, cleaned, and locked. As it was, there were only twenty-two active patients housed on the premises, eighteen in Wing A and the rest in Wing B.

Jack was prepared to charm the nurse who admitted him. He rehearsed his story on the ride, practicing his elocution, his "aw, shucks" tone, his delivery. He brought his family to the lake for a break and to see his poor brother. They build sandcastles on the beach. They tried their hand at fishing. Somewhere between the sand and the boat his wallet must have fallen. He didn't have any identification, but could she see it in her heart to let him see his brother? They had come so far to see him.

Much to his surprise, the nurse didn't even bother to ask for his ID. She was a bored woman, pushing near her pension. The word from the state had already come down, and her care for any state mandate went out the window. The older woman gave him a visual assessment, asked for his name, and checked it against a clipboard. No ID required. She just buzzed him in and had an orderly, another older man who seemed less-than-thrilled to soon be out of a job, escort him to the recreation area. It was the "quiet place," a bland name for a bland opaque room where patients sat and stared out windows or drew pictures with broken Crayola crayons.

Fortunately for Jack, the orderly pointed to where Peter Rothman sat in a high-winged back chair away from the tables. He had no concept of what Rothman looked like and planned to play it by ear if he had to "find" him in an open room such as this.

Rothman wasn't what Jack had expected. Instead of being long haired and drooling, Peter was meticulously groomed. His graying hair cut short and his face clean shaven. At first glance he looked neither wild nor crazy. His eyes were the only clue to something not being right in his head. They looked colorless and heavy and tired.

Jack pulled up a chair beside Peter who glanced at him before returning his stare at the gray cracking wall.

"Peter," Jack said. "My name is Jack Bradford. You don't know me, but I have a couple of questions I think you can help me with. Is that alright? Can I ask you a few questions, Peter?"

The troubled man didn't move. Only his eyes blinked. Jack grabbed a nearby chair and pulled it over and sat down.

"My family and I," Jack pressed. "We rent the cabin you rented. The one at the lake. Remember that one?"

Peter made no sign that he heard or understood what Jack was saying. Jack's hopes started to wane.

"I have a son. He's seen things. Strange things. I don't understand them. Maybe you do."

This time Peter's eyes fluttered. He licked his lips and his eyes looked less hollow and distant.

Jack looked around to see if anyone might be listening. He leaned in close to Peter. "The woods," Jack continued. "The woods are moving. Christ, I know that sounds crazy, but the woods are spreading…"

"They do that," Peter said finally. His voice was quiet and beaten. "You wouldn't think that they could, but they do."

"Why? How?"

Peter still didn't look at him. What he was seeing was not the window in front of him but something farther away in his mind.

"It's a bad place. Very, very bad. So dense, so untamed. A dark place. A bad place."

The words startled Jack. "What about the dark? What's with the darkness?"

Peter slowly turned to him. A broken man, there was no fight in his face. Just a vanquished resolution of events that were forced upon him and rammed down his throat.

"It'll get you," Peter said. "Darkness will always get you. I didn't see it then. I see it now. The Dark breathes. The Dark lives."

Jack didn't understand the man's cryptic remarks. "What happened to your family, Peter?"

The man looked at Jack as if he asked the dumbest question in the world. "The Dark got 'em."

"What do you mean? How did the Dark get them?"

Peter grinned. It was off-putting and didn't fit his character. The smile didn't impart comfort or understanding or humor. It was rooted in pain and irony and suffering. And then he giggled.

"The Dark wants company. The Dark wants to play. Mark saw it first. Kids always see it first. They believe unconditionally, don't they? Adults need evidence. They need to poke their fingers through the nail holes in Christ's hand before they believe.. But they come around, whether they want to or not. But kids… no, kids are the prize…"

Jack tried to focus him. "Listen, Peter, this is important. Where did Mark go?"

"The Dark took him. Took him to the forest. See, the forest is the Dark. The Dark is the forest. So thick with trees and leaves and bushes. The Dark scooped him right up and took him there. It's got a place out there. A place for children."

Jack suddenly thought about the sneaker Joshua found in the woods. It was a lost artifact, misplaced in such a robust natural environment. Like finding a child's stuffed animal in some place you'd least expect to find one.

"Jesus," Jack said. He touched his stomach where an ice ball had formed.

"The forest and the Dark. The Dark and the forest. The Dark forest…" Peter babbled.

The forest and the Dark. They were connected somehow. Jack got a sense of that. But just how they were connected, he didn't know. Joshua told him that the Dark came in through the window, and unless it drove a car, it likely came from the woods.

But the kid was a different matter. Jack took Joshua's story about the kid as his son's attempt to manifest his fear into something real and tangible.

But now he wasn't so sure. Was the kid real? Not in the way Jack or Anne or Joshua were real. But real in the context that the Dark was making itself more accessible to a boy who believed in things that he could not see or touch. It was a subtle seduction, using a mirror like a ten-year-old boy to attract a ten-year-old boy. To draw him close. To ensnare him and draw him to the heart of the forest.

The Dark took Mark Rothman and now it wanted to take Joshua.

Jack had to leave. He had to get back to the cabin immediately. He stood up but not before Peter's hand shot out and grabbed his arm and squeezed. Peter didn't look muscular but the strength in that grip was unmistakable. It didn't come from muscle but from a sense of urgency.

"Bright light," he said to Jack. "Bright light."

"What about bright light?" Jack asked, thinking about the last page of Peter's journal. "What's light do, Peter?"

The sitting man giggled again. He came out in disjointed bursts, as if he was trying to contain the hilarity. "How do you kill the Dark?"

"I don't know," Jack said. "How?"

"Fire," he said, finally surrendering to hysterics. And with that, Peter grabbed a nearby black marker and scribbled frantically on the white tab-letop. It was similar to the image Jack saw at the end of Peter's Journal

"Fire! Fire!!!" Peter shouted over and over until the orderlies came over to restrain him.

# Chapter 14

Jack got back to the cabin just as the sky was turning. Clouds had moved in again, threatening another miserable night, and in its infiltration, easily extinguished some of the less magnitude stars. The weather patterns here were strange at best. Summer months rarely had this much overcast and so little rain to the best of his recollection. It seemed almost – unnatural. Maybe supernatural?

And yet there were signs in the sky of another dark night.

That realization held infinitely more meaning for Jack now.

At the cabin, Anne had already packed up their things. None of her usual meticulousness was evident in their lopsided suitcases. She did not fold clothes as per her custom, making sure there were tight creases and that they lay flat so that they could be strategically inserted. The bags bulged like they bore tumors. She obviously just shoved the clothes inside, pushing the bags' capacities to their limits. And when covers did not zipper easily, she simply sat on the luggage, pushing down the contents until she could close the lid. She brought them down the steps and set them near the front door.

Jack noticed that most of the food in the refrigerator and cupboards had been packed, a decision Anne had made in the hopes of convincing Jack to leave that night instead of the morning, an argument that she ultimately lost.

"First thing tomorrow," Jack promised, fishing out the last beer from the refrigerator and cracking it open. "It's late and we need gas. We'll get up early and get the hell out of Dodge. But I need two seconds to breathe."

He sat down on the sofa. The very depression of his ass on the cushion was the perfect metaphor for how he felt – a heavy sagging feeling. He glanced over at Joshua who sat on the floor in front of the television, playing with his marbles and watching some animated show about kids with powers to twist and turn the elements.

Resigned to not leaving, Anne poured herself a glass of red wine and joined her husband on the sofa.

"How'd it go? Did you get the answers you were looking for?"

Jack pulled deeply from the beer. "I don't know. Maybe? I know he's supposed to be off-his-rocker, but I have to say, he didn't seem completely crazy to me."

"What do you mean?"

Jack looked over at Joshua one more time, and leaned into Anne, lowering his voice. "With what happened to his son, you'd expect him to be, I don't know... withdrawn and tough to reach. Not old' Petey. He didn't hesitate to tell me about things once I got him talking. Once I forced him to remember."

Anne's face drained of color. "What did he say, Jack?"

Jack glanced at the front window. He could make out the forest's tree line through the glass. Limbs stirred and they made Jack think they were laughing at him. "Something in those woods just isn't right. That's for sure. He saw it, but he ignored it at first. Like us." He took another sip of beer. "Whatever is out there, it went after his boy."

Anne looked like she was about to throw up. "What do you mean, it went after his boy? What went after his boy?"

Jack turned to her. His eyes were wide, and honest, and afraid. "The Dark," he said.

It was a ridiculous response but the only answer he could supply. Anne finished the large glass of wine in one gulp. Jack knew that she believed him, but her reason was fighting the only answer that made any sense.

"But the blood on his shirt, his wife? What happened to the wife?"

Jack shook his head. "He didn't say. But I don't think he murdered her," Jack continued.

"Why?"

"It's a feeling is all. If you saw this guy, you'd understand. You've seen the crime documentaries. All those interviews with killers. There's a way they speak, the way they look. You just know. It was an easy arrest for the Podunk police department, but this guy's not a killer. A husband and a father, yes, but not a killer. I don't know how to explain it."

Jack watched Joshua thumb-shoot a large Cats Eye into the circle of marbles, knocking out two orange fire swirls.

"But what he said, about the things that happened?" Jack continued. "They sounded pretty familiar. That's the thing. They sounded like the same things that Joshua's been saying. That can't be just a coincidence. What are the odds of that?"

"I can't wait to get out of here," she said. "I'm sorry I brought us here. I'm sorry for a lot of things, Jack."

Jack grabbed her hand and held it.

"Me too. Nothing like a supernatural crisis to bring a family together."

She smiled and he followed suit. He leaned over and put his head on her shoulder.

"Promise me one thing," he continued. "No more camping. No more outdoors. Only hotels, pools, and all-you-can-eat buffets."

"Done," she said.

***

Jack put Joshua to bed in their bedroom. They would all sleep together tonight. Jack brought in the night light and plugged it into the light socket. Anne had packed her son's bags, conveniently placing them to the side of the bedroom door for a quick and easy exit. Knowing her son's tendency to delay his morning routine, Anne planned ahead, laying out his clothes for the next day on the small desk in the corner. Get up, get dressed, get out, like a highly-trained special force team. End of story. Other than the orange night light, the room looked like it did when they first arrived – spartan and clean. Jack sat on the side of the large bed, bringing the covers up to his son's chin.

"We're leaving tomorrow," he said. "We're done with nature for a while. You ready to get back and see your friends?"

"Yes," Joshua said without a second's hesitation.

Jack let out a laugh. "I bet you are." And then he got more serious. "I'm sorry about all of this, sport. I really am. This wasn't what we had planned."

"It's not your fault," Joshua said truthfully. He glanced uneasily outside the window at the darkness.

"It's a parent's fault when he puts his son in harm's way. Even if it's unintentional. Parents need to be better. I need to be better. In more ways than one. Forgive us, sport?"

Joshua smiled and nodded his head.

"I owe you," Jack said smiling back.

Joshua sat up and grabbed his favorite book from the nearby night table. Jack and Anne had read it to him at least a thousand times. It was the story that kids Joshua's age never got tired of hearing over and over again. Knights, royalty, swordplay, what wasn't to love? There was an obstacle, a hero prince, a huge cataclysmic battle at the end. Good triumphing over evil. The quintessential happy ending and complete package.

He opened the well-worn book and began to read to his son. The pages were creased and yellowed from use.

"Once upon a time in a land far away, there was a prosperous kingdom where people were happy and safe from outside evil forces. But when the king died, shadows infiltrated the land. Crops and livestock died or disappeared. No one felt safe. And everything fell under a deep and unyielding darkness…"

As he read, both father and son gradually immersed themselves in the fable, oblivious to the Darkness that started to unfold and gather outside his parent's bedroom window. If one or both turned to look, they would have seen the unnatural black ooze seep from the forest and through the tree line, growing in volume like the pent-up energy of an encroaching storm.

Unnoticed by either father or son, the Bugs Bunny orange night-light subtly flickered.

***

After Joshua had fallen asleep, Jack returned to Anne on the sofa and collapsed next to her, laying his head in her lap. Anne juggled her third glass of wine, barely managing to keep from spilling any. She took a sip and set it aside. As she stroked his hair, she noticed how her husband's face had aged at least ten years since they had arrived that first day. Sure, stress was a big component of premature aging. Just look at any president's face after their first term in office. And yes, Anne accepted some of the blame for causing Jack stress. Her indiscretion with Selznick did more than its share of causing the creases of consternation under Jack's eyes and around his mouth.

"That took a while," she said, shutting off the television.

"Story time."

"The Last Knight?"

"Remember when we used to get sick of reading him Green Eggs and Ham? God, what I wouldn't give for a fox in a box rhyming couplet."

"I'm just happy he's sleeping. He's got too much on his mind for a ten-year-old," she said with a twinge of guilt.

"That changes tomorrow. We'll get back to normal again."

They sat that way for a few moments, saying nothing and just going over their respective thoughts. Anne caressed Jack's head, brushing his hair with her fingers. He closed his eyes, relishing in the repetition of the motion.

"We're going to be all right," she said quietly. "I believe that Jack. I really do. After everything we've been through, there's nothing that can come between us."

"I'm sorry," he said finally. "I had a hand in driving you to do things. I see that now. It's easy to see the effect, but much more difficult to recognize the cause. Especially when you were it."

"Don't," she said.

"I have to," he said. "I have to own my part."

She reached for his hand and squeezed it.

"We're going to be stronger for this," she said.

"I know."

Anne leaned down and they kissed. It was an honest kiss, not one driven by passion or lust, but love. Anne got up and laid alongside Jack, spooning him. Before long, they were both lost in a deep and heavy sleep, the kind that only happened absent mental or emotional burden. For the first time in a long time, they slept together as a couple.

***

Joshua opened his eyes. He had fallen asleep briefly but woke up because of a strange sensation that someone, something, was watching him. His eyes adjusted to the darkness in the room and immediately looked for the familiar orange glow of the night light. Reassured, Joshua felt more comfortable. He knew that fear played tricks on him, but he also needed verification that his concerns were just that – concerns – and not rooted in the real and the tangible.

What made him turn to the corner of his parent's room, he did not know. But turn he did and what he saw made him want to empty his bladder.

Mark Rothman sat in the chair near the desk. He looked small in an adult's seat, with his feat dangling inches from the floor. Mark sat upright with his hands on his legs staring at Joshua in bed. Joshua's eyes went wide, and he rubbed them to make sure he was awake and seeing what he was seeing.

*Hello, Joshua.*

It took Joshua time, but he caught his breath and managed a response.

"What do you want?" he finally managed. "How did you find me?"

Mark Rothman ignored the question and cocked his head to the side like a dog. *It's time.*

"I'm not going," Joshua said. "You can't make me."

Mark stood up. *We'll be best friends. You don't have a best friend, do you, Joshua? Not like me. I can play all day and all night. And so will you.*

In bed, Joshua instinctively backed away from the eerie boy, his back thudding against the wall. Mark didn't pounce on him or attack him but watched him curiously.

*What are you going to do, run? There's no running, Joshua? Where are you going to run to? Look outside. You see it, don't you? The Dark. The Dark is everywhere.*

"No…"

*Best friends,* Mark said again, as he took a step closer. *Forever, and ever…*

Joshua's heart raced under his pajama top. "No…"

Mark stood before him. The boy steadily transformed before Joshua's eyes. Mark's hand reached out, and Joshua noticed that the fingertips were black and that the black travelled slowly up his hand to his wrist and up the boy's arms. Horrified, Joshua watched Mark Rothman's form become a living shadow, so black that the edges of his form looked like an outline against an already dark room.

*Best friends,* the Mark-shadow reiterated. Only this time the voice did not come out human, but a hybrid sound composed of a guttural croak and the whine of a sharp wind through the trees. What's more was the stench that flowed out of exposed pit of the shadow's mouth, the rancidness of wet leaves and stagnant ponds.

Joshua didn't feel the urine fill his pajamas. Even if he had felt the initial release, there was nothing he could have done to prevent his bladder from evacuating. His eyes couldn't break from Mark's perverted form. Before the shadow consumed him, Joshua did the only thing he could do.

He screamed bloody murder for his parents.

***

Anne's eyes popped open. Like any parent, human or animal, her ears were trained to the sound of her child's voice and cries and any other sound her offspring made. Children stirred in their sleep, they made noises, they fell out of bed. Knowing the difference between these sounds was instrumental to a parent's sleep and sanity.

She wasn't alone. Jack heard it too, and he sat upright, ears attune to any subsequent noise. When he heard none, he was less visibly relieved than more frightened. Three weeks ago, he wouldn't have given his son's scream a second thought, chalking it up to a nightmare.

But that was then, and this was now.

"Jack?" she asked.

Adrenaline-fueled, Jack leapt off the sofa and made the stairs in two large leaps. He sprinted up the steps to their room, and the sick ice ball returned in his stomach. The room was empty; the window was open, and the curtains billowed from the outside storm breeze.

Joshua's pajamas were on the floor and the clothes he had left on the floor were gone. Joshua was nowhere to be seen.

Anne stumbled into the room. The desperate hope in her eyes quickly left. She looked at Jack who just shook his head.

"Joshua! Joshua!" she screamed. She went over to the open window and looked out into the darkness.

"Joshua!"

Jack went to her and held her. She sobbed against his neck.

"My boy," she cried. "Where's my boy? Where's Joshua?"

The porch light provided enough illumination for Jack to see the dark outlines of the trees swaying back and forth. The line itself seemed to have encroached further if that was possible, sending an indelible chill though his body.

"He's out there," Jack said finally. "It's got him."

"What do you mean "it's got him? What's got him."

Jack gestured to the tree line. "The woods," he said. "The Dark."

"Then let's get him back, Jack. We have to get our boy."

They raced out of the room, but not before Jack removed the Bugs Bunny night light from the wall and stuck it in his pocket. It had been a necessary comfort for most of Jack's childhood, and now it was very important to have that security.

That is, if there was any magic left in that old plastic cartoon fixture.

***

Downstairs, Anne rummaged the musty closet. She noticed a faint smell of rotting plaster and wondered how she had missed that and the yellow water stains and whether they were throughout the cabin? Was her judgment so clouded in the desperate attempt to save her marriage that she neglected to see the red flags? Were her eyes now finally opened so that she saw what she needed to see?

She retrieved the flashlights and made sure that they worked. Then she headed into the kitchen and removed two of the larger kitchen knives from the wooden block near the stove. She handed a knife and a flashlight to her husband.

"What's this for?" he said, looking at the large chef's knife that looked like something Michael Myers would use in the Halloween movies, and less practical for the task in front of them.

"I don't know. Because we don't have a gun?" Anne wielded her own large, bladed kitchen weapon.

He tossed the knife to the ground, where it clanged off the wooden floor.

"Jack?"

"This isn't going to do anything out there," Jack said.

He glanced around the room quickly. He saw Peter Rothman's journal on the coffee table.

"This is what we need," he said.

She made a face. "What's that?"

"Something that Rothman said to me before I left him. He asked me how you kill the Dark?"

"How you kill the Dark? I don't know, how?"

Jack turned to the last page and showed it to her. "We don't need knives, Anne. We need fire."

"There may be some gasoline in the shed for the mower," she said.

"Good. We'll need that, matches, rags… What am I missing?"

Anne's face was pale and grief-stricken. "Tell me it's going to be okay, Jack," she said. "I need to hear that."

He grabbed her and brought her close and squeezed.

"We're going to get him back, Anne. I promise you that."

***

Mark and Joshua walked through the woods. Joshua didn't try to run. As much as he wanted to, he physically wasn't able. Whenever he tried to divert from his path, he was instantly drawn back to Mark's side, like a magnet attracted to its polar opposite. Only in this case the pull was stronger than a magnetic connection.

Joshua was afraid, but he wasn't panicked. At least, not yet. He glanced out of the corner of his eye at Mark.

The Dark manifested itself back into the familiar body of Mark Rothman. Joshua could only conclude that its shadow form, while purer in representation, was rejected by the humans to whom it showed itself. One thing had been consistent through the years; humans were afraid of the dark, and that fear never left them no matter how large they grew or how old they got. Children were more susceptible to the dark, and as such, they could be tricked and lured and deceived easily.

The adults largely ignored children, which also helped the thing that was the Dark work unnoticed in the background. If someone came by, they would have seen two kids walking side-by-side in the woods. Nothing odd about that. Only that it was night and pitch dark and two kids that age should not be alone in a place like that. But still – boys will be boys – and who hadn't snuck out of the house after curfew when they were young?

This thing looked like a boy, but Joshua knew that this was no boy. Besides the obvious – the kid could become a shadow! – there was the fact that Mark's footsteps made no sound. The forest floor was full of brown dried leaves and brittle twigs that had fallen and dried out over time. Each footstep from Joshua sounded like he was stepping on tortilla chips, crunching and crackling. Mark's feet were noticeably silent, as if he was an original Native American, knowing how to walk silently across all sorts of terrain when hunting deer.

Joshua adjusted his shorts. He was able to change out of his pajamas before it took him. He looked up trying to see if he could see the night sky through the tree limbs. Flashes of stars could be seen poking through holes in the canopy, desperately trying to shine through the darkness that tried to reclaim the sky. He didn't know why that reminded him of the story about the kingdom in the story his father read to him, but it did. Maybe it was being immersed in darkness. He wondered if the Bugs Bunny night light would have any impact out here.

*I've been wanting a friend for such a long time, Joshua,* Mark said. His voice was soundless, toneless, and more of an expression of thought than the utterance from a living human being. *Such a long time.*

"I'm not your friend," Joshua said, trying to sound brave but his voice trembled. "I don't know you."

*You will,* Mark said. He didn't turn to look at Joshua but kept focused on a distant destination that only he could see. *We have time. A lot of time. There are so many friends you will meet, so many new friends you will make.* Mark then giggled but the sound was more unnerving than mirthful.

"Leave me alone," Joshua said. "Please."

*Do you like hide-and-seek?*

"What?"

*Do you like hide-and-seek?*

Joshua shook his head. "No."

*You will,*" the boy said again. *See, there's so many places to hide out here. So many places to hide in the Dark, Joshua. So many shadows.*

Joshua subtly dipped his hand into his shorts pocket and removed five marbles that he always carried with him. When his parents took him places, he was never sure if how long they'd be there or if there would be something to amuse him. As they walked, he dropped them one after another to create a make-shift trail for someone to follow him.

If they were following him.

***

Anne found the gasoline, a rake, and a shovel in the utility shed on the side of the cabin. She brought them to Jack who surveyed the supplies he had compiled on the kitchen table. Rags, a box of Diamond Blue Tip matches, a half-gallon of gasoline, the flashlights, two cutlery knives (Anne insisted), and now the rakes.

"This is the best I could do," she said.

"They'll work."

"They'll have to."

Jack laid one wooden-handled rake against a chair and raised a foot over it. He slammed it down at the part closest to the chair. The snap was loud like a gunshot. He did the same to the shovel, although that took three strikes before breaking off at the neck. He liberally drenched the rags in the gasoline and secured a few of them around the end of each of the wooden handles, tying them firmly in place. Jack stuffed the remainder of the soaked rags into a canvas shoulder harnessed mail bag. He reeked like a gas station.

"What if we don't find him, Jack?" she suddenly asked. It was the type of question that rose from insecurity and the fear of potentially losing someone close.

Jack's eyes spoke the answer his mouth did not. They were fierce and resolute and didn't waver an instant. He wasn't allowing that kind of talk, and the nonverbal response was exactly what she needed to hear.

"Give me the matches," he said.

They hurried out the door and down the front steps. Jack struck a match and touched it against one of the gas-soaked rags. It ignited immediately into a ball of orange flame casting light in the blackness that had settled around the cabin. He passed it to Anne and lit his own torch. He adjusted the canvas satchel on his shoulder and raised the torch high.

"Come on," he said, walking across the driveway toward the tree line.

Anne paused in her tracks.

"What is it?" Jack asked?

"The forest, Jack…"

Jack thrust the torch forward. Even in the evening darkness, the tree line was obviously closer than it had been the previous day. The high-pitch chirping of the crickets competed with the songs of katydids. The sounds were less celebration than they were threatening.

"Is it me," she continued, "or is it closer??

"It's closer."

"How can that be?"

"I don't know, Anne, it just is."

Anne's face deflated. Jack took another step forward before he stopped dead in tracks. Anne bumped into her husband.

"Jack?"

He saw it. The long branch, the Widow's Hand, stretching out toward the driveway, stretching out toward them. He didn't know how he had missed it before, but there it was now.

"What is it?" she pressed him.

Jack stared at the jawed limb and withered leafless fingers. His spine tingled.

"That's unholy," he said quietly.

With no more time left to waste, Jack took lead. The tree line was fortified with thick blackberry bushes armed with thick sharp thorns that served like razor wire on a military perimeter. Those hadn't been there before, he noted. They sprung up overnight as if the forest was trying to protect something.

Lowering the fiery edge of the torch, Jack touched it to the bush. The limbs twitched and shook as the thorns charred under the heat. A sound that only could be described as a buzzing scream ensued, and a long Ripple flurried up and down the tree line in response to the attack.

"Did you see that?" Anne asked.

"I saw it," Jack said grimly.

"That's not natural, Jack. That's nowhere near natural."

"You still have that chef's knife?"

"Here."

She handed her knife to her husband. Jack hacked away at some of the more stubborn branches, using the torch to help the process of clearing an entry. Anne followed suit, trying to set fire to live, living agriculture. Things didn't burn as much as blackened before being trapped by the flame. The result was the same – a singed odor and a screeching like nails down a blackboard.

Jack and Anne made quick work of the bushes, creating an opening that they could pass through. The gap was short lived, as the branches quickly regrew where they had been cut, stretching out to reduce the size of the aperture.

Once inside the thorny perimeter, a noise reverberated around them. It wasn't a scream like the noise the bushes made when feeling fire for the first time. This was more of a bleat to alert the surrounding area that a breach had occurred.

The woods were not pleased.

Jack pushed forward, holding onto Anne's hand, keeping her close to him. Like animals trying to intimidate an adversary, the plants and shrubs swelled larger, making themselves bigger than they actually were. They had to push past these obstacles, an effort that made every footstep a chore. Gnarled roots sprung up and caught the toes of their shoes, branches snagged their shirt and scraped their skin, drawing blood. Even in the dark, Jack knew they were headed in the right direction. The woods were throwing everything at them to impede the couple's progress.

As the couple trekked, they called out their son's name. Their voices barked out forcefully, but the resonance didn't reverberate. The sound quickly dissipated, absorbed into the surrounding environment until everything remained silent.

For the second time, Jack's spine tingled. "Hear that?" Jack asked.

Anne focused then shook her heard. "I don't hear anything," she said.

"Exactly. When have you been in the woods and not hear anything? Cicadas, crickets, bullfrogs, hell, even rutting deer… There's nothing out here, Anne. It's like a frigging mausoleum."

As fantastical as that seemed, Anne knew he was right. The woods were startlingly silent, watching them, trying to figure them out.

They pushed forward, touching their torches to any of the thick foliage that even looked out of place. Each time, the branches held firm, preferring to hang tough under a scorching flame, willingly accepting and enduring the heat before curling away.

Anne noticed her torch's dying light. "Jack!" Anne shrieked. "It's going out!"

He spun around to see her gesture to the torch. The once bright vibrant flame had subsided, diminished to a few lapping tongues of fire instead of a blazing ball. It was good that the darkness was so vast or else she might have seen the worried expression on his face. Jack dipped into the bag and fortified her torch with a new strip of gasoline-soaked rag. The flame grew and burned aggressively, illuminating Anne's troubled face.

A new noise came to their attention. This wasn't supernatural or foreign, but one that very much belonged in woods as deep and dark as this.

A large cat's snarl was unforgettable in its pure viciousness. It was a threat, a warning, and a promise of pain all wrapped into one chilling sound. You didn't want to be on the receiving end of that snarl. You wanted to get as far from it as possible. Typically, cougars avoided people. Those that didn't were probably infected with rabies. And if they attacked, there was only one thing to do – kill it or it would likely tear you apart, or at least, maim you severely.

And then there were cougars driven by an unseen evil force.

If someone had bet Jack three weeks ago that he'd be in a forest in the middle of the night facing down a large wild cat, he would have been all-in.

And yet, here they were, watching a muscular, very angry cougar with its ears flat against its head, exposing a mouth full of sharp, drool-dripping teeth. From what Jack recalled in his research before coming to the cabin, there were no cougar populations in the state. There had been a large presence, but that was in the 1900s. Despite what he read about and believed to be true, the cougar stood in front of them, one-hundred and seventy-five pounds of thick muscles.

"Holy shit," Anne whispered. The immediate threat of such a predator sucked all the wind out of her lungs.

Jack kept his eyes fixed on the large animal. There was no getting out of this situation. They couldn't outrun a hunter of this caliber. They had to outsmart it or outfight it. There was no other choice.

He grabbed Anne's arm and led her behind him, keeping his torch between them and the pacing cougar. The annoyed cat swiped at the torch, punctuating his anger with piercing and shrill vocalizations. The cougar's yellow eyes trained on Jack's slightest movement.

"Hey, kitty, kitty," Jack said in a low and even tone.

"Jack," Anne whispered. Though soft, her voice was full of fear.

He gestured with his hand for Anne to keep quiet, never breaking eye contact with the large cat. Jack thrust the torch forward, trying to drive the cougar backward and hopefully away. Instead, the predator remained undeterred, swatting at the torch with its claw-exposed paw, waiting for its chance to leap.

Jack remembered Anne's chef's knife. He removed it from the bag and wielded it in his dominant hand, keeping the torch in his left.

"Listen to me carefully, Anne. No matter what happens," Jack said. "Stay behind me, understand?"

"Yes."

Leading with his knife in hand, Jack took a step forward. The cougar growled at him, flashing those sharp teeth. It readied its large front paws, read-ying the retractable claws to attack.

"Ha! Get out!" Jack screamed at the cat. "Git! Get on! Git!"

The cougar snorted, sending mucous and sa-liva flying out of its nose and mouth. It feinted at Jack, gauging his reaction, his reflexes, and his quickness.

Jack fell for the feint, overcompensating for the diversionary attack. This was what the cougar wanted. It closed the distance between them in a mat-ter of seconds. The large paw slashed out at Jack, catching his shorts-exposed leg. The claws cut deeply because the laceration didn't immediately bleed and revealed a flash of white bone.

"Ahhh!" Jack screamed, falling backwards, his leg buckling from the attack. The pain didn't im-mediately come, the shock of being attacked over-whelming his senses. Anne shrieked, rushing over to her husband's side.

The cougar lunged but she thrust the torch in time to stop him.

"Jack! Jack!"

"The knife? Where's the damn knife?"

The cougar hissed and took a different tack toward the fallen prey. Jack jabbed the torch at him as his free hand patted at the ground looking for the knife. He found the handle when the cougar made his next attack.

The cat came on quickly, darting around the torch flame. Jack slashed at the face, an unexpected turn of events for the cougar that retracted its head to dodge the blade. Anne took advantage of the cat's surprise to strike it with her own torch, singing the fur. The large cat yowled in pain, retreating outside the attack periphery. Things had changed. There were two threats with which it had to contend. It retreated a few feet, turning its attention from Jack to Anne and then back to Jack again.

Jack gathered himself, getting to his knees. Torch and knife in hand, he beckoned the cougar, taunting him.

"Come on you pussy," he said through clenched teeth. "Come and get some."

The cat didn't like the tone and expressed it through a strained growl. It looked at Jack and then at Anne who held her torch out in front of her like a two-handed sword. The cat swiveled its head back and forth, reacting to each of the sudden movements that the couple made.

"At me! Look at me, you son-of-a-bitch!" Jack screamed at the animal. "You want me, I'm right here!"

The cat's head snapped to Jack. He released a fierce growl. Challenge accepted.

Jack readied himself. He wasn't an outdoors person by any means, but he had watched enough animal shows with Joshua to know that predators did not make blundering attacks like humans. They were precise hunters. Their existence depended on perfecting their skills and finishing their kills.

But being efficient predators meant that their attacks were standard. Unlike humans, animal predators did not typically approach hunting with improvisation, sticking to tried-and-true tactics. They didn't make awkward rushes or overcompensate because their adrenaline drove them to make mistakes.

When the cat attacked, Jack knew what to expect.

From what Jack remembered from a Nature Channel special, the cougar delivered its deathblow via a leaping pounce that trapped its prey in its big forepaws while sinking its teeth into its prey's neck. And that was what Jack looked for.

The cougar's whole body tensed as its eyes gauged the distance between Jack, the fire, and where Anne stood in relation to the other two. Once it calculated what it needed, the cougar struck.

Watching a pure predator in action was a sublime tribute to nature's construction of an elite animal. It moved in one fluid motion, springing, its body outstretched over a distance that made it look like it was flying. Jack fell back when he watched the cougar contracting before it leapt, further enticing the animal to do exactly that – jump through the air – and in the process, exposing its belly. The cat landed on target, the weight of its propelled body slamming into Jack, knocking him down. Jack landed with a thud, grunting under the force of impact. His body took all the animal's two-hundred-pound frame, fracturing at least three ribs in consequence. Blood flowed down the sides of his face where the sharp claws had lacerated skin.

But the tactic, while dangerous and risky, served its purpose. The chef's knife found its mark. The animal's aggressive attack and the weight it carried had expedited its death. Jack had used both hands to firmly position the twelve-inch knife at his sternum so when the cougar pounced, it went cleanly in between the animal's ribcage, hitting the bottom part of its heart. At that moment of impact, the cougar's eyes shifted from pure anger to genuine surprise. There was no chance for a final strike. The animal's heart pumped out its blood quickly and effectively, killing it a few moments.

Jack groaned as he pushed the animal off him. Anne helped drag the carcass, checking her husband for any additional wounds. Aside from the obvious cuts, scrapes, and torn clothing, there didn't seem to be additional wounds incurred.

"Don't you ever do that again," she said.

"That is a promise," he said hoarsely.

She helped him sit up and checked out the leg wound.

"It's deep," she said. She removed the belt from her shorts and tied a makeshift tourniquet above the wound. Jack tore what was left of his shirt and wrapped it tightly around the open cut.

"I'll live."

"What the hell was that?"

"A cougar as far as I could tell," he said. Then added as an afterthought, "A warning."

"A warning?"

"There haven't been cougars this far north in decades. We're close, Anne. We're close or else the woods or Dark or whatever wouldn't send that thing."

Reaffirmed by the news, Anne nodded. "Let's get our boy, Jack," she said.

***

Mark led Joshua past the place where Joshua had found the boy's sneaker. The path seemed clearer than that day, devoid of any grass or bush or shrub. It was as if the woods purposefully parted to make the trail visible and accessible for those it invited to enter its most inner sanctum.

The trail led to a clearing in which an exotic, gnarled tree grew at its center. It was a genus of tree that Joshua had never seen before. The thick trunk's twisted roots sprouted from the base and entrenched themselves firmly into the ground. They reminded Joshua of octopus tentacles. A black octopus, something from a science fiction novel. Only this wasn't in a book. This was right in front of his eyes, whether he chose to believe it or not.

The tree wasn't tall as compared to the birches and pines that surrounded and concealed the clearing. Those stood up straight and imposing like the sharpened wooden planks that formed the perimeter around frontier forts. But it was unique. Unique and threatening. A series of contorted limbs and branches that bore no leaves looked like the hands of a drowning old woman exploding up and out from that gruesome base. The bark, black as obsidian, shined even in the darkness.

This wasn't a typical tree and Joshua knew it immediately. If the look didn't give it away, the low humming that emanated from the trunk certainly did.

"What's that?" Joshua asked, his eyes glued to the black shine.

*That's a funny question,* Mark said.

"Why is that funny?"

*Because it's the source. The wellspring of all that you see around you.*

Joshua shook his head. "The source of what?"

*Of everything. It's the one forever. The one constant. In the beginning there was a Void, a color-less stretch of nothingness. But that Void was filled and then it grew into what is here and now.*

"Nature?"

*Is one word for it. It's how It's had to manifest itself. To be seen and be accepted. And it thrived. For a long time, It thrived in this environment. But then things changed... the balance shifted... and now It wants it back... The older ones don't see it yet, but the young ones do. The young ones' disappearances will be the voice that informs their elders. We will congregate in the Dark, and then they will know.*

Mark's human voice was slowly fading and being replaced by a primal guttural rasping. It was the sound of stretching roots and vines. Joshua was filled with a burning terror.

*And the Dark will be the instrument by which the Order will be restored...*

"I don't understand," Joshua said.

*You don't. But you will.*

Joshua didn't like the way the boy said it like it was an uncontested fact. "Why am I here?"

*Because we're friends. Best friends. And best friends stay with each other. We're going to play,*

*Joshua, but first you had to see this. You understand? You had to see this first.*

"I want to go home."

*You are home now. You feel It, don't you? You feel It inside you?*

Joshua wanted to walk away but was compelled to stay. Some unseen force gripped him. It didn't hurt, but Joshua knew that It could if It wanted to.

"I feel… something," he said.

*Let It wash over you,* Mark whispered. *Let It know that you are here.*

***

Jack and Anne trudged through the uneven terrain. They exerted themselves, stumbling in places, breaking through large spiderwebs whose thick silk clung to their skin. The unpleasantness of their journey was overshadowed by the significance of the goal in front of them – finding their son and bringing him home. With this inspiration, they moved methodically forward, slower than what they would have preferred, but the woods at night became a complex ever-changing labyrinth. Going fast and carelessly risked them heading in a wrong direction. Jack was no tracking expert and had to rely on his memory for an approximate fix on their location. He knew where Joshua had found the sneaker was the key; that's where his son had to be. Nowhere else made sense. Something was there responsible for all this mess.

Something.

Jack paused from time to time, partly because his leg painfully throbbed and partly to determine if he was leading them in the right direction. He waved his torch around shedding minimal light in deep blackness. Where the light touched was inconsequential; the forest loomed large.

"Joshua! Joshua!" Anne screamed.

"Joshua!" Jack yelled.

Their torches suddenly flickered, assaulted by a robust gust that blew through the tree limbs, rustling the leaves in a haunting chatter. The gust attacked the flames relentlessly, trying to extinguish them. Jack turned his back to the fierce wind, preserving the light like the last of three wishes. Anne tried to follow suit but somehow stumbled, her shoe getting caught up in bramble. She fell to the ground, the torch slipping out of her hand, and skidding across the forest floor. The flame sputtered in the cool dirt.

"Anne!" Jack quickly retrieved her torch and then helped her up. Another gust tried to take advantage of the situation, but Jack shielded the flame, and in the process, allowing the burn to build. "You okay?"

She nodded, although it was obvious that she was shaken up.

"Be careful," he said.

"I'm trying," she said. "But this place… It's fighting us, Jack."

Jack flashed the torch around, exposing the robust growth of bushes. He knew it couldn't be possible, but the undergrowth had bulked up, expanded its roots, become thicker, fuller. Even tree limbs seemed to be longer, their ends sharper, the bark rougher. Everything seemed to be swelling around them.

This realization should have frightened Jack. That was the point after all. The Dark was fueled by the fear of others. It harvested that fear, capitalized on it, used it to fortify and protect its environment.

But if this change was meant to deter them, it failed. Jack wasn't afraid. He was mad.

"I'll burn every inch of this fucking place down! Every tree, every bush. Everything. You hear me? You're going to be ashes!"

He handed the torch to Anne and removed two more soaked strips, wrapping one each around the ends of their sticks.

Jack started to burn everything around him. The leaves and branches cringed under the heat. A strange shrieking pierced the night.

"Hurts, doesn't it?" Jack hissed, spittle flying out of his mouth. Anne mimicked her husband, pressing that fiery tip into everything rooted into the ground. It may have been the darkness or the way it burned, but the woods appeared to separate, creating an opening. Jack jumped at the opportunity, grabbing his wife's free hand, and pulling her through the aperture before it closed.

The woods tried to collapse on them, but it was too late. The determined couple had gotten through, and the bushes shook in anger, seething at their loss.

"Jack."

Anne grabbed her husband's hand. Jack stopped look at her then followed her arm where she pointed the tip of her torch on the ground.

It was a marble, specifically, a Cat's Eye, a transparent sphere with a distinctive blue swirl in the center. It trapped the image of the torch's orange light in its geometry.

"That's Joshua's," he said, picking up the marble and turning over in his fingers.

"Look, there's another," she said.

It was a Tri-Lite. Brilliant splashes of red, blue, and yellow on an opaque base. The others were there too: The Dragonfly, the Sunburst, the Aggie.

"Good boy, Joshua," Jack said. "That's one smart kid we got. He's showing us the way,"

Reinvigorated with this proof of life, Jack dismissed the gnawing pain in his leg and pressed forward. Nothing would hold him back now. It'd have to kill him first.

"Joshua!" they both yelled. They were in complete synch now, motivated by purpose and need. Their voices reinforced one another and made the calls of their son's name an imperative and not a wish. As they both hurried through the punishing underbrush, the sharp deterrence of brambles and pricker bushes were no longer a factor. They became nuisances no more worthy of attention than a horsefly bite. That itself was a victory.

But the victory was short lived.

Jack and Anne abruptly stopped when they saw the figure. An odd break in the overhead canopy allowed the light from the stars to shine through, giving this patch of ground an ethereal majesty about it, accentuated by the orange burn from their torches.

Standing in front of them about ten feet away was a feral-looking woman, dirty and unkempt, with mud-stained clothes and bits of leaves stuck in her hair. She was human, that much was clear, but everything about her indicated that she was wild and uncivilized, a product of the land around them.

"Who is that?" Anne asked.

Jack had never seen the woman before in his life but knew exactly who it was.

"Karen Rothman," he said. "The mother."

Karen Rothman's face was deeply lined. The cheeks were bruised and filthy and the eyes regarded them with malignance, the way an animal would when people stumbled into their territory. Her shirt was slashed and tattered and stained with dried blood. Karen held a jagged branch in her hand that tapered off into a substantially blunt end, which she wielded like a primitive club.

She scowled at them, baring her teeth. If the light was stronger, Jack and Anne could have made out their yellowed tint. If they had been closer, they would have whiffed the stink of death from her mouth.

There wasn't a warning. No parlay. No explanations. Karen Rothman did not give quarter. She only attacked, raising the jagged branch over her head.

For a woman that looked emaciated and lean, her speed was unexpected. Jack got in front of Anne and raised the torch feebly in defense before the surprisingly strong woman knocked it out of his hands with a swing of her club. The torch twirled to the ground in a thump, sending red-hot embers into the air. Most of the orange sparks extinguished, but some caught the dry crust of fallen leaves and dried pine needles. Those embers quickly turned to patches of fire that spread along the forest floor.

Jack was slow to get to his feet. Karen took advantage of opportunity, striking him again in the legs. The blow from the heavy branch sent a searing flash of pain throughout Jack's body; a brilliant white blinded his eyes, rendering him momentarily immobile. Then she struck Jack one more time in the chest to see if he was responsive. As the feral woman stood over Jack, her wild eyes squinted as if trying to understand who he was and what he was doing here. Then Karen Rothman turned her attention to Anne.

Anne's face froze in fear. She had never been in a fight with another woman, no less one for her life, and she could count on two fingers the number of times she saw firsthand the ferocity that women could dole out on one another. In high school, she witnessed her first fight when her friend engaged in an all-out scratch-hair-pulling altercation with a rival over a boy that apparently had cheated on them both. The two girls fought in the school hallway, slamming each other into lockers as they dug their nails into their opponents' arms. It took three teachers to separate them. Both girls bore the marks of the battle – bloody lips, scratches, bite marks on an arm or two. Anne didn't think she could ever do that to another person. The only other time she had seen two women fight was in her living room. Then, the combatants were on the television and in the confines of the Octagon, the ring in which mixed martial artists went *mano-a-mano*. She found women striking women in that way to be less impressive or threatening than comical. Despite all of the blackbelts and fancy submission moves they possessed, these fights seemed to always revert to schoolyard tactics – knock your opponent down, straddle them, and hit them until they cried "uncle."

When survival mode kicked in, Anne knew she didn't have a real choice. She fled on pure instinct. Karen quickly pursued her, closing the slight lead the smaller woman had. Worse, Anne's panic made her sloppy and careless. Looking back to gauge Karen's distance, she did not see the low-hanging tree limb in front of her. It caught her on the shoulder, knocking her off-balance and sending her sprawling face-first onto the forest floor. For the second time that night, her torch flew out of her hands. The ball of flame burned three feet from her outstretched fingers, catching fire to the susceptible branches and twigs.

With Anne down, Karen slowed her pursuit, cautious of the felled prey struggling to catch her breath. The feral woman's eyes never strayed from Anne's body, stepping carefully, ready for anything. When Anne turned over to right herself, she saw Karen looming , wild and inhuman.

"What happened to you?" Anne managed, finally finding her voice. "That was your child."

If she hoped to connect with the woman, it did not work. Karen's face did not register her words. She stared unblinkingly at Anne. Her eyes were sterile, her look a thousand-mile stare. It seemed to Anne that Karen Rothman was listening to the sound of her voice rather than the words that were spoken.

Anne's tears flowed. "Do you understand what I'm saying? For Christ's sake, can you understand anything at all?"

But her words fell on deaf ears. With the resignation that she was going to die in the forest, Anne wept unashamed.

Karen opened her mouth. Her face contorted; her throat gurgled. She tried to speak but nothing coherent came out. Only a strained and craggy sound. She convulsed and a syrupy fluid spilled out her mouth and onto the ground. When she relieved herself of that mess, she tried to communicate once more. The painful catharsis managed one word.

"Dark," she said.

Then Karen raised her branch-club. The light from the nearby small fires illuminated her wild eyes. The person who was Karen was no more. She had been replaced by an inner darkness that had consumed her.

A loud THUNK suddenly rang out, and the crazy woman dropped to the ground without another word. She landed hard, her body collapsing in a lifeless heap. Gray matter seeped where the side of her head was dented and broken. Jack stood behind the dead woman with torch in hand; he was bloody and bruised but fiercely alive. He breathed heavily, looking every bit the savage that Karen Rothman did. Anne shivered with the realization. Jack went over to the fallen women and finished what he had started, pulling out a moss-covered rock from the ground and using it to crush the woman's skull.

Anne got to her feet and hugged her husband.

"Are you okay?" he asked.

She nodded as she held him close.

"Come on," he said.

Anne grabbed the torch, its flame running out of fuel. It was now or never.

# Chapter 15

Mark brought Joshua to the foot of the strange, gnarled tree. Joshua touched the bark and was shocked by how smooth it felt. It reminded him of a dolphin's skin, so slippery and without the roughness and ridges that were typical of more conventional bark. He let his fingers traverse down the trunk and over the twisted roots that dug into the ground and gripped it tightly. His eyes followed the flow of the roots as they disappeared and reappeared in other places, its humps rising and falling like a sea serpent.

He didn't have to be an adult to know that this tree was different, and because of that, it was special. Joshua walked around the tree, stepping carefully and marveling at its extravagant uniqueness. There was a palpable energy pulsing within, and the bark was warm to the touch. There was comfort there, but the boy could sense that the good feeling could turn cold quickly. It was a fickle sensation. Joshua noticed that the night sky wasn't completely blotted about by the forest's dense overhang. Stars could be seen poking through the areas where leaves didn't overlap in a tightly thatched pattern. This made him feel better for some reason.

Mark studied his face, and when he spoke, it was as if the boy knew what Joshua was thinking.

*They're just stars,* he said. *Specks of gas and dust that children make wishes on, nothing more.*

Joshua didn't articulate his response but thought it. Yeah, but they're light.

He noticed patches of shadows collect and move across the ground. Like the malleable composition in the liquid motion lamp in his father's study, once it gained enough mass the dark blobs dispersed on their own travelling until it found another patch and either joined or else bounced off the mass.

Joshua turned to Mark. "What is it? What's the Dark?"

Mark stared intently into Joshua's eyes and then smiled. *What definition do you want to hear?*

"Whatever is the truth."

Mark laughed again. He found a large root and sat down. He swept the ground with an open hand. Here, the forest floor was already pristine, devoid of twigs and dried pine needles. Fallen leaves did not land here. The ground was composted of perfectly flat and compact dirt, making it even more special, if that was possible.

*Dark is older than light, did you know that? It came first. How can you see something if you can't see anything? And being the oldest, it is the stronger partner. Light is only strong enough to show you that the Dark exists.*

"Like a twin."

Mark turned to Joshua. *Yes, like a twin. Dualism. Contrary forces that can be complementary. You don't have to understand the Dark to know its strength. To respect it. To obey it. Do you want to play a game, Joshua? The best way to know the Dark is to immerse yourself in it.*

Joshua shook his head.

*There's nothing to be afraid of,* Mark admonished. *Why do you fear it?*

"Because I don't know what's there."

Mark grinned an unsettling smile. *But you will, Joshua. You will.*

"What if I don't want to?"

Mark didn't have to respond. The tree did it for him. The tree and the surrounding Darkness. The familiar Noise sounded in its customary fashion: low at first and feeding on itself to build in intensity and volume. The circumference of the tree line surrounding the clearing started rippling as the Noise's pitch intensified. Wide-eyed, Joshua watched the Ripple fly around and around, every limb, branch, leaf moving in perfect synchronicity. The thrum was the sound of a million bees coalescing around a large hive. It was all connected somehow – the Tree, the Dark, the Ripple, the Noise.

Nature. It was all a part of nature and yet, weren't natural things, but maybe good things? Nature wasn't bad; it simply just was.

So, why did he fear everything that was unfolding around him?

Joshua blocked his ears with his hands. The Noise had no effect on Mark who stood watching the spectacle before him with the respectful adoration reserved for holy things. Dark blobs accumulated, gathering until they had collectively reached a tipping point before leaking in a steady stream across the clearing.

Too terrified to move, Joshua's face stiffened in a mask of horror. Even if he could scream, the heavy-bass pulse of the Dark would easily drown out any cry that feebly escaped his trembling mouth. Joshua watched as the Dark steadily pushed, covering the ground, and now pooled around his feet, building until it covered his shoes. From there it travelled up his legs, slowly, dripping upward if that was possible. Around him, the Noise escalated, getting louder and eager.

*Do you see, Joshua? Do you see it now? How do you explain something like this? You can't. You just have to feel it...*

Joshua felt the Dark creep up his body. It was not a gentle ascent. The Dark pricked the boy's skin as it climbed, like the teeth inside the suckers on a squid's tentacles; it rose, sunk it, and lifted itself. And that repetition, Joshua did feel, helpless under the probing inky grip.

*We're going to play, Joshua… Play forever together. Forever together… forever together…*

***

The woods had done its best to shield the entrance to the clearing. It had collapsed onto itself, obfuscating the worn path with primitive, natural camouflage. But it couldn't hide the last two marbles on the ground that Joshua had dropped right outside the entrance – a green Corkscrew and an orange Oxblood. Anne picked them up and showed them to Jack who thrust the fiery end of his torch into the bushes.

An unnatural scream broadcasted from the woods. It was one borne of pain and fear. It was a sound the woods were very unaccustomed to making. The bushes tried to repel the flame and fight back Jack's relentless attack, rolling the tip into the thickest parts. The bush caught fire and retreated, exposing the path.

"There!" Jack said.

Anne saw it. She took her own dying torch and used its fire in tandem with her husband's. The brush peeled back from the flame exposing the path more and more. Jack walked in with Anne behind him.

"The roots! Burn them at the roots!" he directed her. Together, they thrust their flames at the bushes' bases, catching fire to the dried twigs and leaves scattered on the ground. The blaze grew quickly and spread equally as fast. As much as the branches tried to regenerate and push back against the flames, they could not. Rooted in the ground, they had nowhere to go.

So, they burned.

Jack and Anne entered the clearing. Although the only visible light source emanated from their torches, the clearing was surprisingly illuminated. The gnarled tree that stood at the center gave off its own murky radiance. Joshua stood next to the tree; half of his body appeared covered in shiny black slime. It looked as if he had fallen in a vat of tar.

"Joshua!"

The boy couldn't speak. He could only stare intently in their direction, hoping his eyes could convey the fear that he felt. The Dark was consuming him slowly, purposefully, blotting out his body inch by inch. While terrifying, it was a relatively painless consumption. The scabrous Dark would cover a portion of exposed skin, pricking him like little Novocain needles and numbing the flesh, before moving on. Gradually, his extremities were becoming pleasantly anesthetized.

Mark stood next to Joshua. *Your parents are here. Do you think they're going to help you? They can't help you. Mine didn't help me. But I didn't need them. I had the Dark.* He leaned in close to Joshua's ear. *You're with me now.*

Joshua tried to shake his head, but his skull felt so heavy that it only lolled around his shoulders. Everything seemed so sluggish, and he was so tired that all he wanted to do was close his eyes and sleep.

Jack and Anne did not see Mark. They couldn't. He wasn't there for them to see. What they saw was their son covered in a dark bile that was spreading like a speedy leprosy.

"Josh!" His father screamed. He limped over to the boy. Jack was immediately struck by the stink in the air. It was acrid and pungent, and it stabbed through his nasal cavity engaging his gag-reflex so that he started to dry heave. The only worse smell he had ever encountered was when he was trying to fix his parents septic system. Other than weeks of fermenting excrement and urine, he couldn't have imagined a worse stench.

Until now.

Jack vomited, spitting up bile from beneath the pits of his stomach. It spilled on the ground over a root bend. It was difficult to collect himself to the task at hand. Every time he inhaled, that wall of repugnance filled his nostrils.

But he had a more immediate problem.

His torch was losing juice, the ball of the flame noticeably shrinking in circumference. Without fire, he couldn't see. Without fire, he had nothing to kill the Dark.

Jack reached out to touch Joshua, but hesitated, his fingers lingering over the strange dark matter that blanketed his son's lower body.

"Joshua? Can you hear me?"

Joshua's face looked impassive; the lids of his eyes sunk at half-mast. The dark mass was sucking his son's strength. Jack's hand instinctively snapped out and slapped the boy's face. The surprise of the sting registered on Joshua's face, his eyes coming back to the now, temporarily.

"What's wrong with him?" Anne called out from behind him.

"I don't know. He's drugged or something."

The boy's head slumped forward to look into his father's eyes.

"The Dark," Joshua croaked. "The Dark, Daddy."

Jack set the torch on the ground on a root, and the appendage emitted a scream as the flame burned the smooth bark. He carefully got his hands around underneath the boy's arms and lifted trying to separate his son from the Dark. He could not.

"Jack!"

The Noises picked up all around him, chirping louder like frenzied chimps. The shadows had become an audience and a witness to the Dark's ceremony unfolding before them.

"Jack!" she shouted again.

He whipped around. "What?" What he saw made his stomach drop. A thick tangle of chickweed had ensnared Anne, entangling her legs, trapping them.

"Anne! Anne!" Jack yelled. His wife and his son were trapped, putting Jack between a rock and a hard place.

"Dad?"

Jack bit his lip but stayed with his son. "I'm going to get you out of here, Josh."

Anne screamed again, and for a second time Jack looked over at her, concerned. As much as he didn't want to, the Dark was forcing him to make a choice he didn't want to make.

"You wanted to leave her, didn't you?" his son asked out of the blue. Joshua's mouth moved, but the voice and its timbre were not his son's.

"Joshua?"

The boy's pallid face bore no recognition of the dire situation. The eyes, normally a warm chocolate brown, appeared detached and untouched by any emotion.

"You did. I know you did. She cheated on you and you got the excuse you needed to let her go."

"Joshua, no, that's not right…" But it was. How did he know? How could he know?

"So, leave her. Let her go. No one will know. It'd be our secret. Let the forest have her and we'll go home. She took another man's tongue in her mouth. What else did she take?"

Jack looked at Joshua. It was his son's face but what burned behind the eyes was not his son. The Dark had him. The boy smiled as if reading Jack's mind, knowing what he was thinking.

Anne struggled with the vines. She regarded the dying torch in her hand and thrust it between her legs into the mesh of the spreading, mat-form weed. The weed resisted but ultimately succumbed to the fire, the thin fibrous strands breaking and giving her enough space to break through its grip. The remaining tentacles of the chickweed pivoted from the attack and wrapped around her other leg digging into the skin around her calf.

Anne screamed again, beating at the strands with the torch. The fiery wrapping popped loose, burning on a patch of empty ground. It looked alone and out of place, like a flare fired from a ship in the middle of an ocean at night in a hopeless call for help.

Jack opened the canvas satchel and touched the torch flame to the remaining soaked strips inside. The bag caught immediately, and Jack swung the fireball around and around.

The Dark didn't like that. The Noises protested. But they weren't confident, intimidating sounds like Jack had heard previously. Their tone was different, softer, questioning.

Afraid.

How do you beat the Dark?

Fire. Lots and lots of fire.

And now it was Jack's turn to smile.

Like an Argentine cowboy twirling his bolo, Jack pushed back the shadows with every arc of the twirling fire ball. His other hand thrust the torch to keep back the patches of black that ached to press forward. It was more than a stalemate; he was winning. Jack made his way over to Anne incinerating the chickweed at its source at the edge of the clearing. Once burned through, the weed immediately died and curled limp on the floor. He handed Anne the torch.

"Burn it," he growled at her. "Burn everything in sight and don't stop until this place is an inferno!"

Anne didn't have to be told twice. She started at the closest green tufts, pressing the red-hot blaze against the leaves and branches. They sputtered and cracked into flame, screeching in agony. Only when she was positive that the torture did its job did she move onto another section of overgrowth.

As Anne set fire to the surrounding perimeter, Jack raced back to his son. The Dark had consumed the boy up to his chest. Jack imagined that this is what the beginning of time was like before there were stars. Just a rich deep black and nothing else. A darkness so complete and limitless that you couldn't place the sounds that were made therein.

Undeterred this time, Jack tried to strip away the black mass spreading over his son. It was sticky like hot tar, and it burned his fingers much the same way hot tar would. Sudden, flashing pain seared through Jack. And yet, his son seemed unaffected. It did not burn him, which made Jack conclude that the Dark was protecting its prey.

Worse, Jack was losing him.

"Mark wants to play with me," Joshua said. "The Dark isn't so bad. I'm no longer afraid of it." He looked at the gnarled tree that was thrumming in all of its glory. "Goodbye, Dad."

Jack smelled the stink around them. He looked at his wife struggling to burn the woods, and he looked at his son being swallowed by the Dark.

He thought of Peter Rothman, so lost and left to the haunting memories of his experience in these goddamn woods where everything that mattered was taken away from him. These thoughts and feelings boiled within him, bubbling up, making Jack mad, his scream building until it exploded out of his mouth.

"No!" Jack yelled.

The sound that he heard at first sounded like a laugh, as if the tree was making fun of his pitiful show of defiance. But that sound quickly changed when the tree or the Dark or whatever was lurking here saw his true intentions.

And it didn't like them.

Jack threw the burning satchel at the tree's base.

The Dark shrieked. Jack ran to the edge of the clearing and ripped the dry branches and brown leaves from the protective natural barrier. If they tried to put up a fight, Jack didn't notice. Adrenaline pumped through his veins like fuel injection and even though he bloodied his palms, he never felt the pain. He ran back and added the fuel to the flames. He repeated this process two more times until the fire grew and the shrieks grew louder.

"It's not burning," Jack said after his third trip. "Why isn't it burning?" He turned to see Anne's progress. She had half the clearing's tree-line burning. The heat had escalated twenty degrees in ten minutes. Smoke started to billow, and Jack knew that was a good sign. The more things burned, the brighter things were, and the less places that the Dark had to hide. The shadow that had consumed Joshua had ceased its ascent. In fact, it retreated from the boy, more focused on Jack's and Anne's immediate threat.

The tree was still intact.

And Jack understood.

The tree for the boy.

The Dark seemed to be making an offer: one for the other, a fair trade. He could try to kill the tree, or he could save his son, but he could not do both. Now, Jack understood. Peter thought he could do both. He tried. He failed. And he lost both his son and his wife.

The Dark might be afraid, but it was still strong. It wasn't beaten. It probably couldn't be beaten without the exact type of sacrifice that Jack was unwilling to surrender.

Not his family. He knew that now. And in recognizing that vulnerability, he got strength of conviction.

"How we doing Jack?" Anne said, rushing over to his side. She saw her son's blank expression and her heart sank. "Oh, God, Joshua…"

"Joshua, can you hear me? Come on, I know you're in there. Speak to me, Joshua."

"Daddy…"

"I'm not going anywhere. Your mom is not going anywhere. We are going home. So, come on. Snap out of it. I need your help here. I can't do it alone."

"Come on, big boy," Anne encouraged. "We're right here."

"Sooooo tirreeeeddd…"

Anne turned to her husband. Her face was hopeless and desperate.

"Jack…," she pleaded.

He cupped the boy's cheeks, focusing the boy's face so that his eyes looked directly into his.

"No darkness will ever dim this light."

The familiarity of those words made Joshua's eyelids flutter.

"What?"

"No darkness will ever dim this light," Jack repeated. "I told you that when we got here, remember? No darkness will ever dim this light."

And with that, Jack removed the night light from his front pocket. He showed it to Joshua.

"Remember this, Joshua? Remember?"

The boy looked at the night light. The recognition slowly took hold, and as the boy remembered, his eyes got more focused, and he became more alert.

"Come on, Joshua," Jack said. "Say it with me. No darkness will ever dim this light. No darkness will ever dim this light. No darkness…

"…will ever dim this light," Joshua said. "No darkness will ever dim this light…" Each iteration was a stronger assertion of a deeper-rooted affirmation.

"Hey," Jack said, smiling as he saw his son return to him. "It's Bugs."

Jack glanced at the tree and the surrounding blaze. His son was free of the shadow. The Dark had released its hold on the boy waiting to see Jack's next move. The tree was there. He could give it another try. The clearing was almost completely lit, and the fires were still burning, but the spreading had stopped. Jack could try to finish the job if he wanted.

If he wanted. The Dark was tempting him. Teasing him.

He could do it…

Jack's attention was drawn by a tug on his shirt. He looked down to see Joshua staring up at him.

"Dad," the boy said. "Your leg."

Jack looked down at the bloody wrap.

"How about we discuss it when we get home, okay?"

"The cabin or home-home?"

"Home-home, sport. We're going home."

"What about this?" Anne asked, gesturing to the fire they had created. The flames had subsided considerably as the nature around them fought back against the fire. She bent over to grab a burning dead branch. Jack stopped her and threw the branch on the ground. "What are you doing?"

"We're done," he said.

"No, this can't happen anymore. It's got to stop, Jack. We have to make it stop!"

He grabbed her by the shoulders firmly so that she felt the seriousness of the words he was about to say.

"We're going home, Anne," he said. "All of us. Together. We're going home."

Joshua stepped from behind his father. He looked pale and small, but he was alive. Anne scooped him up, crushing him against her chest.

"Mom, you're squishing me," he protested.

"You're damn right," she said, burying him in kisses.

The family made their way through the crackling and the smoke to the path that led out of the clearing. Jack ushered his wife and son through but paused for one more look. Although the fire had done damage, the choice made, Jack could see that it was already healing itself. But some parts were not growing back, the result of the purity of an element that helped keep the balance of nature in check.

Slash-and-burn agriculture had been around for centuries and had occurred around the world. It started with areas so inundated with vegetation and overrun with trees and shrubs that it had to be cleared before anything could be planted. The quickest way for that job to be accomplished was through a combination of slashing the density and burning it on the spot on which it was cut, releasing the nutrients needed to fertilize the ground for future crops. The problem with this was that this only benefitted the first-generation crops. Subsequent crop generations never realized the full benefit of those nutrients, relegated to whatever was left. Eventually, this type of farming wore out the land, requiring a relocation to replicate the process from the beginning, leading to deforestation and high carbon dioxide levels.

Fire and nature. Symbiotic enemies.

Jack wasn't sure how many others had tried to burn down that damn tree or tried to keep the Dark at bay with fire. One thing was evident; no one had succeeded. Peter Rothman certainly didn't. He lost his family and his mind. Well, Jack had both. The tree lived. So what? It wasn't going to see them again. He was damn sure of that.

And what about the Dark?

Before Jack left, he knew that he not only did not stop the Dark, but he had also inadvertently played into its hands. By burning the forest around the clearing, Jack had only fertilized the ground from which the unholy gnarled tree grew. He didn't stop its growth; he only fortified it. His and Anne's actions merely sustained the tree and by extension the Dark until the next unfortunate rental family came looking for an idyllic retreat in the woods. And if they had children with them, well, then the cycle could start all over again.

This realization made Jack sick, but not enough to regret his decision.

He had his son and his family.

So, he had kicked the can down the road. So what?

Let the damn town deal with its own headache, once and for all.

# Epilogue

The condo was just what they needed: two bedrooms, generous closet space, two bathrooms, a common living area, a galley kitchen, and a small dining area between the two. The windows looked out into the courtyard and the party room, a place with two large screen televisions, a pool table, and a wet bar – that could be reserved by the residents. The condo was much smaller than their nearly 3,000 square foot house, but what it lacked in living area it made up in function. There was little wasted space and a logical flow to the design, and because of this, the square footage seemed much larger than what it was.

Another important difference from their original house was location. The building was in an up-and-coming section of town where new restaurants and apartment residences were popping up all over, making their new neighborhood a hot commodity. The building was just under ten years old, with good bones. Sure, newer offerings were in the works, but everything worked, the amenities were generous, and the location was in the heart of the neighborhood, a block away from the subway.

There was no question. The cul-de-sac was in the past. The house, the neighbors, past mistakes and indiscretions, everything had been set aside and left behind without a second thought. Now, there was only the future. In the nearly nine months since their summer from hell at the cabin, Jack and Anne had reconnected. More importantly, Joshua had been doing much better. His nightmares had reduced significantly, and although he still liked to sleep with a night light, that was the least of their worries. Jack and Anne had even discussed having another child. All was good and right in their lives.

That night, Jack, Anne, and Joshua had dinner at their favorite local restaurant, a French-German brassiere on the corner of their block. Jack and Anne loved the *steak frites* while Joshua could not get enough of their seasoned French fries that came with an assortment of dipping sauces. After dinner, they got dessert from a shop that specialized in making individualized ice cream with liquid nitrogen. The process fascinated Joshua who watched the staff closely as they donned the thick rubber gloves before pouring the vat of the liquid nitrogen. He smiled as the contents smoked when the liquid hit the bowl. They each got their favorite flavors: Jack got coffee, Anne strawberry cream, and Joshua triple chocolate fudge.

On their walk back, night had settled in, the sky was black as squid ink making the stars pop in their brilliance. The darkness was less intimidating here; streets were lit up through a combination of business neon and streetlamps, and people shuffled about with energy and excitement. Once inside the building, Jack, Anne, and Joshua stopped by the video room, which was uncharacteristically unoccupied, and watched thirty minutes of a Disney film before calling it a night.

Joshua bathed, brushed his teeth, and got into his pajamas, sliding into bed just as his father entered his bedroom.

"Story time," Jack said sitting on the bed beside his son. He held up two books: Joshua's favorite, and one about a cowboy dinosaur. This was a routine he had started, giving his son two choices knowing full-well which one the boy would choose.

"The Last Knight," Joshua said.

"How did I know you'd say that?" Jack smiled. He opened the book and began to read. "Once upon a time in a land far away, there was a prosperous kingdom…"

Joshua listened intently on his father's words. No matter how many times he had heard the story, and by this time it had to be at least a thousand, he never got tired of the tale where a lone knight was able to save a kingdom from an evil spell from a witch that created a veil of darkness that took over the land. Jack did not read the entire legend. He was well versed in the sections that his son liked to hear and knew those parts that could be edited out of the narrative. But most important, Jack never got tired of seeing his son's face as he absorbed the words to his favorite bedtime story. His eyes burned with interest, and he knew that his son's imagination was expanding filling in more and more detail each time he read the book.

Since the episode at the cabin, Jack was thankful to read anything to his son, and vowed never to be distracted or give anything less than his full attention to responsibility of storyteller.

"…and so, the knight defeated the evil wizard, and the thousand years of darkness was forever vanquished from the kingdom. The knight married the beautiful princess and the two lived happily ever after. The end."

Jack closed the book. His son's eyes were heavy with impending sleep. He leaned over and kissed Joshua on the forehead.

"Sleep tight, sport."

"Good night, Dad," Joshua murmured, as he settled under the covers.

Jack got up and walked to the bedroom door.

"Open a crack?" he asked his son.

Joshua hesitated then shook his head. Jack smiled. Since the incident at the cabin, they had been making slow progress with regards to Joshua's bedtime habits. An inch forward was still forward, and as long as they weren't going backward, that was okay with Jack.

"That's my boy," he said.

Jacked walked out of the room, shutting off the light and closing the door behind him. The Bugs Bunny night light immediately turned on once it sensed the absence of light, glowing its familiar orange glow. Joshua stared at it a few minutes until he felt reassured, then he turned over on his side.

Joshua thought about the last few months. It had taken eight weeks with a therapist to get him to sleep at night instead of the day, and another eight to discuss the happenings at the cabin. Dr. Pearlstone seemed nice enough; a woman close to his mother's age, she had a way of getting him to speak about things in a way that even his parents couldn't. She spoke like he spoke, and because of that, he was willing to share things about what he saw, about Mark, about the strange tree, and most of all, about the Dark.

The doctor seemed fascinated with Joshua's descriptions of the Dark. They talked extensively about it – as a natural occurrence, a triumphant force, a symbol, and a personification of living entity. He told her how it moved, how it pooled and collected and then disappeared. How it wanted him.

Dr. Pearlstone was supportive and nonjudgmental. She listened intently and rarely interrupted him with her own thoughts and opinions, waiting until he had spoken and asked her questions to things that were on his mind. She had a way of bringing a practical logic to what he had seen and felt. The Dark wasn't so scary then because it was less about imagination and interpretation. It was simply a natural phenomenon and being so, it was accessible. And anything accessible could be understood, and once understood, the unknown could be peeled away, and its truth, sanitized in the light of day.

Seven months into therapy, Dr. Pearlstone told his parents that Joshua had turned an important corner. At a meeting with the three of them, she emphasized the need to develop something she called "building measures," little victories that would bolster Joshua's confidence in uncomfortable situations. If he continued down this path, she was certain that the unpleasantness that Joshua had experienced would become a manageable memory. The news made everyone happy, and the doctor recommending seeing Joshua once a week, instead of the three times that he had been seeing her.

And on this note, Joshua acquiesced to the sleepiness that had imposed itself on him. It had been a full day with lots of time at the park, and now he was just plain tired. As he drifted off, Joshua thought about his upcoming birthday and the type of cake he wanted and how much fun it was going to be to have his friends over again.

With thoughts of normalcy setting up a night for good dreams, Joshua didn't stir from his slumber. If he had, he might have seen a familiar troubling sight, something that would have turned his blood cold and made him empty his bladder into his new pajamas.

The night light in the socket near the bedroom door flickered, sending orange flashes into the room like a strobe light. Each time Bugs Bunny's face went out, the darkness in the corners grew larger, becoming thick and gaining ground, getting closer.

www.ingramcontent.com/pod-product-compliance
Lightning Source LLC
Chambersburg PA
CBHW061045190726
48286CB00006B/1607